Eye on You - Knights in White Satin

by Joe Hamilton

Eye on You - Knights in White Satin

Book design by Pen2publishing

Copyright © 2020

A Primer

This is the 7th book in the *Eye on You* mystery series. For newbies, The Eye on You Detective Agency was formed in 1979 by Gabriel Ross and his silent partner Ben O'Shea, a Biloxi Police Detective. Jacqueline Cooper was the agency's first significant client (*Eye on You – Murder in Biloxi*), and as luck would have it, she became Jacqueline Ross at the end of the first book.

Over the years, the agency has grown in business, reputation, and employees. The initial office was relocated to a bigger space in Gulfport, and Rachel Henderson was hired as a receptionist/associate. Arnie Sims joined as a part-time associate.

Book One	*Eye on You – Right Place, Wrong Time* (formerly titled *Murder in Biloxi*)
Book Two	*Eye on You – Rock Me like a Hurricane*
Book Three	*Eye on You – Mississippi Queen*
Book Four	*Eye on You – Gimme 3 Steps*
Book Five	*Eye on You – House of the Rising Son*
Book Six	*Eye on You – Born on the Bayou*

This story is a work of fiction. While Charles Lindberg and the America First Movement are well-documented, all other characters exist only in my imagination. Any resemblance to actual people is a pile of hooey.

I hope you enjoy the story. If you do, let me know. Unlike the other books in the series, this book is written from Rachel Henderson's point of view. Some readers might think that the title of this book is based on the Moody Blues song Nights in White Satin. While I love the song, they would be wrong. The title is Knights in White Satin with a "K."

ISBN   978-0-9939999-7-0

People are trapped in history, and history is trapped in them.

-James Baldwin

Cast of Main Characters

Rachel Henderson	Narrator and Private Detective/Office Manager/Receptionist/Secretary for the Eye on You Detective Agency
Jacob Henderson	Rachel's older brother
Edith Henderson	Rachel's mother
Archie Henderson	Rachel's father
Hartley Green	Reporter for the *Herald*
Adrienne Green	Hartley's wife
Don Kittyburg	AKA Don Tittley; Rachel's off-again, on-again boyfriend
Fred Moller	Don's immediate boss at the MBI
Joyce Coogan	Senior Director at the MBI and Don's bosses boss
Professor Beau Snyder	Rachel's former boyfriend
Gabriel Ross	Half-owner along with Ben O'Shea, of the Eye on You Agency

Jacqueline Ross	Gabriel's wife
Benjamin Ross	Gabriel and Jacqueline's two-year-old son
Mayor John Baxter	Former Biloxi Mayor, now a permanent resident at the Mississippi State Penitentiary
Frank Reznikov	Sketchy businessman arrested with Baxter for racketeering, murder, fraud, and embezzlement
Arnie Sims	A part-time associate at the Agency, who recently agreed to take over the New Orleans office
Grace	Arnie's girlfriend
Deputy Weber	Harrison County Deputy Sheriff
Gordie Howe	AKA Gordon Bones, a rat-faced man with rotten teeth. Creep!
Travis Franklin	A teenager Gabriel befriended in the first book
Reverend McGloyn	Pastor at Bay Vista Baptist Church

Barry McGloyn	The Reverend's son
Rod Smith	Local lawyer and Arnie's childhood friend
Sheriff Pardy	Harrison County Sheriff
Corbin Masters	Millionaire who owns most of the trees north of Biloxi
Gladys Mayview	Corbin's former wife
John Dietz	Former President of the Biloxi Chamber of Commerce
Bubba Lange	Owner of Bubba's Shrimp Emporium
Parker Lange	Bubba's brother
Fender	Associate of Bubba's
Hollis Huntley	A key witness against Baxter and Reznikov, who fell off Legacy Towers
Michael Boyle	A client looking for his biological father
Jimmy Hopkins	A young teenager who is helping Rachel
Larry Bremmer	Editor of the *Biloxi Herald*
Angel Garcia	Typist at the *Herald*

Table of Contents

Chapter 1

December 25, 1984

Jackson, Mississippi

Howard Johnson's. I looked around the stark, antiseptic motel room and stomped my feet, hoping to scare away all of the creepy crawlies. At $19.99 a night, I shouldn't complain, but I have a thing about bugs, snakes, and rodents...

I'd arrived this afternoon from Biloxi for the annual Christmas interrogation with my parents. Luckily, they'd recently downsized to a one-bedroom apartment, which meant one of their two kids was going to have to stay in a hotel. I was ten seconds faster volunteering than my older brother Jacob.

I dropped my Samsonite on the bed and went to inspect the bathroom. Flicking on the light, I caught my reflection in the mirror. "Rachel Henderson, you still looking good, girl," I said to my reflection. I pushed out my boobs, "Well, maybe not so much in that department. But girl, your butt still looks good." I angled myself in front of the mirror and was immediately horrified at how stirrup leggings made my ass look huge. "This must be one of those fun-house mirrors," I said dismissively. I nodded approval at the peach-colored cotton blouse with shoulder pads I was wearing, before noticing I'd spilled gravy on my left boob earlier at dinner. Other Christmas dinner low-lights popped into my head while I blotted out the stain with a wet towel.

"You know you aren't getting any younger, Rachel," said Mom. "Most girls your age are not only married but having babies. It would just dill my pickle if you could settle down with the right boy. Your father and I would like to have grandchildren before we slip into dementia."

I looked over at my father, who, despite having long left the military, was wearing his WW2 uniform. *Too late,* I thought, taking a tentative bite of turkey. I was sitting across from Jacob, who was grinning at me. Despite being two years older, and a bachelor, he had somehow managed to elude Mom's nagging. I looked at him and wondered, *Are you gay or just awkward?* I'd never seen him with a girl, not even in high school. I chuckled at the thought of Jacob ever showing up to one of these family dinners with another man - they would likely have simultaneous coronary. *Or maybe they already know, and that's why they don't talk about it.*

"Seriously, Rachel, are you seeing that Don, or is it, Drake? You know, the one with the different names?" Mom gave me a haughty smile.

"I'm not sure. We're taking it slow. By the way, last I heard, his name was Don Kittyburg. I doubt that's true, though. He was petting a cat at the time. A couple of months ago, I met one of his old girlfriends, who had tits out to here," I pantomimed a pair of large breasts. "She told me his name was Don Tittley."

"Oh my," said Dad, pouring a lake of gravy on his plate.

Mom raised her voice in alarm. "Archie, you know what that much gravy will do to your arteries."

"Well, you made it, aren't we supposed to eat it?" he asked, raising his voice.

I shared a look with Jacob. *Like two mules fighting over a turnip.* Both my parents had hearing loss and were too stubborn to do anything about it. Jacob flashed me a smile in return. *I bet he's remembering last Christmas when we took them to Tupelo. The shouting in the car got so bad we almost ran off the road.*

"I didn't expect you would overdose on it," Mom said under her breath. She always has to have the last word.

"What did you say, Edith?" screamed Dad.

"Nothing." Mom rolled her eyes.

"So, what happened to Mr. Tittley? Didn't you measure up?" asked Jacob, trying to change the subject. His grin had turned into a full-blown smile.

3

"He's still around. He's up for some big promotion with the Mississippi Bureau of Investigation."

"You're better off without him," added Mom. "What about that professor? What was his name?"

"Beau Snyder. There was too big an age difference. Plus, my boss said talked like Kermit the Frog."

"Wasn't there a married man in there somewhere?" asked Dad. "You ask me, you're better off with the married ones. Lots of sex and no commitment." He cast a wary eye at Mom.

A couple of years back, Gabriel, my boss, had been separated from his wife, and we'd gone out briefly. There was a big-time attraction, but he was conflicted over what was happening with his marriage. I've often thought I missed the boat on that. "That ship has sailed."

"Do you remember Eldridge Crane? He's such a nice boy, and I think he's still single," Mom whispered, her eyes growing large as saucers. "Maybe I should invite him over. You two made such a beautiful couple in high school."

"No, don't do that," I said firmly, fixing her with a threatening stare. One date, and she'd never t stopped talking about it. All Eldridge had wanted to talk about was how he was going to be a big shot when he took over his father's tire store.

"You know he runs the Speedy Tire store now." Mom spoke with as much reverence as if he'd been elected President.

"Jacob, what's happening with your new job? What is it again?" I mentally begged him to help shift the conversation.

"It's a shit job."

"It's only been a few months. Have you given it enough time? I know when I first started at the Agency...."

"I meant literally," Jacob said, cutting me off. "It's a shit job. My job at the lab is to analyze stool samples. It gets a little hard to maintain focus. There's the dark brown, the light caramel color, and then I had one the other day with bits of corn in it."

"Jacob, I won't have that kind of talk at my table," huffed Mom.

"Didn't you say you got a promotion at work?" Jacob looked at me before jamming a spoon full of corn in his mouth and then turning to grin at his mother.

I giggled before replying. "Gabriel Ross wanted to step back from the day-to-day running of the agency. Plus, he and his partner Ben O'Shea are key witnesses in an upcoming trial, and a couple of other witnesses have died suspiciously. On the advice of the DA, they took their families on an extended vacation, and I volunteered to take over."

∗ ∗ ∗

The evening lasted until 7:30 when Mom started ranting over the amount of whipped cream that Dad put on his pumpkin pie. I wondered how many more years my parents had. One of Mom's expressions came to mind, "*They had so many wrinkles they could screw their hats on.*"

Jacob and I started yawning simultaneously, our signal that it was time to leave. On the way out, I made a lunch date for the weekend with him to discuss the parent situation.

The television at the motel was black-and-white, with rabbit ears. To get my parents off my mind, I spun the dial through the different channels. Playing with the antenna, I finally got decent reception, which of course, went snowy as soon as I let go of the rabbit ears. My attention was drawn to the screen as a news anchor talked about a late-breaking story taking place in Biloxi.

> "*This, just in to the Channel 6 News team. We are following a story unfolding in Saucier, northwest of Biloxi. The body of one of the city's best-known reporters, Hartley Green, was discovered earlier today in a quiet residential neighborhood. The journalist was found by his family housekeeper at approximately 10:00 AM Christmas morning. Harrison County Deputies are not commenting on the case; however, confidential sources tell us he appears to have been the victim*

of foul play. Police are currently looking for Adrienne Green, the young wife of the reporter."

A picture of Hartley Green, along with his youthful African American wife, was displayed on the screen behind the newscaster.

"Green was well known for his hard-hitting stories about crime on the Gulf Coast. The Biloxi Herald recently ran one of his exposes, which uncovered corruption and racketeering in our fair city."

The camera shifted to a different news anchor.

"In other news, residents were woken early on Christmas morning, not by the sound of reindeer, but by the sound of an explosion that rocked a suburban Hattiesburg community..."

The sound of the television faded into white noise as I started to pace. "My God, Gabriel will want to hear this," I said to the television. This past July, Gabriel had disappeared for three days. Everyone had panicked, afraid that one of his past cases had come back to hurt him. We later learned he'd narrowly escaped a kidnapping attempt with the help of a good samaritan. Then, a critical informant in the case against former Biloxi Mayor John Baxter and sketchy businessman Frank Reznikov was stabbed to death in Angola State Penitentiary. And another key witness in the State's case 'jumped' off the highest building in Gulfport. Now a local crime reporter was dead. "Should I call and warn Gabriel?" I asked the television.

The news anchor was gone, replaced by a portly Eldridge Crane leaning up against a black Ferrari. He was wearing a white linen jacket over a blue pastel t-shirt and wearing dark sunglasses, "Make love to the road with a new set of Speedy Tires."

I tried to wipe that image from my mind by thinking about Hartley Green. *Was this some type of retribution for the expose last summer? If it was, could Reznikov get at Gabriel and Ben up north?* I had put the phone number of their resort in my suitcase. Opening the clasps on the Samsonite, I was stunned to find a pair of well-worn white jockey shorts with skid marks. Confused, I looked at the luggage tag and found the case belonged to a P. Jackson. At the luggage carousel, I had been sure that the powder blue hard shell was mine, but clearly, I'd taken someone else's luggage. I picked up the hotel's phone and looked up the airline phone number in the yellow pages. While I was being bounced around and finally put on hold, I berated myself for taking the wrong suitcase.

After about five minutes, a woman's tired voice answered. "Ya'll have reached American Airlines."

"Yes," I blurted out quickly, "My name is Rachel Henderson, I was on the flight earlier today from

Biloxi, and I think I might have picked up the wrong suitcase from the luggage carousel."

"You might have?"

"I'm sorry?"

"Ya'll said you might have picked up the wrong suitcase. Did you, or didn't you?"

"Well, I have, I know I have because the clothes aren't mine. They belong to a man." I held up the pair of jockey shorts as if the woman could see them.

"Ma'am, didn't you check the tags before you took the suitcase?"

"I guess I just assumed it was mine."

"Assumed?" The woman asked with a sigh, "Do ya'll know what you do when you assume?"

"What?"

"You make an ass… out of you … and me."

I was finding her tone less than helpful. "Can you just check to see if my suitcase is still there?"

After a brief moment, the woman responded, "All of the suitcases from that flight have been picked up."

"The two suitcases must look alike. Maybe they took mine."

"Unlikely, most people check the luggage tags," she said smugly. "In all my days of working here, you're the only one that's ever done this."

I find that hard to believe. "Alright I hear you, I should have checked, what can I do to get my luggage back?"

I then heard the woman speak to someone. I could hear laughter over the phone. A few moments later, she returned, still chuckling, "We've had no complaints about a missing suitcase."

"Maybe whoever has it hasn't noticed …"

"Ma'am, is there a luggage tag on the suitcase?" she cut me off.

"Of course, it has my name, Rachel Henderson, and my address in Gulfport."

The woman took another deep breath before replying curtly, "No…. the suitcase you picked up."

"Oh, yes, it says P. Jackson."

"Address?"

"No, just P. Jackson."

"Do you realize how many people with that last name there are in this town? That's why they call the city Jackson," She said condescendingly. "Ya'll will have to wait until they call. In the meantime, you can make up for picking up the wrong suitcase by bringing it back."

"But he must have been on that flight. Can't you just look up the passenger list and contact him? I'd like to get my suitcase back."

I thought I heard what sounded like a growl. A few moments later, she came back on the line. "No one named Jackson on that flight."

"There must have been. Look again."

"No, ah got better thin's than t'be doin' thet," her Southern accent showed before she hung up..

"Wal, thank yo' fo' nothing." I slammed down the receiver.

Her self-righteous attitude had annoyed me. I was already frustrated at picking up the wrong suitcase and not having Gabriel's phone number. I sat down on the bed and looked at the luggage tag again. *What kind of a person would put a fake name on their luggage?* There was a jumble of underwear, pants, t-shirts, and socks, along with a couple of Hawaiian shirts. I was checking the size of the shirts when I felt something icky. Sudden realization hit me when I pulled my hand away. I stifled a scream and flapped my arms in the air, trying not to throw up. My hand was covered in dark red blood.

Chapter 2

I don't know if it was finding blood, picking up the wrong suitcase, or hearing what had happened to Green, but my heartbeat started to skip like a NASCAR on a wet track. I needed to talk to Gabriel but had no idea how to reach him - my address book was in my missing suitcase. I finally picked up the hotel phone and dialed a number. Waiting for the line to be picked up, I resumed pacing. Finally, the phone was answered by a sleepy voice.

"Arnie, it's Rachel," I said quickly into the phone. Arnie Sims was the other Agency associate who had taken over the New Orleans office. Up until recently, the elderly African American had worked part-time with me in Gulfport, moonlighting from his job as the superintendent at the Trade Winds hotel.

"What's wrong, Rachel? You sound upset. Is everything all right with your parents?"

"They're fine. Arnie, something has happened, and I needed to talk to someone."

"I guess you heard about Hartley Green? It's all over the news down here."

"I think we need to tell Gabriel. But I don't have his number."

"I saw you record it in your phonebook. Did you lose it?"

"That's the other thing." I brought him up to date on the mix-up with the suitcase and the blood-covered shirt.

"And the lady from the airlines said there was no one with that name on the flight?"

"Right, doesn't that sound strange?"

"I suppose someone could have borrowed a suitcase."

"But the blood…do you think this could be somehow connected to what happened to Green?"

"I don't follow, Rachel," said Arnie. "I guess I'm still a little sleepy."

"The suitcase was on my flight from Biloxi that got in this afternoon. What if it belongs to the killer?"

"Okay, I get it now. It's probably nothing, but to be safe, you should call the police. They aren't releasing details to the press, but my cousin in the Harrison County Sheriff's Department said there was a lot of blood at the scene."

"Did he say how he died?"

"Multiple stab wounds."

Chapter 3

It was almost 10 PM by the time I ended the call with Arnie after he made me promise to call the police right away. He also gave me the phone number of a resort on Mackinac Island where Gabriel was staying. I decided to dial that number first.

It took a few moments for the call to go through, but eventually, a man with a smooth sounding voice answered, "Pine Resort, Front Desk, you've got Wilford."

"I'm sorry. I know it's late, but I need to speak to one of your guests. It's very important."

"Who might that be, young lady?"

"His name is Gabriel Ross. He's traveling with his wife."

"Yes, of course. He and his friends, the O'Sheas, went out to dinner and haven't returned. We don't have telephones in the rooms, but I can take a message if you want. He can call you from the public phone in the lobby."

"Yes, please, let me give you my number. It's Rachel Henderson, and he should call as soon as he gets in." My voice started to quiver. "The number here at the Howard Johnson's is 601 …492-6532. Tell him not to worry about the time."

"Are you all right, Miss?" His voice sounded concerned. "He didn't say which restaurant they were going to go to, but I could call around."

"How many restaurants are there up there?"

"About twenty that you'd want to eat at."

✳ ✳ ✳

After the call, I took a few deep breaths and tried to calm myself. When I'd agreed to take over the *Eye on You* office, I had been brimming with confidence. Now, I was racked with uncertainty and doubt. I picked up the phone to call the police and, after a moment, put it back down. The murder had taken place in Harrison County, but the suitcase was in Jackson, part of Hinds County. I stewed over who to call.

I finally decided to call the Harrison County Sheriff's Department. I identified myself to the receptionist and asked to speak to someone about a murder. Ten seconds later, I was put through to a Deputy Sheriff.

"Deputy Weber. Can we start with your name and location?"

"Rachel Henderson, I'm staying at the Best Western in Jackson, Mississippi. The one near the airport."

A tired voice replied, "If this is related to an investigation in Jackson, you should call the Hinds

County Sheriff Department. My badge says Harrison County Deputy, different thing altogether."

"But, it's related to what happened to Hartley Green."

"Green? Why didn't you say so?"

I cut him off. "I know you. You're the guy I met while we were investigating the Mardi Gras Killer a few months ago."

There was a momentary pause on the line. "Oh right, I remember. You work for that outfit, the one with the strange name, Eye on You something. Yeah, I remember. I never forget a name. You were with that guy from the MBI, Mr. Kitty-something."

"Kittyburg." I went on to tell him about the suitcases and how I had found blood on a shirt.

"Hmmm. Likely a nosebleed. I remember once in high school, I had to go to the hospital because my nose wouldn't stop bleeding…"

"It's not a nosebleed," I interrupted. My frustration was starting to boil over.

"Wouldn't this be something for the airlines, Miss… Henderson? Besides, I don't see how picking up the wrong suitcase sheds any light on a murder investigation."

"I called the airlines, Deputy Weber, and the tag on the luggage says it belongs to P. Jackson, yet there were no passengers named Jackson on the flight. It suggests that whoever owns this suitcase is traveling under an alias."

"Or, maybe he borrowed someone's suitcase. So, let me get this straight. You got it into your pretty little head that there's this big conspiracy going on. What, you think the person who did Green, made his escape on a commercial flight to Jackson after he wiped his bleeding nose on his shirt?"

"It wasn't a bleeding nose," I repeated. "There was a lot of blood found at the murder scene. The killer might have got it all over himself."

"How do you know there was lots of blood at the scene? We haven't released any information on the cause of death to the media."

"I have confidential sources that told me."

"Who?"

"It wouldn't be confidential if I told you."

"You're coming very close to interfering with a murder investigation."

"No, I'm not. I'm trying to help you with the investigation. There might be fingerprints, clues about this, Mr. Weber."

"Fine, Miss Henderson. There's not much I can do from my end but, I'll put in a call to Hinds County. What room are you in at the Howard Johnson?"

* * *

Despite Arnie saying not to touch the suit-case, I told myself to get a grip and start acting like a detective. I started sorting through the contents.

There was nothing but clothes and the shaving kit. I looked in the kit and found an electric razor, some Aqua Velva, a tube of Brylcream, and a disgusting toothbrush, but no toothpaste. I rooted in the pant pockets and found a few coins and a package of Hubba Bubba bubble gum.

I was just about to give up when I noticed a tear in the inside lining of the case. It looked like it had been torn open and then hastily repaired with tape. I pulled off the tape and, reaching in, found a small plastic baggie with a five and a quarter inch floppy disk inside.

I put the clothes and shaving kit back in the suitcase but left the baggie on the nightstand to show the police. Finding the baggie hidden in the suitcase added fuel to my suspicions. Could Green have been killed because of something on this floppy disk? I lay down on the bed, suddenly feeling overwhelmed with everything that happened. I kept staring at the phone, wishing Gabriel would call.

I woke up sweating, finding that I had kicked the covers off the bed. I picked up the phone, "Gabriel?" All I heard was a dial tone. The alarm clock read 12:30, which didn't make sense. The room was bathed in light coming from the window.

I crept out of bed and went to the window. Slowly pulling the curtains back, I took a quick peek outside. An old pickup truck was parked facing the door, its headlights illuminating my room. It was too dark to see into the truck, but I could see the glow of a cigarette held by someone behind the wheel.

* * *

I stewed and paced the room until I heard a knock on the door. "Who is it?"

"Suitcase." There was a chain on the door, so I opened it a crack. A tall man dressed in a Minnie Mouse t-shirt and jeans was looking at me. His dark hair was greased back like he was an extra in a John Travolta movie. Red marks on his cheek looked as if his cat had scratched him.

"You don't look like a Deputy Sheriff to me."

"Just here to pick up a suitcase that don't belong to you." The man had a rat-like face with beady eyes and was looking at me through the chain holding the door. I sensed him calculating just how hard he'd have to push to break in. "Listen, it's late. Are you Rachel Henderson?" he read from a piece of paper he'd pulled out of his pocket.

"Who are you?"

The man looked up at the ceiling as if the answer was somehow written there. "Gordie."

When I continued to stare at him, he added, "Howe."

"How what?"

"What do you mean, how what? Just Howe. You know, with an 'E.'"

"Wait a minute, your last name is Howe?"

"Gordie ... Howe. Listen, Miss, just open up, and I'll take the suitcase and be gone, unless, of course, you want to invite me in. You all alone?" He stepped closer to the door; a lecherous grin washing across his face as he tried to look into the room.

I looked down at the suitcase at my feet and made a decision. "I'm a private investigator, Mr. Howe, and I have a gun. Get back in your car, and I'll put the suitcase outside the door."

The man shook his head before replying. "Did you take anything out of it?"

I thought about the floppy and crossed my fingers behind my back. "Nah, there's just some dirty men's clothes and shaving stuff." The man smiled, showing off his rotten teeth. He then stepped back to his car. I gauged the distance as being less than five feet from where he was standing. "I said, get in your car."

When he did, I pushed the suitcase out the door and locked it again, letting out a sigh of relief.

* * *

My nerves frayed, I turned on the television again. I tried to come up with a logical explanation for everything, but the nagging in the back of my mind spoke of nothing but danger. I jumped at the shrill sound of the motel phone.

"Sorry for calling so late, Rachel. How are you?"

I almost started to cry when I heard Gabriel's voice. I began jabbering away about what I had learned about Hartley Green, as well as the mix-up with the suitcase and the bloodstained shirt. "I'm worried about you, Gabriel. Do you think this is related to what happened last summer?"

Gabriel ignored the question. "You called the Harrison County Sheriff Department?"

"They said they'd pass a message to the local cops. There was a guy, now that I think of it, clearly not a cop, he was creepy. He said that he was sent to pick up the luggage. He scared me."

"So, you gave him the suitcase?"

"Yes, and no. I gave him the suitcase. But Gabriel, when I was looking in the case for something that would tell me about the owner, I found a tear in the lining. I pulled out a baggie with a floppy disk in it. I'm sorry, I had to make a snap decision. I held that back."

"You still have it?"

"It's right here on the nightstand."

"How long ago did the creepy guy pick up the suitcase?"

"Maybe ten minutes."

"I want you to get out of that hotel," he said urgently. "Now."

"Why?"

"Just do what I say, Rachel. Get out. I'll be home tomorrow."

"No, Gabriel, you and Ben need to stay where they can't get you."

"I'll discuss that with Ben. This is what I want you to do. Hide the disk in your purse and check out of the motel. I've always trusted your instincts. If that guy was a phony, then, chances are, he's discovered you held back the disk. Have the hotel call you a cab. Go to the bus station and buy a ticket to Biloxi. Before getting on the bus, call me back. There are no phones in the rooms here, but the guy that owns this place will make sure I get the message. I'll try to get Arnie to meet you at the bus station."

Hanging up, I jumped off the bed, grabbed my purse and the disk, and ran out of the motel room.

The office for the motel was at the end of the building. When I opened the door to the office, I found a young man reading a Playboy magazine. "Listen, I'm in room seven, and I need to check out. I also need a cab."

There must have been something in my face that warned the young man that he'd better move quickly. Checking me out at the register, he gave me a puzzled look. "You just checked in this morning, is everything okay with the room?"

"Yes, the room's fine, but I have to go now." I heard a noise in the parking lot. A pickup truck similar to the one that had been parked outside my door rumbled by and stopped with a screech in front of my now vacant room.

"I wonder what's got into that guy?" The kid strained his neck to watch.

"Here's $30 bucks," I said, looking at the guy getting out of his truck. "Forget the cab. I have to go." I watched as the rat-faced man went to the motel room door and started banging loudly. After a moment, the man played with the doorknob before turning towards the office.

"Listen, kid, I'm not here," I whispered as I got down and hid on the other side of the counter. The kid was still looking down at me with a puzzled look when I heard the little chime of the office door opening.

"I'm looking for the woman that was in room seven."

I looked up at the kid who was looking at the man with a blank expression on his face. The kid shook his head and then shrugged his shoulders.

"I said I'm looking for Rachel Henderson," the man said gruffly.

"I haven't seen her."

"Give me the spare key to her room then."

I realized that when I'd entered the office, I'd set my room key on the counter.

"I can't …you know, do that. It's not your room." I heard the kid scream out in pain. "My hand, c'mon man, that hurts."

"Then, give me the fucking key."

I watched as the kid reached into a cupboard with his other hand and handed the man the spare key. After the door chime went off again, I breathed a sigh of relief. I smiled up at the kid who was looking back at me with terror on his face.

"Thank you," I whispered.

Chapter 4

December 26, 1984

Biloxi, Mississippi

It was 4 AM when my bus arrived at the Biloxi station. Arnie was waiting for me with a warm hug when I stepped off the bus. "Oh, Arnie, I was so scared, I didn't stop shaking until we were an hour out of Jackson."

Arnie walked me to his van. "Gabriel wants me to take you to my apartment. It'll be safer there."

"Why?"

"Since you ended up with the wrong suitcase, and yours is also missing, it stands to reason the other guy has it and knows where you live."

It hadn't occurred to me that my troubles might follow me home. "Alright, but I need a few things tomorrow." I looked out the window as the first drops of rain splashed down on the windshield.

* * *

"What do you think this is all about, Arnie?" I asked, sipping the hot tea Arnie made me. I was sitting on his couch wearing a pair of his flannel PJs. Bourbon, his orange tabby, was on my lap.

"If you're asking who killed Green, I don't know. I suppose we'll hear more in the next day or two."

I looked around the living room and noticed a couple of cardboard boxes. "Moving?"

"Yeah. I gave my notice to the Trade Winds. They need the apartment for the next super. I have a line on a place in the French Quarter of New Orleans near where Ben lives."

"Are you sad to be leaving Biloxi?" I asked, petting Bourbon, who, in response, raised his backside and started purring.

"I think it's time for a new adventure."

"How's the new office?"

"I'm still getting used to it. I'm looking to hire someone to help out. For now, it's pretty much a one-person show. I just put up a sign on the door telling people to make an appointment through the answering service."

"Have you been busy?"

"I get the odd call, mostly from cops wanting to talk about what happened with Rutledge."

Rutledge was the original manager hired to run the New Orleans branch of the Agency. He'd had forty-five years of experience with the NOPD before he retired to take the job, only to be murdered by a serial killer named Charles Bouvier this past summer.

Arnie poured more tea in my mug. "I received a call from Rod Smith, the lawyer."

"I know Rod. We helped clear one of his clients last year. He also helped us figure out Bouvier's estate." The serial killer, who had been thought to have drowned two years ago, had surprised everyone by resurfacing and continuing his bloody reign of terror. His estate had been worth over a million at the time he was believed to have drowned. "I don't know if we would have caught Bouvier if it wasn't for Rod's information."

"Rod wants my help in a paternity case."

"That's great, but Rod's office is in Gulfport. Why wouldn't he call me? Is the client living in New Orleans?"

"No, Biloxi. I'm sure Rod appreciates your work, but we've known each other since Grade Two. How's it been for you?"

"I still have reference checks coming in. Travis Franklin helps out the odd time after school and on Saturdays. A few walk-ins, but when they hear that Gabriel's gone, they look over my head for someone other than me. It doesn't seem to matter that I'm qualified. They just smile and say they might come back. But they never do."

"You grew up in Mississippi, and you know how some people can be. As a black man, I've had to learn to deal with it."

I bit my lip and gave Arnie a serious look. "I just don't know if I made the right choice. With everything that happened today, I'm second-guessing everything I'm doing."

Arnie moved to sit with me on the couch. "You know Gabriel once said that he didn't look at being short as a handicap, even though many people remark on him being five feet tall. He said it leads people to underestimate him. You have a lot of great things going for you, Rachel. You're smart, quick, and your youth and beauty will lead people to underestimate you. Remember when you single-handedly broke up that stolen car ring?"

"I think Kittyburg helped on that one."

Arnie shrugged his shoulders. "So what? I have an appointment with Rod Smith this week. Do you want to tag along?"

"Absolutely."

"Speaking of Kittyburg, is he out of the picture now?"

"Yes and no. No, and yes...he's a mystery. I haven't heard from him for a while. I was going to pay a surprise visit to the MBI while I was up in Jackson." I looked at my Casio. It was almost 6 AM. "You know what, I need a shower, and then maybe we can stop by my apartment for some clean clothes."

Chapter 5

When I got out of the shower and put my clothes back on, I found that Arnie had made breakfast. "Oh, you read my mind! I had a hankering for flapjacks."

"Well, sit on down, girl, and they'll be right up. I spoke to Gabriel while you were in the shower. I told him everything was fine and that we'd be roommates for a few days."

"Alright. Did he say he was staying up there?"

"That's why he was calling. He said he spoke to Ben, and even though it's a holiday, they were going to try to talk to the Mississippi District Attorney today."

"We talked about Kittyburg last night, but I'm sorry I never asked you about your gal. Are you still seeing Grace?"

"Yes, we both enjoy each other's company." Arnie lifted a stack of flapjacks onto my plate.

"How does she feel about you moving?"

"She loves New Orleans. She's pretty busy during the week with work, but she's talked about weekends in the Big Easy. Of course, the other benefit is we'll be away from Bernice Cross. She moved into an apartment on this floor and is constantly knocking on my door." Arnie rolled his eyes and smiled. Bernice and Arnie had known each other since childhood, and her love crush had been going on sixty years. She'd recently announced her desire to divorce her husband and had been throwing herself at Arnie.

I'd once snuck a peek at his employee file and seen that Arnie was 63 years old. He took pride in his appearance, stayed in shape, and taught martial arts to kids at the YMCA. His best feature was his voice - warm and comforting, or was that just because I was one step away from losing it?

"What about Bourbon? How's he going to take to a new place?" I asked in between bites of pancakes.

"I don't know. Lately, he's been playing in the empty boxes, trying to imitate a lion protecting his lair. Not sure what that means. But I think he'll be fine." Bourbon had become the Agency mascot when Gabriel first started the business. Back then, he used to show up on the fire escape and meow until Gabriel let him in and gave him a treat. I'd become concerned about where the cat was spending his nights when I'd found a piece of his ear bitten off, and had asked Arnie to take him home. Since then, they've been bachelors together.

It was almost 8:30 when we finished cleaning up after breakfast. "I was thinking about that disk. The public library just had some computers installed. Want to head there first?" asked Arnie.

"Let's go, partner. I'd also like to stop by the Sheriff's office and lodge a complaint about that

Deputy who took my call, and find out who he talked to about the suitcase."

It was a crisp sunny morning. White fluffy clouds hung high like pillows floating in the sky. The high for the Gulf Coast was expected to be a chilly 48 degrees. "We're going to have to convince Gabriel to buy a computer for the office," said Arnie as he pulled into the library's parking lot.

"I, for one, would need to take a course on how to use it. Plus, I would have to bring in some business to pay for it."

We walked up to the front doors of the library just as a young African American man was unlocking them. After checking the layout inside and finding no computers, we approached the young man, who was now engrossed in sorting through the overnight returns.

I read his name tag. "Excuse me, Jimmy?"

Jimmy looked at me with a blank expression through John Lennon glasses. He was slim and appeared to be in his late teens. His sports shirt was buttoned all the way up to his neck under a sleeveless plaid sweater.

I showed him the floppy disk. "We desperately need to see what's on this. We're told that you have a computer."

Jimmy looked at me and then Arnie. "It's not for public use. The library is using it for cataloging."

Arnie was just about to flash his PI card when I jumped in. I gave him my best smile. "Would you even know how to read it?"

"Sure, I'm taking a DOS course at the local… college."

"DOS, I know nothing, what's that?"

"It stands for Disk Operating System. It's the language interface to get the computer to work."

"Wow, you must be smart. I wish I had your brains." The kid looked down in embarrassment. "I wouldn't even know how to start a computer. Tell me, Jimmy, do you need a key like on a car?"

"It's not that complicated. You just press a button; then, when it boots up, you put the floppy in the drive."

"Boots up?" I cocked my head.

"Computer talk for waking up."

"I bet you have to be pretty clever to take that course."

"No," then he corrected himself. "You have to memorize some stuff."

"I bet it would take hours to see what's on this disk."

"No, the computer is really fast. Since it's already booted up, it would take less than a minute."

I looked around the library. A few people were checking out the bookshelves, but there appeared to be only one other staff member. "Jimmy, it would mean so much to me if you could just take a quick peek. It's very important."

Jimmy looked around the library before addressing the other employee, "Rob, I need to look for something in the back, can you keep an eye out?"

As Jimmy turned and walked to a door behind the counter, Arnie nodded to me, mouthing the words, "Well done."

* * *

Jimmy returned ten minutes later carrying sheets of printer paper. When he got to the counter, he whispered that there wasn't much on the disk. "I was able to use Lotus to put the data into a spreadsheet format. There's another file, but the library doesn't have the program to open it. It's a CAD file."

"A CAD file?"

"It stands for computer-assisted drafting. You know, for blueprints. If you went to an architect, they might be able to read it."

"Thanks so much, Jimmy," I gushed, looking down at two sheets of computer paper. There was a column of names followed by another with addresses. Most of the addresses were in Mississippi, but a few were spread out over several states. Once again, Jimmy looked away and said it was nothing. "Seriously, thank you, Jimmy, what's your last name? Maybe we can grab a coffee sometime."

"Hopkins, Jimmy Hopkins. I don't drink coffee, but I like root beer."

"I'll call you, Jimmy Hopkins, and thanks again." I gave him a final smile.

* * *

"That was masterful," said Arnie as we got back into the van. "You had that kid eating out of your hand."

"I may just call him up. We might need a computer geek."

"What do you make of the printouts?" Arnie pulled out of the parking lot, heading to my apartment.

"I don't know. Some of the names on this list sound familiar. Hey, Mayor Baxter's name is on here!"

"Interesting. Green did that story last fall on municipal corruption. I wonder if that's a list of people he was looking into?"

"Maybe, but my pastor's also on the list." I chewed my lip and looked over at Arnie.

"Maybe this has nothing to do with Green," said Arnie.

Chapter 6

We stopped at my apartment so that I could pick up some clothes. After about ten minutes, I got back in the van. "I packed enough for three days, after that, you'll have to get a new roommate."

"Let's go. Where to?" Arnie asked, putting the van in gear.

"There's an architect off Beach Blvd. I'd like to know what's on that other file."

✳ ✳ ✳

The firm of Brown and Lewis was located on the second floor of a tall building. As we took the stairs, Arnie asked if I was prepared to use the same technique to finesse the people in the architect's office.

"Whatever works, Arnie."

When we opened the door to the office, we were greeted by a teapot-shaped woman with limp brown hair hanging down to her shoulders, wearing a frumpy gray tunic. She scowled at us from the moment we walked in the door. "Over to you, Arnie," I said, handing him the disk as I went to sit in the waiting area.

"Good morning Ma'am," Arnie said, approaching the desk. "I wonder if I could speak to Mr. Brown?"

"Are you a psychic?" When Arnie shook his head, she added, "Jerry Brown died six years ago."

"Oops, I meant Mr. Lewis, of course." Arnie detected a not-so-thinly veiled hostility in the woman.

The woman raised a man-brow, "Is he expecting you?"

"No, but I think he'll see me." He handed her his business card.

"Arnie Simms, Private Investigator. Will he know what this is about?"

"He will once I tell him."

"Mr. Lewis is a very busy man. He doesn't appreciate his time being wasted."

"Neither do I. He'll appreciate it even less if he reads about all this in the papers." For a second, I thought the woman was going to lunge at Arnie. She told him to sit down and wait before heading down a short hallway and going into a room on the left. Arnie looked over at me, and I flashed him the thumbs-up sign.

After a few minutes, the scowling lady stomped back and looked at Arnie, "I told you to sit down."

"I didn't want to." Arnie held her gaze.

"Mr. Lewis said he could spare a couple of minutes. If you take any longer than that, I'll be dragging your ass out of there."

Arnie walked quickly down the hall to the door he had seen her go in. When he opened the door, he found an older black man sitting at a drafting table engrossed in some drawings. He didn't look up but said, "The clock's ticking. I'd get on with it if I were you."

"Mr. Lewis, I'm here because of the murder of Hartley Green. This isn't a police investigation at this point, but I believe you are uniquely equipped to help apprehend the killer." Lewis's curiosity must have been piqued, as he put down his pencil and looked back at Arnie.

"How's that?"

Arnie handed him the floppy disk. "There's a file on this disk which we retrieved from a suspect. On it is a spreadsheet with a list of names and addresses. More importantly, there's a second file. A CAD file that might yield a clue to the identity of this person."

"A CAD file?"

Arnie looked over at the man's desk. He had a Commodore 64. "I'm told it stands for Computer-Assisted Drafting.

"I know what it stands for. You want me to tell you what's on this disk?"

"I'd like your professional assessment."

For a minute, it looked like the man was going to say something and then thought better of it. He got up and opened the office door and spoke to the scowling woman, "Bea, I might be a bit longer with Mr. Simms. Don't worry, I'll be done the drawings on time."

Once the man inserted the disk, his fingers tapped away at the keyboard. After a moment, he said, "I'm not sure what you were expecting, but this isn't architecture. To me, this looks like an electrical schematic." Looking at his screen, he said, "12 DIP switch, 400 MGZ …I failed electronics, but it might be a garage door opener."

"How do you know that?"

"Because it says garage door opener right here," he said, pointing at the screen.

Arnie wondered why someone would go to such lengths to hide a schematic for a garage door opener. "Are there any notations on the file that might explain what the device might be used for?" asked Arnie, looking over Lewis' shoulder.

"I assume, opening a garage door." Arnie nodded, and then Lewis pointed to something at the bottom left of the screen. "It says 91% RDX, 5.3% Sebacate, 2.1% Polyisobutylene and 1.6% Motor oil."

"Does that mean anything to you?"

Lewis shook his head and smiled, "I failed chemistry too."

"Could you print that file out for me?"

"What does this have to do with that reporter getting murdered?"

"I wish I knew. This is all confidential for now, but that disk was recovered from the reporter's house. Something he'd been working on. Something that might have got him killed." They watched as the dot matrix printer started to work.

"Once this is done, you best be getting out of here," said Lewis. "If I don't get those drawings done, by this afternoon, Beatrice Brown," he said, nodding to the outer office. "She's the managing partner," he said, gulping. "She's going to have my balls."

Chapter 7

After the waitress brought our salads, Arnie explained what Lewis had found. We were at the Friendship Diner, a place that Gabriel and Ben frequented regularly.

"What do you think about the drawings for the remote control?" I asked.

"I'd like to show the drawing to someone I know at Keesler Air Base. Maybe we can swing by tomorrow," he said before taking a bite of his salad.

"How does this all relate to Hartley Green?" I took a sip of water, waiting for Arnie to confirm my thoughts.

"One possible theory would be that someone found out he had this disk, and didn't want to read about it in the paper."

"What about Adrienne Green, where do you think she is?"

"That's a mystery. My guess is that she was out at the time and came home to find her husband. Maybe she even saw the killer. She could be holed up somewhere too scared to come out of hiding."

We finished our salads, likely both thinking about the danger of possessing something that might have gotten someone killed. "I think we had better turn over the disk to the Sheriff," said Arnie, leaving a few bills on the table.

"Thanks for lunch. I'm okay with giving the Sheriff the disk, but I'd like to keep the copy of the list until we know what we're dealing with." As we headed out to the van, I added, "Do you think we can stop by my church? When I call Mom later, I know she's going to ask me whether I attended Christmas mass."

* * *

The sign in front of the Bay Vista Baptist Church read, 'Our Lifeguard Walks on Water.' "Thanks for the lift Arnie, I won't be long," I said as I got out of the van. The front door of the church opened to a large room with chairs, neatly arranged theatre style in front of a communion table. After taking a seat at the back, I thought about my family. *Is Jacob a homosexual? If he is, should he keep it from our parents? Is it time for them to live in a retirement home? What if that means they'd have to live apart?*

My rambling musings were interrupted by a handsome man wearing a gray tunic approaching me from the front. As he reached my row, he smiled at me, "Welcome to God's house."

"Thank you. You're Reverend McGloyn, aren't you?" I stood up. He was tall and had a kind face. His salt and pepper hair suggested he was north of fifty.

"Yes, I am," his eyes squinted, "Are you a member of our church?"

"Yes, my name is Rachel Henderson. I'm sorry, I don't come as often as I should."

"That's all right, Rachel. Only the Lord keeps score." There was an awkward moment of silence before I asked if he had time to talk. "Of course, why don't you come to my office?"

* * *

"Rachel Henderson," the Reverend said as we sat down. "I see you wear no wedding ring."

"I'm not married."

Reverend McGloyn nodded. "Do you know the origins and meaning of your name, Rachel?"

"I think at one time my mother might have told me. She's an elder of the church up in Jackson where they live."

The Reverend looked impressed. "Rachel was the wife of Jacob and the mother of Joseph and Benjamin. She's described in the Bgible as petulant, peevish, and self-willed." McGloyn looked closely at me, gauging my interest in the topic. "Now, I'm guessing you're not here for a bible class. What would you like to talk about?"

I told him about what was happening with my parents. He listened intently before asking me what I thought God would want me to do. "I think he would want me to talk to them. He'd want me to be honest."

"Honest and compassionate?"

"Yes, of course."

"Relinquishing control is a difficult thing to do, especially for a man. You might want to involve someone from the church to give them spiritual guidance."

"Good idea, Reverend McGloyn."

"Please call me Sean. You know Rachel, I believe that most people are more aware of their circumstances than we might think. Sometimes they just need to ask The Lord for the courage to act. Was there anything else you wanted to discuss?"

I was tempted to bring up my brother's situation, but I couldn't remember the current views of the church on homosexuality. Finally, I decided to brave the real question that had brought me. "Sean, I work at a detective agency. In the course of an investigation, I happened to have seen a list of names and addresses. It concerned what happened recently with that reporter. The one that was killed."

The Reverend looked at me, his eyes wide with interest. "And?"

"Well, I happened to notice your name was on this list."

"My name?" A cloud came over the Reverend's face. "What's the nature of this list?"

"See, that's the thing, it has many names, and at this point, I don't know the connection. There are several politicians and business leaders on the list. One name that stood out to me was our former Mayor, John Baxter."

"Oh my. And are you thinking there is something nefarious about this list?"

"I don't know what to think."

"Where is it? Let me see the list," he demanded.

I saw that something had changed in his face, and made a split-second decision not to show him the list. "I gave it to the Sheriff."

Reverend McGloyn's face relaxed, and his smile returned. "You probably saw a list of community leaders. My name is often on such lists. Usually, it's to get my support for some worthwhile cause. If I were you, I wouldn't give it a second thought."

"I won't," I said, getting up. "Thank you for your time Reverend McGloyn." As I was leaving, I turned back to ask a final question. "What percentage of your congregation is white?"

He thought for a moment. "It's blackened a lot over the years. I'd have to check our registry to be sure, but I guess it might be about fifty-fifty now."

* * *

"Hey, you were in there for a while. I hope you said a prayer for me?" Arnie asked as I got in the van.

"Sorry, I got talking to Reverend McGloyn. Remember, I said I recognized his name on the list?"

"Ah, so this wasn't just about missing mass."

"Yes, but he wasn't much help."

"How was he when you brought up the list?

"At first, when I was telling him about my parents, he was all churchy like you'd expect. But then I told him about finding the list with his name on it, and his manner changed. He got really serious and demanded to see the list. There was something … I can't explain it, but I decided not to show it to him. When I told him I gave it to the Sheriff, he seemed to recover and said it was probably someone making a list of donors to various charities."

"Do you believe that?"

"No. Plus, he said something odd as I was leaving. I asked about the racial makeup of the congregation, and he said it had 'Blackened a lot over the years."

Arnie nodded and then looked at his watch. "Strange expression. You know it's almost 4 o'clock, and you must be working on adrenaline. How about I make you dinner, and you turn in early?"

"Sounds wonderful. I'm tired, and it's been a long day."

When we arrived at the apartment, Arnie went to work on supper while I picked up a purring Bourbon and settled in to call Jacob at work.

When he answered, I explained that something had happened at The Agency, requiring me to return home.

"That's too bad. I was looking forward to telling you all about my shit job."

"So, it's a lab thing. Do you get to wear one of those white coats?"

"Yeah, but that doesn't make up for the rest."

"What do you mean?"

"Never mind."

"Talk to me, Jacob." Ever since we were kids, Jacob had a habit of saying something controversial and then making me tease it out of him.

Jacob lowered his voice, "I'm bored with the work, and my supervisor isn't helping." Jacob let out a big sigh. "He's been hitting on me, making me feel uncomfortable. It's nothing I can't handle, but when I told him I wasn't into it, he started treating me…like, I was like one of the lab specimens. But Sis, none of this matters because I applied for a new job at another lab. They do real science over there, processing DNA samples."

"DNA, isn't that what they use for paternity testing?"

"It stands for deoxyribonucleic acid. DNA mapping is a technique developed in the sixties by some guys up in Cambridge. Think of it as a genetic fingerprint. The uses go way beyond paternity testing and are almost limitless."

"Is your supervisor going to give you a recommendation?"

"He said he would. I think he's embarrassed about what happened and would like to see me gone."

"Good luck, I hope you get it."

"If I do, you'll be seeing me more often as the lab is in Mobile."

"Really? That would be wonderful. Call me and let me know. Before I let you go, do you think Mom and Dad are getting worse?"

Jacob started to chuckle. "Mom thinks Dad is past his best-before date. Dad, of course, refuses to see a doctor. They're constantly sniping at each other, but that's not new. I think he knows he's not right, but he's scared. A couple of weeks ago, I took him for lunch, and on the way home, we stopped by a nursing home Mom had mentioned. He freaked out and started yelling at people. He called it Auschwitz, and demanded that Jews be liberated."

I ended the call feeling more uneasy about my parents' situation. I took a deep breath and dialed my parent's telephone number. As usual, Mom answered. Dad had long since given up using the phone, thinking there was a link between phone usage and Alzheimer's. "Hi Mother," I repeated the excuse I'd given to Jacob.

"That's too bad, dear. We aren't getting any younger, you know. There may not be many Christmas dinners left."

"I'm going to try to get up there in the new year," I replied, trying to deflect the guilt trip she was laying on me.

"That would be nice, dear. Did you make time for Christmas services?" Her question hung in the air for a moment.

"Yes, I went today. I actually spoke to the Reverend. How's Dad?" I asked, wanting to change the subject before Mom started asking about scriptures.

"Not well. I told your brother that he's slipping into Kooksville. You know how hard I work to clean up after him, to cook for him. And I never get a thank you."

"I know Mother," I wanted to say living with an elderly person can be difficult, but I didn't want to risk my mother thinking I was referring to her.

"He bought a gun, you know."

"Gun? What kind of gun? Who would sell him a gun?" I asked, my voice rising with concern.

"Rachel dear, sometimes you can be so naive. If you've got money, you can get a gun at the corner store. I've been hiding the ammunition in my jewelry box."

"Why does Dad think he needs a gun?"

"Because of all the Nazis running around."

* * *

Once I had finished the call, I took a long hot shower and put on a pair of pajamas I'd brought from my apartment. When I came out of the bedroom,

I discovered that Arnie had made his famous chili, served with fresh bread right out of the oven.

"Just what the doctor ordered," I said, sitting down at the table. "How will I ever repay you?"

"Gabriel said to keep you safe, and that's what I'm going to do."

I told him about the conversation with Jacob, and then the call to my mother.

"Sounds like you have a lot to deal with."

"Reverend McGloyn suggested that I be honest and compassionate about how I feel. We can't have my father brandishing a gun and thinking there are Nazis everywhere."

Arnie nodded. "Sounds like something that you and your brother should do together, and for everyone's sake, sooner rather than later."

"Jacob said he freaked out when they went to check out a home. He'll get his back up."

"I understand. It must be hard when you realize that you're starting to slip. The thought of going into a home can be scary. My dad passed away before we had to deal with that. I think if it were me, I'd start by telling him how worried I was and reassure him that he doesn't need to make any rash decisions. A good first step might be for him to talk this over with his doctor. Maybe that's a middle ground that would be acceptable to him."

"That's good advice, Arnie." Bourbon startled us by jumping onto a spare chair. His eyes were at table level, shifting back and forth between our plates, looking at our food longingly.

"I think I forgot to feed someone," said Arnie.

Chapter 8

The weather called for clear skies and a blustery day with highs in the mid-fifties. I put on a white turtleneck, a tweed jacket, and a pair of navy twill pants.

"This is quite the facility," I said, as Arnie drove up to Keesler's main gate and identified himself. He told the male guard that he had an appointment with Master Sergeant Geiger. After checking his log, the man directed Arnie to park in the visitor lot and go to the main building, where they'd tell him where he could find the master sergeant.

"You never mentioned how you know this man."

"Lucius Geiger is another guy from the neighborhood. We were close when we were in our teens, just when World War 2 was getting started. The U.S. wasn't in the war yet. Geiger lied about his age and went to fight in Spain. He fell off my radar for a while. Later, after Pearl Harbor, the U.S. declared war, and I was swept up along with everyone else and joined the Air Force. I got sent to Keesler for basic training. That's when we reconnected. I was a wet-behind-the-ears airman while he was a technical sergeant working on the planes."

"Did you ever see any combat?"

"No, Lucius pulled some strings once he saw me. He had me transferred to his squad, and I learned how to repair planes."

I thought about my Father and the conversation that morning, "Were you disappointed that you didn't see any action?"

"Sometimes. But in my sane moments, I'd say to myself that I did my part by keeping the planes flying."

✳ ✳ ✳

We were escorted to a small office where a barrel-chested black man was sitting behind a desk. When he looked up and saw Arnie, his face broke into a wide grin. "Airman First Class Simms."

The two friends hugged, and Arnie introduced me as his colleague at the *Eye on You Detective Agency.*

"You know, I got it when you said you were going to work as a building super. I have to admit I didn't see this detective thing coming."

Arnie laughed and asked about Geiger's wife.

"Samantha's fine. She still dyes her hair blonde every month. It'll be thirty years next month. She's put up with me so far, so I guess we're good for another thirty."

The phone on Geiger's desk rang, and a frown came over his face. "Sorry, I have to take this." Geiger listened for a few minutes and then said, "It shouldn't take long." He hung up the phone, shaking his head at us. "President Reagan is coming to visit the troops. Everyone's in a panic."

"We won't keep you," Arnie said. "I know how busy you are." Arnie pulled out the paper copy of the CAD file and handed it to him. Geiger nodded and started examining it.

"I know it says garage door opener," said Arnie. "But I was wondering about the legend in the left corner. Do those chemicals mean anything to you?"

Geiger was silent for a minute before putting the paper down on his desk and looking back and forth between Arnie and myself. "Where did you get this?"

I spoke up and told him about the suitcase and my suspicions about Hartley Green's death.

"I heard about Green. My advice is to surrender this drawing to the authorities. It's material evidence of a crime and an even worse crime being planned."

"What do you mean, Luc?" Arnie leaned forward.

"It's called C-4. It's a chemical explosive with roots going back to World War 2. The British originally came up with it, and it went through various improvements to make it more stable. There's C-2,

C-3, and then C-4. It has the consistency of modeling clay. You can set fire to it, throw it against a building, stomp on it, and nothing will happen. But, and it's a big but, attach a detonator to it, and lookout. They use something called an RE factor. It stands for Relative Effectiveness. C-4 has an RE a third more powerful than TNT. Someone is planning to blow up something big."

✳ ✳ ✳

It was a hub of activity when we walked into the lobby of the Harrison County Sheriff Department. I stepped forward and approached an older woman at the front desk. "I'd like to speak to the Sheriff."

"Ya'll have an appointment?" She looked past me and spoke to Arnie. "This place is a zoo today."

"No, Ma'am, but we have information about the murder of Hartley Green. I think the Sheriff will want to talk to us." Arnie handed her his card.

She spent a few moments staring at his card and then looked at me. "Deputy Sheriff Weber is assigned to that case. Can he help you?"

"No," we replied in unison.

"Let me see if Sheriff Pardy will spare you a few minutes. Please have a seat."

Once we were seated in the waiting area, I leaned over and whispered, "I've decided that I don't like Deputy Weber. He's so by the book. Plus, he's always looking down at me. You know how some men don't take women seriously? Like we're trespassing on their turf."

"You don't get that vibe from me, do you?"

"No, just the opposite. You're the protective type. You're always bending over backward to prop me up and make me feel good about myself."

Arnie deflected the compliment. "What do you think about what Lucius had to say?"

"I'm scared. I'm glad we're turning the disk over to the Sheriff. I'm convinced that this is the reason Green was killed."

We waited the better part of twenty minutes before the woman ushered us into an empty interview room. After another few minutes, a big-bellied man wearing a Sheriff's uniform waddled in, followed by Weber. "Good morning, folks, sorry to keep you waiting, but you can imagine how hectic it is today." He held up Arnie's card and squinted as if having difficulty reading it. "Arnie Simms, private investigator. Well, that's just fine. Now how can we help you two?"

I spoke up first. "As I'm sure Weber has already told you, I have what I believe is evidence material to the investigation of Hartley Green's murder." Deputy Weber moved uncomfortably in his seat, avoiding eye contact with me. "I spoke to Weber last night, and he was less than helpful."

"Deputy Weber is one of our smartest," replied Sheriff Pardy, a perplexed look on his face.

"That doesn't speak highly for the department," I replied. "I've met tree stumps that are smarter. I had dealings with him regarding the Mardi Gras killer. He was less than cooperative."

The Sheriff waved the comment off like he was swapping at a fly. "I understand you have a suitcase."

"I did, but it was picked up from my hotel room after I called Mr. Big Brain here. He said he was going to call Hinds County." I turned to face Weber. "So, who did you call?" Sheriff Pardy turned to Deputy Weber with a questioning look.

"I called Hinds, but because it was late, I left a message with dispatch." He looked over at Pardy, "I followed up this morning and was told that by the time they went out to the hotel, Miss Henderson had already checked out."

Pardy then looked at me. "You don't have the suitcase?"

"A man came to the hotel and said he was sent to pick it up. I assumed Boy Gnius here sent him, and I gave him the suitcase."

"Let's dispense with the name-calling, Miss. You assumed?" asked the Sheriff. I rolled my eyes and nodded. "Did this man look like a Hinds County policeman?"

"Not really."

"What was his name?"

"Gordie, Gordie Howe." A smile flashed across the Sheriff's face.

"Did he have identification?"

"I didn't ask, but I could give you a pretty good description of him."

"Okay, let's see how observant you are."

"He was big. I mean, tall. He had greasy brown hair. His face was kind of rat-like, and he had rotten teeth. He was wearing a Minnie Mouse t-shirt that was way too small for him, and blue jeans. Oh, and he was driving an old pickup truck."

"And you gave a man like that the suitcase?" Sheriff Pardy shook his head.

"I probably shouldn't have. I'm sorry, it was late, and I was scared."

"So, you don't have this evidence that you think is going to help with our investigation?" asked Weber.

I ignored him and pulled the floppy out of my purse. I slid it across the table to the Sheriff. "I was looking in the suitcase and found a rip in the lining. In it, I found this floppy disk. Because the guy was so creepy, I held it back. I think it's important."

Sheriff Pardy picked up the baggie and squinted at the floppy. He held it up to the lights as if he would be able to read it. "What's on this?"

"We don't know," Arnie said quickly. The Sheriff looked at Arnie. "We don't have a computer," Arnie explained.

"If you believe this is material to what happened to Green, you must have an idea what's on it."

Both Arnie and I shrugged in unison.

The Sheriff leaned back in his chair. The buttons on his shirt were ready to pop from the strain of his protruding stomach. He stared at Arnie, then turned to Weber, "Anything to add?"

"Yes," a smug look appearing Deputy Weber's face. "Last night, she told me that she knew there had been a lot of blood at the crime scene. Since we still had not released any information to the media, I asked her how she knew about the blood. She refused to tell me."

Sheriff Pardy turned to me, a questioning look on his face. When I ignored him, he turned back to Weber, "Deputy, I want you to take Miss Henderson's written statement. Next, I want her to sit with a sketch artist. Show her some mugshots; maybe she'll recognize this …rat-faced man." The Sheriff got up to leave. At the door, he turned back to me, "Thank you for coming in. I'd like to give you a bit of advice. I know you're in the investigation business, but we have it now, and despite your opinion of Deputy Weber, most of us are pretty good."

❊ ❊ ❊

It was after 2 PM by the time that Arnie and I walked out of the Harrison County Sheriff's Department. "I hope I never have to look at another mugshot."

"When you were going through all the books, I was thinking to myself if I was going to arrange a murder, I wouldn't use local talent. I bet our guy's in some database somewhere, just not here," Arnie suggested.

"You think we should contact the MBI or the Feds?"

"That probably wouldn't be well received by the Sheriff. I think he was pretty clear. Besides, we learned recently that the Feds are reticent to get involved unless the local authorities make a request." Arnie drove towards downtown Gulfport and our appointment with Rod Smith and his client. "When we were talking to Sheriff Pardy, I was tempted to tell him what was on the disk."

"Why didn't you?" I asked.

"Just a feeling. That guy didn't just show up at your motel room looking for the suitcase. Someone told him your room number. What happens if the killer finds out that you not only know what's on the disk but that you kept a copy?"

Chapter 9

Rod Smith's office was in Legacy Towers, the tallest building in Gulfport. The same building that Hollis Huntley had fallen to his death from last summer. Since Huntley had been prepared to give testimony against Mayor Baxter, everyone at the Agency had thought his death was suspicious. Deputy Weber had maintained that there was insufficient evidence to press charges because a poker chip was found on the dead man, and a witness had said that Huntley was seen losing heavily at Lucky's Casino. Hollis Huntley's death had been ruled a suicide.

As Arnie and I rode up to the fifth floor in the elevator, I asked about Rod Smith's client.

"You know as much as I do. The client wants to sue someone for lots of money over a paternity issue. Our job will be to help Rod prove it."

We followed the plush carpeting off the elevator to an oak door with a brass nameplate announcing the occupant, Rodney J. Smith, Attorney at Law. "Kind of beats the handwritten sign I taped to the agency's front door," remarked Arnie as he opened the door.

We were met by an attractive African American woman introducing herself as Emma Lawrence, Mr. Smith's associate. "Mr. Smith will be with you in a moment. In the meantime, please have a seat. Can I get anyone a coffee?"

We respectfully declined. While Arnie took a seat in the waiting area, I walked over to a picture window with a view of the parking lot. I looked up and then down as if expecting a body to fall at any moment. I winced at the thought of Huntley hitting the sidewalk below.

Rod Smith came out of an office and greeted his old friend with a warm handshake. "Thanks for coming Arnie, the client will be here soon," he said, looking at his watch.

"You remember Rachel Henderson, my associate?"

"Of course, welcome to my office. Let's go inside where we'll be more comfortable."

Once we were seated, Arnie thanked Rod for the referral.

"You know, that business last summer with Charles Bouvier, the families of the missing girls ditched their representation and agreed to my services. I would never have had that business if it wasn't for your agency's fine work."

"Anything else you can tell us before the client gets here?" I asked.

"He was a walk-in. He saw my name in connection with the award the families received." Smith opened a thin legal file in front of him. "His name is Michael Boyle, and he lives in town. I'll let him tell you the story, rather than spoil it for you. I'd like your take." Once again, Rod looked at his watch just as his secretary announced that Mr. Boyle had arrived.

A couple of moments later, a tall man dressed in jeans with a tweed sports jacket and wearing Reeboks, came in. "Mr. Boyle, nice to see you again. Let me introduce you to my associates, Mr. Arnie Simms and Miss Rachel Henderson. They're from the detective agency we discussed."

The client shook hands and then took a seat in front of Rod's desk. As he sat down, he mentioned that he had read favorable things about Gabriel Ross. "I was kind of hoping to meet him."

I spoke up and smiled at him. "Gabriel is away…taking a break from the day-to-day running of the business. In the meantime, we're looking after things, both here and in New Orleans."

Boyle shifted uneasily in his chair. After a moment, he nodded and turned to Rod.

"I'm going to let you tell your story in your own words," said Rod. "They'd like to hear everything from you."

"Well, my name is Michael or Mike Boyle. I go by both. I approached Mr. Smith to help me sue the richest man in Mississippi." He paused for effect before I gestured for him to continue. "My mother passed last year from throat cancer. There wasn't much money; however, before she died, she told me that the scumbag I thought was my father, wasn't. She said when I was conceived, she had been having sex with several men. A dozen, according to her. One of these men is my real father."

"Was the man you thought was your father, one of these dozen men?" asked Arnie, who had started taking notes on a legal pad.

"His name is Owen Boyle, or maybe I should say his name was Owen Boyle, and no, he wasn't part of the team, so to speak. You see, Owen's from a wealthy family and his parents didn't approve of his ... lifestyle." Boyle made a limp wrist gesture before continuing. "He and my mother met in the bar where she shook her tits, and they hatched up a plan. They got married. Strictly a marriage for appearances, and to keep his name from being scratched out of the will. Meanwhile, Mommy Dear got knocked up by someone else on the team, and nine months later, I was born."

"You said his name <u>was</u> Owen. Did he die?" I asked.

"I have no idea, and I don't care. You see, the marriage of convenience was fine, but Mr. Boyle never signed up for both a nagging, sleazy wife and me, a screaming baby. He told his parents to go to blazes and left town with his homo. I haven't heard from him since."

"I don't get something, Mr. Boyle," said Arnie looking at his notes, "You said you wanted Mr. Smith's help in proving your paternity. If you already know Owen couldn't be your father, then what would be the point of suing his parents?"

"I couldn't give a damn about the Boyles. I want to find my real birth father."

"One of the other members of the football team," I offered, catching on.

"Yes, but I've narrowed it down. You see, when Candy or as I called her, Momsy finally coughed out her last breath, I had to look after her shit. I found a diary that mentions a man around the time I was conceived. Have you heard of Corbin Masters?"

"The lumber guy that owns most of the trees north of Biloxi," replied Arnie.

Mike Boyle snapped his fingers. "Daddy."

"But how do you know it wasn't one of the others?" I asked, trying to keep the skepticism out of my voice.

"Because I have this picture," Boyle said slowly, enunciating each word. He reached into his briefcase and put two photos on the desk. One was a file photo of an elderly Corbin Masters, shaking hands with then-Mayor Baxter. Beside it, he put a driver's license photo of himself that had been enlarged. "You see what I mean?"

Arnie and I took turns looking at the two photos. The two men looked nothing alike. The client had a long thin nose, almost aquiline with an average chin. Master's nose was short and pudgy, and he had a protruding jaw. We shared a look. The client picked up both photos and held them up on either side of his face. "You see what I mean, right?"

"You're a tall man, Mr. Boyle. You must be six foot two," said Arnie. "Looking at this picture of Mr. Masters, he's much shorter."

"I get my height from my mother."

"How old is Corbin Masters?" Arnie asked.

"That's the thing. It's the reason I'm bringing this forward. He's 76, and I'm told he is not in good health."

"And how old are you?" I asked, cluing in on where Arnie was going.

"I'm 29 years old."

"And how old was your mother when she died?"

"She was 45. She'd have been 46 next month."

"So, you were conceived when she was 16?" I asked.

"And Masters would have been 47," added Arnie, looking over at Rod. "That would have been in 1956."

For a moment, there was silence in the room. Finally, I spoke up, "This is relatively straightforward. Corbin Masters does a DNA test, and that'll prove it once and for all.

"DNA," repeated Boyle.

"Yeah, it stands for …I don't know what it stands for, but some genius came up with it the sixties as a way of comparing genetic fingerprints," I explained.

Again, the room was enveloped in silence. Boyle finally spoke up, "I know what DNA is. The problem is he won't do it. At least not according to his two creepy kids. Andrew and Elizabeth live with him. Since their mother is out of the picture, they stand to inherit everything. They don't want to split their nest egg with me."

"But have you spoken to Masters? I mean, with your dad?" I asked.

"Yes, and I've written to him. I've offered to pay for the test. I have had other lawyers write to him. I have been thrown off that property more times than I care to remember."

* * *

When Boyle finally left, Rod looked at Arnie. "Judging by your expression, you don't buy it."

"Just because the guy's rich, and Masters' name is in the diary … that hardly makes him the father."

"What do you think, Rachel?" asked Rod.

"Did you see the pictures? Masters has more in common with Jay Leno."

"I hear you." Rod leaned back in his chair and closed his eyes, a pained expression on his face. "Are you guys going to turn this down?"

Arnie was about to respond when I jumped in. "We'll give it our best shot, but we get paid even if it turns out that Masters isn't his father."

"Absolutely, he's already given me a retainer."

* * *

"I don't know, Boyle seemed a little sketchy to me," Arnie said as we got on the elevator.

I smiled at Arnie and pressed the button for the first floor. "You have Rod's cheque for the retainer, and you heard him say, it doesn't matter what we prove."

"Right, but we have to prove something. You can't force him to take a paternity test. Do you have any other way to prove it?" I shrugged, and he continued, "A notation in a diary is not sufficient grounds for the courts to compel him to take a DNA test," When I didn't reply, Arnie's eyes squinted suspiciously. "You have a plan? Don't you?"

"It's not fully thought out."

As the elevator opened to the lobby, Arnie struggled to keep up, "Even if you go through all of Mommy Dearest's papers and find Corbin Masters' name a dozen times, and even if you find a polaroid of them having sex, it won't prove he's the father."

"Of course it won't."

"Then how are you going to prove it? I don't want to let Rod down."

"That's the part I haven't fully worked out yet. But don't worry, Arnie." Arnie stood in the parking lot, clearly wondering what I was planning. When I was getting into the van, I turned around and called out to him. "Are you coming? We need to earn that retainer."

Chapter 10

On the way across town, I was deep in thought and answering Arnie's questions with one-word answers, so he turned on the radio. The local station was carrying a live broadcast from City Hall, where Sheriff Pardy was giving an update on the Hartley Green murder.

"While there are details about the homicide that I cannot divulge at this time, the key points are that a reporter of the *Biloxi Herald* was found murdered on Christmas morning. There's no question that foul play was involved. A potential witness has come forward with a description of a suspect we are calling a person of interest." I looked over at Arnie, a look of satisfaction on my face.

"The man we are looking for is colored, and there is credible evidence that the Greens might have been having marital troubles. We have put out an all-points bulletin on a 1984 silver Mercedes, license plate PHP 578, belonging to Adrienne Green. Mrs. Green has not been seen or heard from since Christmas Day. Anyone seeing this vehicle or having information concerning this matter is asked to contact our department. At this point, I am prepared to answer a couple of questions."

Arnie looked over at me and saw my mouth wide open in shock.

"Peter Benz, Eyewitness News. Sheriff Pardy, have you labeled this a hate crime, and if so, have you been notified of the FBI's involvement?"

"At this point, there is no reason to believe this has anything to do with race. So, no need to involve the FBI."

"Sheriff, just a follow-up," said Benz. "I mention race because the Greens were in a mixed-race marriage, and you said you have a person of interest who is also colored."

"At this point, we don't even know whether the person of interest is involved. It's too soon to speculate about motives and whether this has anything to do with race."

"Candy Morrow from the *Herald*. Sheriff, speaking of labeling, Hartley Green recently wrote that Hollis Huntley, the man who died after a fall from the Legacy Towers building, was likely thrown to his death by someone wanting to silence his testimony. Your office had labeled his death a suicide."

"I was on administrative leave last summer. I have since looked into Mr. Huntley's death, and there was no credible evidence to support homicide, but there was evidence that he had lost heavily that day at a local casino. That's all the time I have for questions. I will update you as more is learned."

Arnie looked over at me. I was still in shock. In the space of a few hours, everything that I had told the Sheriff had been discounted.

"You never mentioned that Mr. Rat-Face was black."

"Because he wasn't. If anything, he was a redneck. Sheriff Pardy is going out of his way to make this seem like Adrienne Green killed her husband."

"Listen, you have a mixed marriage, which until recently was illegal in Mississippi. You have the wife gone missing. You have a witness who says they saw a black man. There are rumors of an affair…I'm starting to believe it myself."

"That's exactly it, Arnie. You're supposed to believe it," I was angry about the elaborate attempt to pin the murder on Adrienne Green. "Let me ask you a question, Arnie. To what lengths is Sheriff Pardy willing to go to avoid having the FBI sticking their nose into everything?"

"I don't know that I follow."

"If this was ruled a hate crime, then the FBI would be here in no time."

The point hung in the air as Arnie turned into the parking lot of the Trade Winds. As we were getting out, I grabbed Arnie's arm. "Before I forget, there's one more name on the list that we should discuss. It didn't register until I heard it from Boyle."

Arnie looked over at me, waiting.

"Corbin Masters."

* * *

"What should we do about this?" I asked as we walked into the apartment building.

"Not sure there's much that we can do. Sheriff Pardy is in charge of the investigation. We've turned over the evidence to him."

I gave Arnie a disbelieving look. "I'd like to talk to this eye witness. Find out if someone put her up to saying what she said."

"Stay out of it. I know you're upset. Why don't you concentrate on how to get Masters to agree to a paternity test?"

I stood in silence as we rode up the elevator. I wondered if Arnie could hear my teeth grinding.

"Can you get past this?" He asked me as the elevator door opened.

"I don't know."

"I'm starving. I have a surprise for you tonight. Maybe that'll help."

* * *

A couple of minutes later, we walked into Arnie's apartment and immediately smelled the sweet odor of cooking coming from the kitchen. Grace stuck her head out of the kitchen, "Your timing is perfect as usual honey. The lasagna you ordered is just about done."

"Lasagna…oh, you are too good to me, Arnie. How did you arrange this?"

"When you were in the shower this morning, I made a couple of calls. Invited a couple of friends…"

"And you kept this secret all day." I playfully slapped his shoulder. "Wait a minute, you said a couple of friends. You didn't invite Kittyburg?"

As if on cue, Travis Franklin came out of the kitchen carrying a bowl of Caesar salad. "Hey, Rach, I hope you're hungry."

"Travis, I didn't know you were a cook." The sixteen-year-old boy was wearing an apron with a picture of a fat tabby cat and the slogan "God, if you can't make me thin, then make my friends fat."

"I love the apron," said Arnie.

"Mom gave it to me for Christmas. I've become a pretty good cook. Mom calls me Master Chef Travis."

"This is a very nice surprise, Arnie. Thank you!" I hugged him. "After what happened in the last couple of days, I need some friends."

✳ ✳ ✳

Travis did the honors and served the lasagna, while Grace poured red wine into everyone's glass. Arnie clinked his glass and said, "A toast everyone…

To good friends, good health, and no more days like we've had recently." While we ate, Arnie and I took turns, bringing Travis and Grace up to date on what had happened since the discovery of the suitcase.

When we finished the story, Travis said he only had two questions. "It sounds like the Sheriff doesn't believe that the suitcase has anything to do with the case. Why are you so sure it does?"

"Call it intuition. Travis, if you could see that man at the motel looking for me. He was frightening. That's not the anger you get from losing a suitcase. So, if it's about the disk, then that tells me it has to be important. We're pretty sure that one of the files on the disk had the ingredients on how to make a bomb."

"Okay, fair enough. Your intuition is good enough for me. Next question, why would Sheriff Pardy lie about all this and say it was a marital problem?"

"I don't know. Arnie and I talked about that earlier. A skeptic might say he doesn't want this to be classed as a hate crime because that means the Feds."

Arnie spoke up. "Or, it could simply be, he's getting bad information from someone."

"Too bad Don's not around. We could use his help on this," said Travis.

"I should give him a call tomorrow. I was going to surprise him when I was up in Jackson. But with everything that happened, I had to leave in a hurry."

"Do you remember when he called the Agency looking for you last summer? Everyone was out looking for the Mardi Gras killer, so I had to take a message. He was totally plastered, but he called because he cared about you and had a lead." Travis started laughing. "He kept going on and on about how much he wuvs you."

"Thanks for the memory, Travis."

The ensuing laughter was interrupted by the sound of the phone ringing. Arnie answered, and a few moments later, asked, "Everything okay?" He listened for a minute then said, "We've had a full day, I'll let Rachel fill you in." He then held the phone out to me. "It's Gabriel."

I brought Gabriel up to speed with what happened. When I was done, he asked how safe I felt. "I'm alright; I admit, yesterday I was a little unsure of myself and a little out of my depth. But today, with Arnie's help, and the company of some good friends, I'm catching my second wind. What about you Gabriel, did you speak to the DA?"

"Ben and I had a conference call with her this afternoon. She's insisting that we stay away until our testimony is required. The trial judge has ordered a delay for a week. That's why I'm calling. If we stay up here, I won't be able to stop worrying about you," his voice trembled before he added, "It sounds like you're in the middle of something down there."

I was silent for a moment, processing everything. Then I said firmly, "Stay up there, Gabriel, we have this."

"Call me if you need help, and I'll be on the first plane home. Are you still going to open the agency on Monday?"

"Absolutely, I have to start putting some business on the books. How's everyone up there?"

"We took Benjamin for a sleigh ride today. It's beautiful up here. It's kind of the best of both worlds. We're spending a lot of quality time with him, but when he starts getting fussy, they have an excellent babysitting service, so the four of us can go out."

"Jacqueline must be missing it here?"

"Nope. Well, maybe her parents, but they talk every day." Jacqueline was originally from Chicago, and her parents had moved to Biloxi once they retired. I told Gabriel about the client interview and that Corbin Masters was believed to be the father.

"Not sure how you get a guy like Corbin Masters to take a paternity test if he doesn't want to."

"That's just it. We need him to want to take the test."

Chapter 11

"Thank you again for a lovely evening last night," I said the following morning to Arnie and Grace as I sat down at the kitchen table. "After the last few days, my mood was getting pretty scary. It was good to unwind and have a few laughs."

"Don't be too hard on yourself, Rachel," said Grace. "I can't imagine what kind of a wreck I'd be if I had gone through everything that you did."

"Thanks, Grace."

"What would you like to do today?" Arnie asked, pouring the coffee.

"Before he left last night, I told Travis I'd see him sometime this morning at the Agency. You know Arnie, you've been wonderful, but I think it'll be okay to go home today. I haven't bought groceries in ages, I have laundry to do, and I want to start researching Corbin Masters."

* * *

The temperature wasn't expected to rise above 40°F. I borrowed Arnie's lumberjack coat and wore it over a polo shirt and Jordache jeans. Arnie and I got in the van, and I told him about a call I had made after breakfast. "I called the number Don gave me for his office at the MBI. I guess it was all this talk last night with Travis. I wanted to explain why I didn't stay in Jackson as I'd planned. Anyway, the call was answered by someone named Fred. He told me that Don no longer worked at the MBI. It kind of took me by surprise, and I told him that there had to be a mistake as Don was up for a big promotion. All the man said he could tell me was that Don hadn't got the promotion, and hadn't taken it very well. He said Don quit to get a 'real job.'"

"A real job?"

"That's what he said."

"You'd think he would tell you if he was going to leave the MBI."

"Any normal boyfriend would. This Fred guy said I should forget about Don and get a 'real' boyfriend."

"Might not be a bad idea."

✳ ✳ ✳

My apartment was on the 8th floor of a building in Gulfport, not far from the *Eye on You Detective Agency*. We stopped to pick up a few staples, and Arnie insisted on carrying them up to the apartment.

As we were walking down the hallway, Arnie stopped suddenly. "Your door's open," he whispered, gently pushing me behind him. He paused at the door and put the groceries down. We shared a look as we stood on either side of the doorway. There was no sound coming from the apartment. Arnie nudged the door open and looked into the living room. Shaking his head, he nodded to the living room. I peeked around the corner. The place had been thrashed. Books were on the floor; pillows were cut open, and a framed photo of my family lay smashed on the floor.

"Somebody's here," Arnie whispered as we stepped into the apartment. We crept into the hallway. The noise was coming from the bedroom. As we entered the room, we saw a man with his back turned to us, holding something in his hands. "Hands up, I have a gun," shouted Arnie.

The man held one hand up, "I'm just going to put this down, okay?"

When the man turned, we saw Don Kittyburg holding a photo album. "What the hell?" I noticed my mattress had been flipped and cut open. Most of my clothes were pulled out of the dresser and scattered across the floor.

"Listen, it's not what you think. I went to the agency and saw your note that it was closed for the holidays, so I came here looking for you. I found the door open."

"Why should we believe you?" asked Arnie.

"Because I'm telling you the truth. By the way, where's the gun?"

"A little lie, something that you're familiar with."

"What were you doing with my photo album?" I asked, looking at the album Don had put on the dresser.

"I came in and saw your place had been tossed. I wanted to make sure whoever did this didn't take your photos."

I frowned and then glared at Don, "I don't believe you. I haven't heard from you in two weeks, and just when my apartment gets vandalized, you show up, looking for photographs?"

"I've called you just about every day…. I didn't do this," he said, his mouth gaping. "I found the door open and the apartment empty. What were they looking for, Rachel?"

"It doesn't concern you," I said, giving Don a once over. He was wearing a ball cap, a turtle neck, and jeans. "You're not even an MBI agent anymore."

Don ignored the answer. "Who did this? Are you in danger?"

When I didn't answer, Don turned to Arnie. "Is she in danger, Arnie?"

It was Arnie's turn to ignore him. He turned to me, "I think we'd better call the police."

Continuing to ignore Don, I replied, "I think that's a good idea. I'll call Sheriff Pardy."

"What's this all about?" I could hear Don ask Arnie after I had left the bedroom. "I'm not leaving until I get answers." I could hear their conversation continue while I was on the phone in the living room.

"You're not with the MBI anymore?" asked Arnie.

"It was time for a change. I was thinking about getting a real job. I have an interview today with a company down here."

"It sounds like you got poopy pants over not getting that promotion and quit in a huff."

"Nah, I was planning on leaving anyway. The new job is going to be great."

"Yeah, what kind of job is it?"

"It's working for a local company - a seafood company. It's a ground floor kind of thing to start, but lots of advancement potential. The great thing is, I'll be close to Rachel."

I came back into the bedroom just in time to see Arnie raise a Spockian eyebrow and nod his head as if he was impressed, but I knew he wasn't. "They're sending a car. Whoever did this, went through everything. Even the cereal boxes in the kitchen." I looked at Arnie uneasily. I turned to pick up some of my clothes off the floor. Holding up a blouse up to my nose, "Arnie, whoever did this urinated on my clothes."

✳ ✳ ✳

"I'm going outside to check the perimeter," said Don nervously, looking at his watch.

Once he left, Arnie put his arm around me, seeing I was upset. "It's going to be alright; I think we'll be roommates for a little bit longer."

"I feel violated. What kind of person would do that to my clothes?"

"Someone who wants you to know it's personal. You know the way Don was acting nervously, looking at his watch, makes me think he didn't want to be here when the cops got here."

"Why do you think that is?"

"I don't know, but it seems odd that he would be here just after the apartment is trashed, and we find him looking at a photograph album. I think a good question is, why was he looking at photographs?"

"I don't follow. What do you mean?"

"I couldn't help notice that there are no photos of him or the two of you in the apartment. You have all kinds of pictures of your family and your friends, but no pictures of him."

"He'd always say he was camera shy. He would hold his hand up every time I wanted a photo. But I surprised him one day when he was on the can, and I took his picture."

"Where do you keep it?"

"In this photo album," I said, picking up the book. "You think he broke in and got into all my stuff because he was embarrassed about that photo?"

"He's kind of guarded about his identity. Maybe there's some reason he doesn't want that picture out there."

I looked through the album, "And, it's not here," I said, looking at Arnie. "He's a bullshitter, and yes, maybe a bit of a sicko, but I can't imagine he would ever urinate on my clothes."

"Tell me what you know about him."

"Everything I know about him, he told me. So, it might all be a load of hooey. Let's see, he told me that he grew up in Natchez. His mom and dad passed away when he was young. He has no brothers or sisters, just an uncle that he talks to on the phone. His driver's license says he's 36. He has a couple of scars, one on his arm and another on his belly. He said he got those when he was in the Marines. Allegedly, he did some work in Cambodia at the end of the war. When he got out of the service, the MBI was expanding, and he was recruited. I met him at a party and then learned that he was working undercover at Huedunit painting investigating the car theft ring."

"Any idea what his real name is?"

"Actually, I peeked in his wallet when he was sleeping. I found his Mississippi driver's license. Don Kittyburg."

"I bet he can get whatever identification he needs. Did you find anything else?"

"Other than a bunch of condoms? No"

✳ ✳ ✳

We were interrupted by Deputy Weber knocking on the apartment door. When I answered, he said. "You should get after the landlord to replace this lock. I'm a Deputy Sheriff, and I'd be able to open it in less than five seconds." He pointed to some markings on the door frame. "Whoever broke in, used a pry bar."

Weber walked into the living room and whistled, "Sure did some damage. Too bad, looks like a nice apartment," he said, looking out the living room window. "How much do you pay in rent?"

"That's not important," I snapped.

Weber ignored the comment. "I live about two streets over, surprised I haven't seen you around the neighborhood." The sound of broken glass made a crunching sound as he stepped into the kitchen. "I see you like Captain Crunch. I'm more of a Fruit Loops kind of guy." I was thinking of a snappy retort when Arnie came out of the bedroom. He nodded to Weber.

"Anything missing?" asked Weber.

"I don't think so," I replied.

"We've seen a lot of this lately. Punks looking for whatever they can pawn to get a fix." He went into the bathroom and started looking through my medicine cabinet. Picking up my birth control pills, he looked like he was doing some mental math. "Yeah, definitely, punks," he said, putting them back.

"I don't have anything worth stealing," I said, feeling my anger mount.

"How would they know until they broke in?"

I looked at Arnie and rolled my eyes. "Whoever did this urinated on my clothes."

"Punks do that. Believe me, I've seen my share. They were probably high on meth."

"Deputy, we both know who did this. And we both know what he was looking for."

Weber shook his head and chuckled, "I knew you'd bring that up. You think the guy with the suitcase you stole, the one with the bloody nose, did this?"

"Oh, my God!" I said, raising my voice. "Listen, I heard your press conference. The man in the sketch was a redneck, not a black man."

"We've decided that what happened to you in Jackson has nothing to do with Green's death. You angered someone when you stole his suitcase. That's it."

"And what about the disk?" I asked my hands on my hips.

"Our techs tell us that it's a list of donors to the Cancer Society."

"At the press conference," said Arnie, "Pardy implied Green's murder was some kind of adultery thing."

"Of course, it is. She was having an affair; a witness identified a black man near her house. And here's a newsflash, we found the wife's Beemer in long term parking at the airport. After she and her lover killed Green, they drove to the airport and took off. We have a warrant out for her arrest."

Chapter 12

Once Weber left, Arnie asked me if I was going to be okay. "I was doing pretty good this morning, but after this, I don't know."

"That's understandable."

I looked around my apartment and started to cry. "This is so frustrating. The cops have it all wrong." I grabbed my purse. "Let's get out of here."

* * *

Back in the van, I said I wanted to make a stop at the *Herald* and pay my respects.

"I didn't know you knew Hartley Green."

"I don't. I want to talk to his boss and find out what he was working on."

"Don't you think it would be wise to let the Sheriff complete his investigation?"

"Seriously, Arnie, do you believe Adrienne Green is responsible for her husband's death, and that the suitcase, the disk, and the rat-faced man are just a big coincidence?"

"No. But I am worried that you are getting mixed up in something dangerous."

* * *

The receptionist was multitasking - chatting on the phone, filing her nails, and smoking a cigarette, all the while ignoring anyone who came to her desk. "I'd like to speak to the editor," I yelled at her.

"Hold for a moment, Agnes." The middle-aged woman with recently dyed black hair held the phone against her big boobs, giving us a frown. "Do you have an appointment?"

"No, we don't. We're here because of an urgent matter involving the murder of Hartley Green," I tossed one of my business cards at her. "Believe me. He'll want to see us." I looked at Arnie, who was wincing at my tone.

"Mr. Bremmer is currently in an important meeting. But I'll see if he can spare a couple of minutes."

When the woman got up from her desk, Arnie whispered, "Tart words make no friends."

I watched as she walked over to a door and knocked. After a brief moment, she entered, closing the door behind her. A couple of minutes later, she stuck her head out of the office. "They'll see you now. Come this way."

When we were escorted into the office, we found a tall bald man with a beard sitting at a desk. He was wearing Levi's and a tie-dyed t-shirt. Facing him was Sheriff Pardy. The bald man stood and smiled as we came into the room.

"Shit," whispered Arnie when he noticed the Sheriff.

"Well come on in, Miss Henderson, Mr. Simms. Join the party," said Pardy, not getting up. "We were just here discussing that very matter that we talked about yesterday."

"Have a seat, folks," the bearded man gestured to a couple of chairs. He extended his hand and introduced himself as Larry Bremmer.

Once everyone was seated, "Now, Miss," said the Sheriff. "Was there something you neglected to tell me yesterday?"

"No. No, I uh,"

"You know I distinctly remember giving you some advice."

Arnie jumped in, "We wanted to offer our condolences to Mr. Bremmer on the tragic passing of one of the paper's best reporters. I've lived in this city for a long time, and Hartley Green was very respected. After having read the articles last summer about our investigation into the Mardi Gras Killer, I felt I had come to know Mr. Green."

There was a moment of silence as everyone waited for more. "I believe you told the receptionist that you had something urgent to discuss involving the murder of Hartley Green," said Pardy.

"It is, in a way… I mean, we wanted to express our condolences, and I…wanted to give you my card in case you ever need our services."

Once again, there was another awkward moment before Bremmer said, "That's very nice of you, folks. I appreciate your kind words. What type of services do you specialize in?"

"We do a lot of reference checks for new employees. We do investigative work for some local lawyers, some insurance work, and the occasional missing person," I replied.

"I have something that might fit," said Bremmer, before turning to the Sheriff. "Are we just about done, Jim?"

"Sure," Pardy said, getting up. "It's been a while since I grabbed a Po'Boy and knocked back a pint."

"Or two?" corrected Bremmer.

✳ ✳ ✳

After Pardy left, Bremmer turned to us, holding up my business card. "*The Eye on You Detective Agency.* That's Ben O'Shea, right?"

"Yes, Ben and Gabriel started the business. I manage the Gulfport office, and Arnie looks after New Orleans."

"You guys do good work. A lot of Hartley's information on the *Corruption in the City* article came from Ben O'Shea. Now, why don't you folks tell me why you're really here."

"How much did the Sheriff tell you about the suitcase?" I asked.

"Suitcase? He didn't say anything about a suitcase."

"A floppy disk?"

Bremmer looked intently at us. "What floppy disk?"

I flashed a look at Arnie. "We were hoping we could help each other out. We have some information that your readers should know, and you might be able to fill in some blanks for us." I looked at Bremmer, hopefully.

"What about Pardy?"

"His idea of working together is a one-way street," replied Arnie. "Did he ask what Green had been working on?"

"Yes, but I told him I didn't know. Hartley was kind of a lone wolf that way. Sheriff Pardy was in today because he had a team going through Green's stuff." Bremmer pressed a button his desk phone and told the receptionist to hold his calls and to push back an editorial meeting about the weekend edition. "What's this all about?"

I told him about the suitcase, the rat-faced guy, the bloody shirt, and the floppy disk. "The disk must be important because someone ransacked my apartment looking for it."

Bremmer listened intently for about twenty minutes. When I had finished, he asked, "Where's the floppy?"

"Before I answer that, it's your turn. Do you really not know what Green was working on?"

"He came to me a couple of months ago about an idea. He wanted to do an expose on the Klan, which is old news. He believed they were making a resurgence here in Mississippi and had recently become more militant."

"Where was he getting his information?" asked Arnie.

"Hartley always has sources. Every source is 'Deep Throat' as in Watergate. Deep Throat said this, and Deep Throat said that. He won't share names unless they're willing to go on the record."

"Do you think he and his wife were murdered because he was about to expose something he'd found?" I asked.

"I don't know. The Sheriff implied it might have been an adultery thing."

"Were the Green's having problems?" Arnie asked.

"I like to keep my nose out of my people's personal affairs." Bremmer paused. "However, I'd be lying if it hadn't crossed my mind. She's twenty years younger, and well … very attractive. Now your turn, where's the disk?"

"I gave the floppy to Sheriff Pardy this morning," I said, adding, "But before I did, we made a copy." Arnie pulled out the computer printout and passed it across the desk.

Holding up the sheets, Bremmer put his sandaled feet on the desk and leaned back in his chair. "My my, some of Biloxi's finest, including our former mayor." He checked through each page before saying anything else.

"What do you think, Mr. Bremmer?" asked Arnie.

"Call me Larry. If we assume the suitcase did, in fact, belong to the killer, then I think this is the smoking gun. What I mean is, if this disk came from Hartley's house, it would be logical to say this is related to something he was investigating. But there are three big problems. One, we are assuming that this belonged to the man who killed Hartley. Second, there's nothing on these sheets that indicates this is a list of Klan members or even sympathizers. Thirdly, I know people on this list, and they're not Klan."

* * *

I left a copy of the printout with Bremmer. "I was hoping we could look at Hartley's office."

"Knock yourself out, but as I said, deputies have already been here. They took everything, including his computer."

"I'd like to have a look anyway."

I shook Bremmer's hand. "Can we keep our little arrangement confidential for now? I've already been accused of trying to obstruct their investigation."

"No problem. Jim Pardy is a good man, but I know he can get a little territorial."

* * *

Hartley's office had been sanitized. Not only was the computer removed, but every bit of paper you'd expect to find had been carted away. I busied myself going through the bookcase looking for loose papers. Arnie started going through the drawers of his desk. After about twenty minutes, we gave up. "If there was anything here, the deputies have it," I said.

"Did you notice everyone looking at us when Bremmer brought us here?"

"I think we're likely the subject at the water-cooler."

"I think we should join the discussion." Arnie went up to a group of employees that were huddled together speaking animatedly.

"Good afternoon folks, my name is Arnie Simms. You're probably wondering what my associate and I are doing here. I'm not a cop. I'm just a guy looking into what happened to Hartley. If anyone has information to share about the murder, or what Hartley was working on, I promise I'll be discreet." Arnie handed out his business cards to them before moving on to another group.

I decided to do likewise and approached a group of people in the typing pool. It took thirty minutes to canvas the whole office.

* * *

"How did you make out?" asked Arnie once we were done.

"It was a good idea. I get the impression that they didn't have much to say to the deputies."

"Sometimes, people are reluctant to talk to cops."

"Hartley kept to himself. No one I spoke to had any knowledge of his wife or what he did outside of work. I got a warm vibe by a couple of women in the typing pool. One was pretty torn up about things and angry that the paper wasn't closed. The way she took my card suggested that she had something to say. How about you?"

"I think a couple of the brothers might call. There's something out there. Maybe they'll just want to talk, but it might lead to something."

Chapter 13

As we pulled away from the *Herald*, Arnie's eyes were drawn to the rearview mirror. "Sorry, Rachel, what color was the pickup? The one the rat-face man was driving when he picked up the suitcase?"

"It was dark outside. It could have been black, maybe blue."

"Did it have Mississippi plates?"

"The truth is that I didn't notice. Although since the truck was facing my door and Mississippi doesn't require license plates on the front of vehicles, I wouldn't have been able to tell anyway. Why?"

Arnie took a quick left without signaling his turn and stepped on the gas. He raised his voice over the sound of the van's engine. "When we left the *Herald*, I noticed someone sitting in a black pickup parked down the street. It might be nothing, but there's a black truck back there that just turned left."

Arnie started weaving dangerously in and out of traffic. I turned and looked behind us. "Whoever it is, they're about three cars back."

"Do you recognize the truck?"

"I don't know." My hands were in a death grip on the dashboard.

Arnie took a quick right on the next side street, causing the van to fishtail. "Hold on, this might get rough." He gunned the van through the next intersection, cheating a yellow. We heard cars screech to a stop behind us. When I looked back, the driver of the pickup was stopped at the traffic light. Arnie took another right and pulled into a narrow alley adjacent to a grocery store.

Arnie turned around and watched the street for a couple of minutes. "There he goes, now the real game begins." He put the van in reverse, and to a chorus of horns, he backed out onto the street.

"There he is," I said, pointing up the block. Arnie floored it, and the van raced ahead, narrowing the gap.

In another minute, we came up behind the pickup. "Write this down somewhere, AHP 521. It's a Ford F150, maybe a 1980."

I dug in my purse until I found a pen and scribbled the license plate on my hand. "Looks like there's just the driver."

Arnie pulled into the left lane and sped up. As we drew adjacent to the truck, I got a good look at the driver. "Hold it, Arnie," I said, slamming my fist on the dash. "It's Kittyburg."

* * *

Arnie passed the van and slowed down, waving from his window for Don to pull over.

"What the hell are you doing?" I yelled, getting out of the van. I was getting angrier than a puffed toad.

"Nice to see you guys," Don said, getting out of his truck. "I was just going to a job interview when surprise, surprise, I see you two."

"Give it a rest, Don," I said. "You were following us. I want to know why." Arnie rolled down the van window and listened.

Don stared at me for a half minute. "Okay, I was following you. So, what? That's because no one is telling me what's going on. Here I go visit my girl-friend, and I find her door open, and her apartment ransacked."

"I'm not your girlfriend." I crossed my arms.

"Settle down. I followed you because I was wor-ried about you. Judging by what someone did to your apartment, you're mixed up in some serious shit."

"I don't need your help."

"I think you do. What happened with the cops?"

"None of your business."

"Why did you guys go to the *Herald?*"

"None of your business."

Don turned to Arnie, "Help me talk some sense into this girl." Arnie picked my side by rolling up the van's window.

I looked at Don, who was wearing a gray base-ball cap that said, 'Make the South Great Again.' "I didn't realize you had those sympathies," I said, pointing to his hat.

"Good southern boy. Natchez, remember?"

I started back to the van. "We're leaving now, and if you know what's good for you, don't follow us anymore."

Chapter 14

It was almost 3 PM when we arrived at the *Eye on You Detective Agency*. The closed sign had been removed from the front door, and Travis was at his desk sorting through some faxes. "Good morning Travis," Arnie said as we walked in.

"Hey, guys. Great night last night."

I nodded. I was still upset over the confrontation with Don. Arnie filled Travis in about the apartment being ransacked, and how we had surprised Don.

"I hope you don't think it was him. He would never do that," offered Travis, looking over at me. "Sounds like he's legitimately worried. Do you think this is the same guy that picked up the suitcase?"

"Any sane person would, that's why the cops think it was a bunch of strung-out punks. Even though I have nothing worth stealing." Sarcasm dripped from my voice.

Travis handed me a bunch of pink message slips. "I just listened to the answering machine."

I flipped through the messages. The first one was from Don on the 25th. The message was, *Welcome to Jackson, did you want to introduce me to your family?* The second was from the 26th, again from Don, *why haven't you called?* The third, from the 27th, *Did you get my previous messages?* At 8 AM that morning there was another, *I'm worried, call me.*

I felt a pang of regret about the way I'd spoken to him. The fifth message was from someone named Angel, with a local phone number. I handed Arnie the stack of messages and told Travis that Arnie was going to drop me off at the Biloxi Public Library so I could start researching the paternity case we'd discussed at dinner.

"It's kind of like the Michael Jackson case. It was in a *National Enquirer* that Mom brought home the other day."

"I'm way behind on my trashy supermarket tabloids."

"A woman who calls herself Billy Jean Jackson is saying Michael is the father of her two children. She claims that he proposed to her and then changed his mind. She wants $10 million in child support, five for each kid."

"Isn't Billy Jean the title of one of his songs?"

"Yep, check out the lyrics." Travis started singing, "*Billie Jean is not my lover, she's just a girl who claims that I am the one. But the kid is not my son, she says I am the one, but the kid is not my son.*"

"First, I find out you are a master chef, and now I learn you're a singer."

"Her real name is something like Lavon Powlis. She's an unemployed legal secretary. She's made similar claims about other rich millionaires."

"Are you suggesting that our client is trying to scam Corbin Masters?"

"If he doesn't even look like him…"

"You might be right, Travis, but I don't care because we're going to get paid regardless. That is, as long as I can find a way to get Master's DNA tested."

✳ ✳ ✳

I walked into the library and waived to Jimmy, who was talking to a customer at the front desk. I sat down at a table and pulled out a legal pad and thought about how best to start my research. Corbin Masters was not only on the mysterious list, but he was also the alleged father of Mike Boyle.

Jimmy, dressed in a sports shirt under a dark blue cardigan, came over once he'd finished with his customer. He pointed at me, "Rachel, right?"

"Do you remember all of the girls, Jimmy?" I smiled at him.

He returned the smile awkwardly, "I don't…I don't know many girls, so it's easy to remember. Can I help you with something?"

"I want to do some research on a man named Corbin Masters. Can you suggest anything?"

"Corbin Masters? He repeated to himself. "I'd start with the abstracts back there," he said, pointing to a row of books. "They list all of the periodical references alphabetically."

"Back there?" I asked, my brow furrowing as I bit my lip.

"Tell you what, I'll start you off. Wait right here." He returned ten minutes later with a stack of books and magazines. "There's quite a bit on him. Start with these." he put a bunch of magazines and newspapers in front of me. "There's even an old copy of the *National Enquirer*. I was surprised to find it because the library no longer subscribes."

"Thank you, Jimmy. This will keep me busy for a while."

"If you need anything, let me know," he said eagerly.

I thanked him again, fluttering my eyelashes and giving him a grin. The first magazine on top of the pile was the *National Enquirer*. There was a black and white photo of Corbin Masters holding a whiskey glass. He was a handsome, debonair man, wearing a dark tuxedo, and black hair slicked back. He was smiling at the camera with his arm around a young, dark-haired woman. The issue was from November 1968 and had a typical trashy headline.

Marriage on the Rocks?

Inside the messy divorce of one of America's wealthiest families.

I turned to page three, where the reporter gave a brief synopsis of Masters, beginning with how, after the Second World War, he and his brother Chester inherited a tree farm near Saucier, Mississippi. The timing for the brothers couldn't have been better. With the local economy in recovery, the demand for lumber had been brisk. The brothers had wisely turned their profits into buying more and more land. They also purchased lumber mills along the Mississippi. As Corbin's wealth grew, so too did his celebrity status. He was always in the public eye, seen regularly at parties given by the Biloxi elite. But it was after his marriage to wealthy socialite Gladys Mayview that his celebrity status took off. The happy couple had two children, Andrew and Elizabeth, in the first three years of their marriage.

The essence of the article was that after four years of marriage, Gladys Masters had had enough. The official reason for their divorce was irreconcilable differences, but the reporter hinted that Gladys had grown tired of her husband's drinking and philandering. The writer predicted the divorce would be ugly, with the question of custody of the children hanging over the proceedings. The reporter speculated the divorce settlement would be the largest in the history of the State of Mississippi.

I looked at the *Biloxi Herald* next and found a story buried in the society pages. It had been written six months after the *National Enquirer* article and said that a settlement had been reached in the divorce case. Gladys, now reverting to her maiden name, had relinquished custody of her two kids as well as any claim on Master's estate, in return for unspecified considerations. I asked myself why a mother would give up custody of her children as well as her claim to the estate. I wrote, *"Huge Settlement? Why? Was she was already wealthy?"* on my legal pad.

There was a more recent article in *Forbes* magazine from 1979 that listed the Masters family as the third wealthiest in the state. It went on to say that the family had diversified from lumber to shipping and financial interests.

A *Times* magazine article was old, dating back to April 1940. The only reference to Corbin Masters was in the fine print, under a photo of him shaking hands with Charles Lindberg. The article was about the rapid growth of the America First movement. Another *Times* article covered a political movement called the White People's Party. Corbin's name was mentioned in the article as one of its financial backers.

When I had finished reading, I looked down at my notes. I had written two pages about Masters but felt that I'd only captured the tip of the iceberg. I wrote down a few questions on my legal pad.

- *Why would Gladys Mayview give up custody of her children? How big was the settlement?*
- *What's the significance of Masters' name being on the list?*
- *What is the connection to the other names on the list?*
- *What is the White People's Party?*

- *How can I make Masters want to submit to a DNA test?* I circled this last question a couple of times.

I pulled out the list from the floppy disk again and counted the names. In addition to Baxter, Masters, and McGloyn, there were fifteen other names. Separating those who lived out of state, there were eight that lived near Biloxi. I went to the abstracts but found references to only three of the names.

The first name was John Dietz, the former President of the Biloxi Chamber of Commerce and a successful retailer. The *Herald* had a short write up of a speech he'd given last year on the affirmative action policies of the Federal Government. The essence was that the pendulum had swung too far, and the rights of those most qualified were being violated. In his speech, he referred to Ronald Reagan as someone who had pledged to eliminate the insanity of the current system.

The second name was Steve Schaffer, who had run for State Legislator and lost. In a brief article in the *Hattiesburg American,* he blamed his loss on uneducated minority votes. Paradoxically, he had argued that had he been elected, that unemployment amongst Negros in the state would have virtually disappeared. Another short article in the *Herald* had Schaffer presenting the case against adopting a public holiday in honor of Martin Luther King.

He'd argued that Confederate General Robert E. Lee would be a better choice.

The third name was Paul Crossman, an editor for the *John Birch Society*. Crossman had written an article advocating a strong U.S. military, and the abandonment of foreign excursions in places such as Lebanon and, more recently, Grenada. Once again, I made a note on my legal pad.

What do a corrupt former mayor, a Baptist pastor, and a multi-millionaire entrepreneur have in common with a magazine editor, a failed senator, and a local retailer?

I saw Jimmy over at the front counter and headed over to him. "I'm done and wanted to thank you again for your help today, Jimmy."

"No, problem." Jimmy smiled.

"I was wondering if you would like to make a little extra money?"

Jimmy cocked his head and pushed up his glasses. "Sure, but if it's more research, you don't need to pay..."

"No, it's not research," I interrupted. "I was thinking of buying a computer for my business, and I don't know the first thing." I handed him my business card. "Maybe you can help me get it set up and even show me the basics."

Jimmy's face lit up, "Sure, I'd still do it for free."

"That's okay, Jimmy. I want to pay you. Do you have a day off next week?"

Chapter 15

I had arranged to meet Arnie for dinner at a local pizzeria, a short walk from the library. "How was the research?" Arnie asked once the waiter had taken our order.

"Like everything else, …frustrating. It seems the more I read, the more questions I have." I filled him in on how Masters had made his fortune, his family, and his involvement with the America First movement.

"In terms of our client Mr. Boyle, any further thoughts?"

"Not really. Masters' marriage broke up over his philandering. I'd like to talk to his ex-wife, Gladys Mayview, and see if she might remember anything specific about Boyle's mother. Any idea of how I can find her?"

"If she has a Mississippi driver's license, I can call my cousin."

"That would be great, Arnie." When the waitress came for our order, we ordered a vegetarian pizza. "I have a date next week with Jimmy."

Arnie frowned. "Aren't you robbing the cradle?"

"Relax, I'm paying him to help me buy a computer for the office. To automate our files and help with scheduling and billing."

"Good idea. Maybe I'll tag along."

"He also said he would help me get it set up."

"Sounds like a good idea."

When the pizza came, we dug in. "I remember the last fight I had with Don, was what to have on our pizza."

"Any more thoughts on what happened today?"

"I've thought about it on and off all day. I'm still angry at the cops for being so stupid, and I'm scared to go near my apartment." I heaved a long sigh. "But I don't think that was Don. He's given me no reason to trust him, but I can't believe he'd do that to me."

We'd finished our meal when I decided to tell Arnie about researching the other names on the list.

"I thought you were going to let Sheriff Pardy do his job."

"I would if I had more confidence in him."

Arnie shook his head. "What did you find out?"

"Not much. A man named Dietz gave a speech against affirmative action, Steve Schaffer is a politician who couldn't get elected and blames minorities, and Crossman is a hawk who thinks the U.S. should stay out of other country's wars."

"The only name I recognize is Dietz. He's not a popular guy with the brothers. He owns a couple of gambling houses on the strip, like Lucky's, as well as a few hotels like the Tivoli, where Travis' mother works. Thankfully he doesn't own the Trade Winds, because he doesn't like renting to non-whites. He's also very anti-union. When he heard union reps were meeting with some of the staff, he closed the business down only to re-open a couple of months later with new staff."

"So, he's a racist. That fits in with what Green was likely working on."

"Remember, this is Mississippi. The views of any of these three men are hardly uncommon." We argued over the bill before I won out by giving the waitress my Visa card.

After we got back to the Trade Winds, I remembered the message from Angel and that I was supposed to return the call. As I dialed the number, I tried to recall if I knew anyone named Angel.

"Angel Garcia," my call was answered by a woman's voice.

"Hi, it's Rachel Henderson, you left a message for me?"

For a moment there was dead air. Finally, she spoke, her voice barely above a whisper, "I really shouldn't be doing this, but you said to call if there was something about what happened to Hartley."

I tried to summon up an image of the woman. "Are you the woman in the typing pool?"

"Yes, and I don't want to be overheard. I might get in trouble."

"Did you want to meet somewhere?" When she didn't answer right away, I asked, "It's Saturday, I didn't know whether you'd be working."

The woman seemed to relax. "I work Saturdays and get Mondays off."

"What time do you get off work today, Angel?"

Once again, she hesitated, letting the silence fill the call. "I'm doing this for Hartley. Do you know the Port City Café on Pass Rd?"

"Yes, I've been there."

"Give me half an hour to finish things up."

* * *

Arnie drove me to the diner. On my suggestion, he agreed to wait in the van. I told him the woman had been skittish.

In the coffee shop, I looked at my watch while my coffee grew cold in front of me. I was reminded of a story Gabriel had told me about meeting with an informant called Chinky that he'd had never met before. Gabriel had arrived early and, after minutes of hesitation, approached a Chinese man and asked if he was Chinky. After the blow-up, the real Chinky showed up, and he wasn't even Chinese.

It was over an hour after I'd spoken to Angel on the phone when a heavy-set, middle-aged woman wearing black polyester stretch pants and a Rudolf the reindeer sweater entered the diner. Her hair was straight, and dyed red like spilled ketchup. I recognized her right away. She walked over to where I was sitting. "We shouldn't stay long."

"Angel?"

The woman took a seat across from me. "This business with Hartley, oh boy, it's thrown everyone for a loop."

"Was there something about Hartley's murder you wanted to talk about?"

"It's just all …." I waited for her to finish. "Fucked up." I cocked my head and nodded encouragement. "I watched that press conference, we all did." She stopped again to look around and see if someone might be listening. Luckily there were only a couple of other people in the diner sitting up at the bar. "One thing I can tell you is that the Greens were happily married. I don't know why they would say all that crap about Adrienne having an affair." Her voice was rising with emotion. "They were nice people."

"It sounds like you knew them well." The waitress suddenly came up from behind and interrupted, causing Angel to jump noticeably.

"I'm sorry. I just wanted to know if you wanted anything?"

"Coffee, yes, coffee. Nothing else, I need to get home and make supper."

"You were saying…Angel?" I asked once the waitress had left.

"I do his typing. I mean, I did," she explained, giving me a sad look that said everything. "Adrienne would stop by to visit every once in a while and would bring cookies for the office. On my birthday, they both brought me here for lunch."

The waitress brought the coffee and gave me a fresh cup.

I waited until she was gone. "As his typist, you would know what he was working on."

Once again, Angel looked around and then whispered, "Ed Harper, he's my supervisor. He told us all to keep our mouth shut about that. He said it was nobody's business, but I thought since you're a detective, that you might be able to figure out something. I don't think he was killed like they said at that news conference." Her hands shook as she lifted her coffee cup. She paused mid-air and then put it back down.

"I was told that he was working on an expose of the Knights of the Klu Klux Klan."

She nodded, "He felt that they were responsible for what's happening at the synagogues, you know, the burnings and the vandalizing."

I had read about a couple of recent church burnings that the police had labeled arson, but they hadn't yet figured who was responsible. "This is common knowledge. Certainly not something that would get him killed."

"Hartley got death threats."

"Death threats?" I repeated, finally sipping my coffee.

Angel nodded. "A few weeks ago, he got excited about something. All he would say was that he had a breakthrough. Someone from the inside had told him about something big that was going to happen."

"Like the Klan was planning something?"

"I don't know. Maybe. He said something like that pastor that was shot.

"Martin Luther King?"

"I don't know. He said it would be like that. I don't know anymore because he planned to work on it from home." Angel's eyes were misting over, her complexion growing paler. She hadn't touched her coffee.

"Was that unusual for him? To work from home?"

"No, he often did that when he got rolling on a story. He said it was more productive."

"Let's tell the Sheriff about the death threats."

A look of fear washed across Angel's face. She said something under her breath in Spanish that I didn't understand. She gathered up her coat and stood up to leave. "I told you this in confidence."

"Wait, Angel! I'm sorry, I didn't mean to …"

"Don't tell anyone you spoke to me." She put some coins on the table. As she was leaving, she said, "Talking to the wrong person is what got Hartley killed."

✳ ✳ ✳

When I got back in the van, I filled Arnie in on what Angel had to say. "I told you all this business about a love affair was crap. That woman was terrified. We need to do something about this, Arnie."

Arnie nodded and started the van. "This seems to be getting bigger and bigger. First, there's the issue of Green's death. Who killed him and why? Where is Adrienne Green? Why was her car found at the airport? Then there's the garage door opener; clearly, someone is planning something on a large scale that frightened Green and probably got him murdered. That brings me back to the list. We have a lot of questions. I know I said to leave this to Sheriff Pardy, but I take that back. We need to get some answers."

When we got back to the apartment, Arnie listened to a message on his phone. He turned to me and said, "It's my cousin, he found a Gladys Mayview in Ocean Springs. I have her telephone number."

Chapter 16

December 29, 1984

Biloxi, Mississippi

I had a terrible night. I rarely remember my dreams, but always my nightmares. This one was filled with men with bad teeth and weak bladders chasing me.

Arnie was in the shower when I awoke, so I helped myself to coffee and dialed the phone number he'd given me for Gladys Mayview.

"Why would you be looking for that old bat?" answered a woman who sounded like she was still in bed.

I gave a glance at my watch. It was 10 AM, Sunday morning. "My name is Rachel Henderson. I'm a private detective in Gulfport, and I wonder if Gladys Mayview could spare a few minutes today. I have questions about her former husband."

There was a sound like someone clearing their throat and spitting. "Corbin? Everybody has questions about him."

"Are you Gladys Mayview?"

"I am she, but I'm afraid you called me a little early. What time is it where you are?"

"I'm in Biloxi. I can be there in thirty minutes. How about breakfast?" I asked, hopefully.

"I usually don't book appearances until later in the day, but if you're willing to buy…"

* * *

Arnie dropped me off at my apartment and made me promise to go straight to the parking garage for my car. Sitting in my AMC Pacer for the first time in days felt good. I knew I'd have to face the apartment eventually.

* * *

I knew it was Gladys Mayview as soon as the old woman walked into the coffee shop in Ocean Springs. She bore little resemblance to the young beauty that had been on the cover of the *National Enquirer*. In addition to some hard miles, she had an eccentric look about her. Despite temperatures expected to be in the mid-sixties, she wore a mink coat over a pink terry cloth bathrobe. She wore bedroom slippers and shuffled to where I was sitting. Her black hair had long strands of gray, ruining the effect of her Betty Page hairstyle.

"I bet you're Rachel. You don't look like a private detective. You look more like a cocktail waitress. Not that there's anything wrong with looking like a cocktail waitress unless you don't have any cocktails." She took off her mink, asking out loud why the restaurant was so fucking hot. She called over to the waitress, who was serving a young man at the counter. "You'd better turn down the heat, dearie, or I'll have to peel off another layer or two." Gladys turned to me, "They may not be impressed with what I have under this robe."

I didn't know what to make of her. The waitress came by to take our order. "Isn't it a little early for you, Gladys?" she asked.

"Not if you've got a little brandy down behind the counter."

"You're thinking about the bar down the street. We don't serve liquor."

"This ain't a bar? Who picked this place? Well, whatcha got honey?"

"The coffee is fresh."

When she'd left after pouring coffee into our mugs, Gladys reached into her mink and pulled out a silver flask. Giving me a wink, she poured a healthy amount into both of our coffees. I started to protest, but she held up her hand. "I refuse to drink alone. If you want to ask me any questions about old what's-his-face, then you'll need to loosen me up, dearie."

I smiled and took a tentative sip of the coffee. "First question Mrs. Mayview, do you ever see Corbin anymore?"

"Why so formal, if we're going to talk about that old fucker, you'd better call me Gladys. Oh, and I haven't seen him in ten glorious years."

"When I was researching your family, there was very little about your ex-husband's brother Chester."

'That's not surprising Chester's a dim bulb. He's what they call in polite company, a retardo."

"Is he institutionalized?" I asked, shocked by Gladys' language.

"He lives with Corbin. I guess that qualifies as a loony bin."

"Do the brothers get along?"

"Not really. It's one thing to be an idiot, it's another to be constantly reminded of it."

"Was Chester ever involved in the business?"

"Sure, he was the VP of fuck-all. I don't think Corbin would be willing to share the limelight even if Chester hadn't been an imbecile."

"Is that why Chester never got married?"

"I don't know. Would you marry a wealthy idiot? Corbin wouldn't have approved. He'd have taken the woman for a gold-digger. But not to worry, Chester got more than his share of women. Corbin takes care of things."

"Do you see Andrew and Elizabeth?" For the first time, I detected emotion wash across the old lady's face.

"What's with these questions? I thought this was about Corbin?"

"My company has been hired to look into a paternity claim against your ex-husband. I'm just trying to get some background information before we ask him to do a paternity test."

"Good luck with that. If there's one thing that Corbin values over pussy, it's his money." Gladys took a long drink of her coffee before pulling out a silver, monogrammed cigarette case and offering one to me. When I shook my head, she shrugged and lit her cigarette with a silver lighter. She sat back and blew a smoke ring towards the ceiling. "So, who's your client?"

I avoided the question, "His mother was an exotic dancer, claims to have met him that way."

"Well dearie, he had more than his share of those. But you could have said maids, cooks, cocktail waitresses, other people's wives, and I wouldn't have been surprised."

"Is that why you divorced him?"

She started to cackle, which turned into a throaty cough. "In the four years we were married, he must have fucked half the town. The only reason I say half is because the other half didn't have the right parts."

I gave Gladys a serious stare. "I'm curious about why you gave up custody and any claim to the estate."

"There it is. The $64,000 question as they say. I was wondering when you'd get to it. I don't see much of Andy or Beth. They're a little resentful. I guess the whole giving up custody thing and walking away with a pile of money might have been too much for their little hearts to bear. I've made attempts to stay in their lives, but sadly what Corbin wants, Corbin gets."

I waited for her to continue as she gulped down her coffee. The waitress brought eggs, bacon, grits, and toast.

"That must have been a difficult time for you, Gladys." I reached out and put my hand on hers.

The woman shrugged it off. "You don't know the half of it." She butted out her cigarette in the remnants of her coffee, making a fizzing sound, and started in on her food.

"Was Corbin ever involved in any movements?"

"Movements?"

"I was thinking of political groups."

"Not sure what that has to do with a paternity suit, dearie." She held up her coffee cup and called the waitress. "Hey, I found a cigarette butt in my coffee!" After a moment of glaring at the waitress, she turned back to me. "He was caught up with the war protests, but that was before my time."

"What about white supremacists?"

Gladys cackled again and said, "Like the Knights? Are you asking if Corbin Masters is a member of the secret army?" I nodded. After pulling out the flask, she took another swig before answering. "Corbin was a member of many organizations.

Nothing would surprise me. He was fascinated with the whole Nazi thing, the superiority of the white race, the swastika, all that bullshit. I wouldn't be surprised if Andy and Beth don't do the Heil Hitler before eating their strudel each morning."

"Do you remember him playing an active role in any Klan activities?"

"You mean dress up in those ridiculous outfits? No. He's more of a behind the scenes kind of man. It's funny, his belief in the superiority of the white race didn't stop him from fucking the black house-maids. The last straw was walking in and catching him getting a blowjob from a Negro maid."

"That's when you filed for divorce?"

"Couldn't take it anymore. It was becoming the talk among our friends and had gotten back to my mother."

"Are you going to tell me why you gave up custody?"

Once again, her face tensed, and she glanced away. "No. But you seem like a nice girl, and I would tell you if it would help you, but it won't." I waited and then put my hand once again on hers. This time she didn't shrug it off. 'Listen, I'll tell you a story. Call it an X-rated fable. You can't repeat any of this," she said in a solemn tone.

"Once upon a time, there was a King and a Queen. The King was the ass, and the Queen had to have a hole in her head to put up with it. The King and the Queen started a family. First a handsome Prince and then a beautiful Princess. Well, to be honest, not that beautiful, kind of homely. The King ruled the Kingdom with an iron fist and felt entitled to fuck anything in his kingdom. The Queen initially tried to satisfy his insatiable desires, but when she couldn't, she realized that she was powerless to stop him." She stopped for a moment to light another cigarette.

"This made the Queen very sad, and she took solace in some things that were not strictly legal but could dull the pain. The King knew she was sad but didn't give a hairy rat's ass. He was too busy getting blow jobs from the peasants. Around the same time, word got out that she had had enough and was planning to leave the King and take her share of the kingdom. This made the King very unhappy."

"One night, the sad and utterly stupid Queen went to a party on her own, where she enjoyed herself too much. When it was time to go back to the castle, she shunned her driver and decided to drive the carriage herself." She stopped the story for a moment as the waitress brought a fresh cup of coffee.

"An accident happened, and the next thing she knew, she woke up in bed in the castle. Standing beside the bed, looking down at her was the Sheriff of the Kingdom. He told the Queen the carriage she had been driving went off the road and had killed a young black servant. She had no memory of the accident or how she had arrived home. She was very distraught about what he said she had done. The Sheriff told her she could look forward to a lengthy jail sentence for manslaughter." Gladys stopped again to butt out her cigarette in the yolk of her egg.

"Rather than suffer the bad publicity that the news of the accident would bring, the King, with the help of his friend, the Sheriff, interceded to cover up the accident and dispose of the body. The carriage was repaired so that no one would ever know. The body of the boy would never be found, leaving his parents to believe he'd run away."

"When the Queen recovered, she found that the King had continued fucking the staff. So, she decided to continue with the divorce. Once again, the King was furious and threatened the Queen. Scared, she ran home to her mother, who lived in a neighboring village. To make a long story short, the King eventually agreed to the divorce as long as she agreed to renounce her rights as Queen and custody over the Prince and Princess. For his part, The King agreed to a cash settlement, and to not disclose what had happened the night of the accident." Gladys paused for a moment and munched on a piece of toast.

"But if it ever came out, the King would be in serious trouble for the coverup, would he?" I asked.

"The King is a very powerful man. In addition to the Asshole Sheriff and the Asshole Judge, there was an Asshole Mayor. They were all his friends."

* * *

After I paid the bill for breakfast, Gladys thanked me for being such a good listener. As she was leaving, she turned back to me once again, "You should talk to Chester. He's an okay guy for an imbecile. I hear he doesn't like Corbin much."

Chapter 17

December 26th, 1984

Jackson, Mississippi
MBI Headquarters

Don sat alone in the MBI Director's office, eagerly anticipating his boss' arrival. After months of interviews and budget meetings, he'd been told the decision on the Senior Agent position had been made. Fred Moller, his boss, had scheduled an appointment for 4 PM to discuss the role. Don looked at his Timex and frowned, seeing that the meeting was already ten minutes late. Don thought he was a shoo-in for the job. The part he'd played in gathering evidence against Frank Reznikov was reason enough to select him over Carol George, the other agent in the competition. He didn't even know what Carol did at the MBI. Probably something to do with paperclips. There was no contest.

Fred Moller finally walked into the office, along with Senior Director Joyce Coogan. *Wow*, Don thought, *they're bringing out the big guns.* He had met Coogan once before at a Christmas party. The details were a little hazy, but he remembered partying a little too hard and making a pass at her. To make it worse, he hadn't realized that they'd been sitting with her fiancée, another MBI agent. He wondered what impressions he might have left with Coogan. She was a fifty-something, pant-suit-wearing woman, with her blonde hair tied severely in a bun.

Once everyone was seated, Coogan spoke up. "How have you been keeping? Uh…Don?" she looked down at the file she had brought with her.

"Fine, I've had a pretty good run, if I say so myself."

"Yes, I've read your reports." She patted the file. Don wondered why his file was so thick. "How are you feeling? I mean, you've been through a lot."

"Good, yep pretty good, well maybe a little tired," he said, looking over at his boss. "Kind of burning the candle at both ends."

"Right, of course." Coogan crossed her legs and shared a look with Fred. "We both wanted to thank you for your interest in the Senior Agent role. You've come a long way in your … skill set. I can't think of too many other agents with your …," she paused for a moment, unable to think of the right word and then sharing a look with Fred.

"What Joyce means," said Fred, is you seem to be able to roll with the punches."

"You understand the big picture," added Coogan. To drive the point home, she pointed to the MBI logo of a wheel on the wall behind Fred. "You're an important cog."

"Well, Carol George is an excellent agent." Don volunteered, leaning back and crossing his legs.

"As you can imagine, Don," said Fred, taking over. "This is a critical decision for the Bureau. We're still a very small organization with only one open position at this time."

"At this time," repeated Coogan. Don shifted his gaze between the two, wondering where this was going. "We're prepared to extend a job offer....to Carol George. But I wanted to say it was a close call."

"Damn close," repeated Fred.

"What?" Don yelled, thunderstruck. He felt like someone was squeezing his heart. He struggled to maintain his composure. "I mean, what?" He told himself to remain calm.

"You said it yourself, Carol George is an excellent agent, and with her experience, she'll make a fine supervisor," Fred said.

"Wait, I was lying about that. This is a joke, right?" Don laughed. "Surely, you aren't seriously picking her over me?"

"Don," Fred leaned forward, "You know how these things go. You're both qualified, but the bureau is under the gun to have more women in key positions. It's called affirmative action."

"I can't fucking believe this!" Don stood up and glared back and forth at them. "I'm the most qualified. What I'm hearing is, I just don't have a vagina."

"Sit down, Don," replied Fred. "That wasn't the only reason. We considered everything. I'm sure you'll get another opportunity in the not too distant future."

"In the not too distant future," repeated Coogan.

"This is all fucking politics. I bring down Reznikov. What has Carol the Vagina ever done that didn't involve paper clips? Seriously, has she ever gone undercover? No, of course not. What the hell am I supposed to do now, Fred?"

"Don, you're upset, I get it. I'm sensitive to it," replied Coogan. "But I didn't expect this reaction from you."

"Upset? Do you think I'm upset? I told everyone I had this. Well, now what? I can't work for Carol, the Vagina." Fred looked over at Coogan, who just shrugged her shoulders.

He stared at his boss, waiting for his face to crack open into a smile. Finally, when it was clear that it wasn't a joke, Don's face fell faster than a corpse in cement boots. "I guess I'm going to quit."

"Well," said Coogan, "we were actually hoping you would."

Chapter 18

Gordie turned up the heat in the Chevrolet Caprice. He slammed his fist on the dash when the heater started blowing cold air. "If you're gonna steal me a car, then steal one with a fucking heater," he said out loud. He blew on his hands as he looked at the fancy-schmancy homes in the neighborhood. He was wearing a denim jacket over a Hawaiian shirt. "Who the fuck ever heard of ordering a hit on Christmas Day?" He popped a piece of bubble gum in his mouth.

"Don't worry, they're Jews," the creep on the phone had said. Gordie hadn't realized that Hartley Green was a Jew name. Part of the problem was that he didn't know the creep. It was a subcontract job. Maybe even a subcontract of a subcontract. That's the way it worked these days. Gordie didn't like it, but the cash was good and paid upfront.

"The job has to be done precisely at 8 AM on Christmas Day," the creep had said.

"Why's that?"

"The Jew is an editor for the *Herald*. Since they don't publish on Christmas, then he's bound to be home. Plus, while everyone else is busy opening gifts, they'll just be sitting there doing whatever Jews do on Christmas morning."

Gordie popped the cap off a bottle of coke using his Bic lighter and took a long swig. "Do I get a bonus for working on a fucking holiday?" he had asked.

"The wife's a nigger, so that's your bonus," said the creep.

Gordie didn't care for the man. He spoke to an imaginary person in the rearview mirror. "The fucker's uptight and doesn't treat me with respect. He made me read back his fucking instructions over and over again like I was some kind of moron. I'm a fucking professional. That job I did in November went off like silk, and still, I have to put up with this shit." Gordie went over what he had been calling the twelve rules of Christmas. "One, I park a couple of blocks away, so no one remembers the car. Two, I walk to the house and ring the bell at precisely 8 AM. Three, when they answer, I say Merry Christmas. Four, pop, pop to the head. Five, I make sure I get both of them. Six, I drop the gun. Seven, I find the guy's study and load all the stuff he's working on into the suitcase. Eight, I trash his computer. Nine, I get some rope out of the suitcase and hang her black ass from the tree in the backyard. Ten, I spray paint a swastika on the front door and drive this shitbox to the airport and park in the long-term lot. Eleven,

I find Locker 742 and put everything from the suitcase inside, throwing the key in the garbage. Twelve, I go to the ticket counter, and there will be a ticket for me under the name P. Jackson. Fucking Easy Peasy, Lemon Squeezy." Gordie put on his gloves and stepped out of the car.

"Jingle Bells, Batman smells, and Robin laid an egg," Gordie sang to himself as he trekked over to the Green's front door. He didn't feel very Christmassy. The Green's lived in a big-ass house with a candy apple red Beemer in the lane. He loved red cars.

The nearest neighbor's house was a football field away and was all done up with Christmas lights, and a nativity scene pointed directly at their Jew neighbor. He held the Luger they'd given him, down by his right side, and carried the Samsonite in his left. It was a nice suitcase; the powder blue was cool. Maybe he'd keep it and transfer his stuff from the garbage bag in the back seat.

As he climbed the steps to the front door, he checked his Casio. It was two minutes to eight. He hopped up and down in place on the porch as he waited. At the stroke of eight, he rang the doorbell. "Good, no dog," he muttered, putting his ear to the door. He rechecked his watch. *C'mon you fucker, I don't have all day.*

Finally, after repeatedly banging on the door, Gordie heard movement. The door was opened seconds later by an older man dressed in a plaid housecoat, staring at him over the top of his glasses. The man looked at Gordie and his Hawaiian shirt. "Can I help you?"

"I've come to wish you Merry Christmas."

"Merry Christmas, yourself," Green looked past Gordie, up and down the street before fixing him with a smile. "You looking for a donation or something?" This confused Gordie. In his mental walkthrough, Green hadn't had a speaking part. "I donate to the homeless at work." Green started to close the door, only to find that Gordie had put his foot in the way. Gordie pushed back on the door. For a brief moment, the door went open, close, open, close in a battle of strength. Finally, Gordie won out, and the two men spilled into the foyer. "What the hell?" Green said before he saw the gun in Gordie's hand.

"Back the fuck up." Gordie struggled to catch his breath from the exertion.

"What? You're robbing us on Christmas Day?" Green's eyes narrowed.

"You're a Jew, so fair game, right?" He was holding the gun flat like they do in those badass movies.

"Take it easy. I have some cash in my wallet. It's in my pants in the bedroom. I'm just going to turn around and get it, okay?" As the man turned, Gordie leveled the gun at the man's back. Before he could pull the trigger, there was a scream, and he was hit and knocked sideways. He fell onto the hardwood floor, the gun sliding down the hall. He scrambled to get up and realized that it was a woman. As he was getting to his feet, Green threw himself at Gordie and knocked him back into the front door. Both men fell to the floor and started to struggle. The woman was now on her feet and started hitting Gordie with a living room pillow.

Gordie kneed the older man in the groin, which took the wind out of him. The woman dropped the pillow and went for Gordie's face like she was a cat using a scratching pole. He got his right hand free and punched her in the nose. She backed away, shocked by the blow. Her husband was curled up in the fetal position holding his balls, when Gordie sprang his switchblade. He gave the woman a quick warning look before sticking the blade in Green's back. Green yelled out in pain. The wife started to scream for help. "Shut up, bitch," he said as he rammed the knife repeatedly into Green's back. When the woman continued to scream for help, Gordie grabbed her husband's head and slit his throat. As blood pooled on the floor, he stood up and wiped his bloody hands on his shirt. "I told you to shut the fuck up."

He felt his cheek burning and tasted blood trickling down his face. The wife and Gordie locked eyes, and she started to back away. She almost made it to the back door before Gordie caught her and rammed her head into the buffet. She dropped like a sack of sweet potatoes. He looked down at her. She was wearing pajama bottoms and a Minnie Mouse T-Shirt. Despite the broken nose and the welt on her forehead, she was a fine-looking woman.

* * *

"It's me," Gordie said, calling the number he'd been given.

"Where are you calling from?"

"The house. Green's fucking house."

The creep took a deep breath. "What did you do?"

"They fucking both came at me. They must have known judo or karate. But it's alright. It took a little effort, but it's done."

"Both?"

Gordie looked down at the woman wearing the Minnie Mouse t-shirt. Her big breasts were stretching the black ears. "Yeah, both."

"Did you get the stuff he was working on?"

"I grabbed all the papers on his desk, and I took a leak on his computer." He decided not to mention the floppy. It might be worth something extra.

"You know what to do now."

* * *

On the stand in the hall, he found the key to the Beemer. He went outside and looked around. There was still no sign of anyone on the street. He opened the trunk and then went back inside and gathered up the woman. He carried her fireman style and put her in the trunk.

Getting into the car, he relished the feel of the BMW's leather seats. He turned on the ignition, a look of satisfaction on his face when he felt the heater blowing hot air. He backed out of the lane and stopped where he had left the Caprice. Gordie retrieved his garbage bag and then drove off to a little place he knew.

Chapter 19

"You want me to quit?" Don repeated, his eyebrows rising.

"That's right," repeated Coogan. "We'd like you to get a real job."

"What's going on here? You give my job to someone less qualified and then tell me to get lost?" Don's eyes bulged as he stood up again.

"Sit down, Don," Fred repeated.

"Let me explain," Coogan continued. "We want you to start working for an outfit in Biloxi called Bubba's Seafood Emporium."

"Is this another undercover thing?"

"Here, read this." Coogan handed him a letter.

November 13th, 1984

Confidential Assessment of Klan Activities

In my opinion, Klan membership has grown dramatically on the Gulf coast since starting this assignment. Many of our country's major cities have seen torch-bearing fascists shouting slogans about Jews, and telling immigrants to return to their own country. Evidence, however, shows that racist views like these are more prevalent on the Gulf Coast. Judging by right-leaning talk shows, views once buried, are now more commonplace.

This new militancy is driven partly by the Nazification of traditional Klan organizations. I plan to attend a paramilitary training facility called The Camp. A man named Schaffer told me that he had recently extended an offer to a Washington senator, to have representatives of this paramilitary group patrol the country's southern border to keep undesirables from entering the homeland.

As I indicated in my last report, a large gathering of Klan, Neo-Nazis, and white supremacist groups was held in Saucier. At that event, I overheard people discussing something big currently being planned that would embolden white supremacists and spark a race war.

The President of the United States has openly talked about his sympathy for this movement. While publicly he has been pressured to disavow bigotry, the Imperial Wizard of the Klan, Bill Wilkinson, a special

speaker at the gathering, not only endorsed the Pres-
ident but also bragged that the year's GOP platform
looked like a Klansman had written it.

I have made contact with a man named Hartley
Green. He writes for the Herald and has an informant.
For my next report, I will assess the quality of the
paramilitary training and try to get more information
on what they're planning. WM

After Don had finished reading the document,
he put it down on the desk. "So what? A bunch
of tattooed baldies meeting up with a bunch of
sheet-wearing idiots is hardly a surprise."

"We're concerned about what's happening down
there, and what this big event is," said Coogan.

"So, you have this 'WM' undercover down
there. What does this have to do with the price of
tea in Biloxi?"

"William Morrison."

Billy had been Don's trainee once he joined the
MBI. "I would have thought he was a little inexperi-
enced, but he'll be a good agent."

Fred took a deep breath, "No, I'm afraid not."

"What does that mean?"

"Attempts by his uncle to contact him have gone
unanswered."

The news hit Don like a ton of bricks. He tried
to respond a couple of times but, in the end, sat
there speechless.

"At this point, we feel he's been compromised. That's why we want you to get a real job," Coogan continued.

Don's frustration with losing both the promotion and now his trainee fizzed up inside him like Mentos in a Coke bottle. He stood up again, "No. No, and no. Send Carol the Vagina. I'm sure she'll do a good job."

"Sit down, Don. We considered that, but as you mentioned, she doesn't have your experience."

Don shook his head. "She gets a promotion because she's less qualified, and I'll probably end up shark bait in the Gulf. No."

"There's something you don't know," said Fred. "Carol, the …, well, she's pregnant and due in March next year. It's a high-risk pregnancy. We can't put her in the field. Assuming the operation is over by March, we intend to give you the senior role with a significant increase in pay."

Don was silent for a moment before shaking his head. "How do you know these people would hire me, let alone trust me with anything?"

"We don't," replied Coogan. "We want to put you with another member of their group. A man named Bubba who runs the seafood company. We've added to your resume, and we'll give you a crash course on the business."

"Would my name still be Don Kittyburg?"

"We don't see the need to change anything." Fred started to chuckle. "By the way, how did you ever come up with that name anyway?"

"I was petting my girl's cat. It just popped into my head."

Coogan and Fred shared a look, and then Coogan said, "Are you in, Senior-Agent-in-Waiting Kittyburg? That has a nice ring to it."

"No, I'll take door number two, and get my own job."

Coogan nodded that she understood. Don was getting up to leave when once again, Fred spoke up. "Sit down, Don. There's one other thing you should know."

"What's that?"

"Rachel Henderson." Fred read from a file in front of him. "It appears that your girlfriend has somehow gotten involved. We think her life might be in danger."

Chapter 20

Biloxi, Mississippi

"Meeting in this parking garage makes me feel like deepthroat," said Dietz.

"Not sure we have much choice," said the white-haired man standing in the shadows. "It wouldn't surprise me if the Feds have bugged all our phones." Masters took a drag from his cigarette.

"Fuck this."

"We're just a few weeks away, and I'm not going to call it off." The white-haired man started to cough heavily.

"You might want to give those up." Dietz nodded at the cigarette.

"Fuck you. You should know better than to lecture me. If you'd been a little more careful in your hiring, we wouldn't be in this position."

"I dealt with that."

"Like you dealt with Green?"

"What the fuck does that mean?" asked Dietz.

"It means that your guy fucked up. Don't you listen to the news? We don't know what happened to the wife. She was supposed to be hanging from a tree. Plus, no swastika. Now it doesn't look like a race thing at all. Because he took all the stuff out

142

of the den, it looks like Green was killed because of what he was working on."

"But if he took everything, no one will know what he was working on."

Masters looked at Dietz as if he had lost his mind.

"He said she was dead."

"Well, of course, Dietz. I'm sure he thought she was. She probably popped up like a fucking terminator, dragged herself to her car, and drove to the airport. Maybe she's on her way to fucking Disneyworld right now."

Dietz put his hand to his head, trying to rub away the headache.

"Who's this guy anyway?"

"I know a guy who knows a guy. He's the one that took care of the state cop in November," said Dietz.

"Let's hope that this one stays dead." Masters lit another cigarette from the butt of his last one. "Listen, Dietz, it gets worse. Some chick handed a floppy disk to Pardy. She says it was stolen from Green's house by the killer."

"He was supposed to put everything in the locker," Dietz whined.

"Supposed to? Listen, Dietz, you and your guy have created a mess. People were supposed to see this as a race thing. Swastika, Luger, nigger hanging in the backyard? A lot of people went to a lot of effort to coordinate things. My contact in the Sheriff's office said the floppy has everyone's name on it. Mine, yours, everyone's."

"He was supposed to leave everything in the locker. So now, this chick knows everything?"

"She told the Sheriff she didn't own a computer."

"Then, she might not have seen the stuff."

"You're a fucking idiot, Dietz. She obviously did, why else would she give it to the Sheriff?"

Dietz was angry, mostly at the way Masters was speaking to him. After Gordie had taken care of the MBI agent, he'd thought he had found someone he could trust to fix things.

Masters started hacking again. Between coughs, he said, "I'll fix the investigation." Dietz hoped that the old man would cough up a lung and kill himself. All of a sudden, he stopped coughing and turned to Dietz as if he could read his mind. "Fix this Gordie thing, or I'll be looking for a tree for you."

Chapter 21

"That's quite the fable." Arnie put a cup of coffee in front of me. I had stopped by his Trade Winds apartment to give him the Coles Notes version of my meeting with Gladys Mayview. "So how does all this fit into getting Corbin Masters to play ball with the DNA test?"

"Still haven't worked that out, but I think knowing about this could give us leverage."

"If it's true. Keep in mind, he would have to willingly let us test his DNA for a judge to rule it admissible."

"I know."

Arnie turned on the local news to see if there were any new developments. The first thing we saw was Eldridge Crane once again leaning against a Ferrari saying, "The only rubber I need, comes from a set of Goodyear tires."

"Guy thinks he some kind of sex symbol," Arnie commented.

"I went out with him once."

"Seriously, him?"

"He was a little slimmer and didn't wear a toupee."

The news came on, and the anchor was speaking with a picture of Adrienne Green behind him. I ran to the television and turned up the sound.

"This just in from the Harrison County Sheriff's Department. The hunt for Adrienne Green has now shifted to Florida. Representatives for the Department have told this station that a woman matching Green's description was seen on a flight to Orlando the day her husband's body was found. It is believed that the woman was traveling under the name Jayla Lowe. Deputies from Harrison County are coordinating their efforts with their counterparts in Orange County."

I looked over at Arnie, "Seriously? They found some young black woman flying from Biloxi to Orlando, and they're now going to pin it on her?"

Arnie changed the subject. "What else do you have planned today?"

"I'd like to speak to that witness who just happened to see the 'suspicious' black man lurking around. I wonder if that same neighbor was the one that told Sheriff Pardy that Adrienne Green was having an affair."

"Hold on," Arnie said, holding up his hands. "What do you think happened here?"

"I know what happened. So do you. Someone ordered rat-face to kill Green because he was getting too close to something. Angel said she thought that he was looking into some major plot like the Martin Luther King assassination."

"Where's Adrienne Green?"

"I don't know."

"Maybe it was her on that flight to Orlando?" Arnie took a sip of his coffee. "Is this the way you normally spend your Sundays?"

* * *

Arnie drove me to my apartment. As we sat in the car, he reached into his coat pocket and handed me his .38 revolver.

"What's this for?"

"In case someone breaks in and wants to urinate on more clothes."

"Arnie, is this your gun?"

"I rarely touch it. Half the time I forget it's even there. I'm only lending it to you. Once the peeing bandit is apprehended, you can give it back."

"Guns scare me Arnie…. but thank you, this is a very nice of you."

"Gabriel told me to keep you safe.

"I don't know how to use it."

He showed me how to load the weapon and how to take off the safety. "Let's go out to the range next week, and I'll give you a real lesson. Just aim for the chest, and don't stop shooting until you've put him down."

I put the revolver in my purse and kissed Arnie on the cheek.

As I approached my apartment, I noticed that someone had fixed the door and replaced the lock. The only problem was I didn't have a key to the new lock. I went down to the basement and knocked on Mr. Hufnagel's door. The door was opened a couple of minutes later by an older woman dressed in a robe, her hair in curlers. Mrs. Hufnagel gave me a sympathetic smile. "I saw the mess that someone made of your apartment. Do the police know who yet?"

"I don't think so, Mrs. Hufnagel. I see the lock has been changed, does Lou have a key for me?"

"Yes. Lou is out doing whatever he normally does on Sundays, probably wasting time with his buddies at a coffee shop. He left a new key for you. Let me get it." When she returned, she handed me a shiny new key.

"Please thank him for fixing the door. I feel safer now."

"Don't waste your breath thanking him. He's just doing his job. Besides, it was that nice man with the funny name that did most of the work."

"Funny name?"

"German, I think. If I heard it again, I'd recognize it. Lou said he thought he served with the man's father in the Navy."

"Kittyburg?"

"Yep, that's it. Funny name. He said his father was a U-Boat captain."

✳ ✳ ✳

I ran up the stairs and tried the key. Opening the door, I found that someone had been there. The cushions had been duct-taped, and the pictures were back on the wall covered in Saran Wrap in place of glass. I went into the bedroom and saw that the bed had been put back together and made. There were three Sears boxes full of ladies' clothes on the bed. A card was taped to one of the boxes. *"Merry Christmas, I thought you might need a few things. I threw out the stuff that was on the floor. I tried to clean up a little. Sorry about the other day. I was just worried about you. You can call me at 682-4597 if you want to talk. Love Don"*

I sat down on the bed and had a good cry after I finished reading the note. It had been a long few days, and I felt overwhelmed. Hopefully, this was a sign that my luck was about to change. I opened up the boxes and found a selection of slinky underwear, see-through tops, a pair of jeans, and some miniskirts. At the bottom of one of the boxes, there was a red satin bustier.

I went to the living room and dialed the number on the card. It rang three times before the recording came on, asking the caller to leave a short message. I blurted out a quick thank you, telling him how sweet he was. "Very original using duct tape on the pillows. Oh, and thank you for the clothes. You have an interesting sense of style." I ended the call by inviting him over for a non-vegetarian dinner on Monday night.

I took a look in the fridge. "Well, Don, you might have to settle for limp celery along with some yummy cheese slices." I started making a list but gave up, realizing I needed just about everything. The Piggly-Wiggly was closed, so I decided to go the next day.

The telephone rang. Thinking it was Don, I answered: "What was on your mind when you went shopping?"

"I'm sorry. Rachel? It's Beau Snyder. Is everything all right?"

"Oh. I'm sorry Beau, I was expecting a different call."

"I'm calling to wish you Merry Christmas."

"Merry Christmas to you too, Beau." As he spoke in his nasal voice, I couldn't help but picture Kermit the Frog.

"I haven't heard from you for a while. Did you go home to Jackson for the holidays?"

"I had Christmas dinner with my brother and my parents. How about you?"

"I didn't do much, just read a new book on the American Revolution. Did you know that the French helped the rebels from the very beginning?"

"Uh…No, I didn't." We'd met while I was taking his American History course. The man was in his fifties and acted even older. While he was nice, the relationship was never going to work, and I'd ended it.

"How's Gabriel? Are you guys putting more bad guys behind bars?"

"Gabriel and Ben took their families on an extended vacation. They're set to testify at an upcoming trial, and the DA strongly suggested they leave town." I had forgotten how long it had been since I had spoken to Beau.

"I read something in the *Herald*. That journalist, the one that they're talking about on the news, wrote about Mayor Baxter and the corruption at City Hall."

"Yes, that was pretty horrible." I felt a tinge of sadness for Beau, as he was likely spending the holidays alone. "I'm now in charge of the office, and Arnie Simms, my associate, is responsible for the office in New Orleans."

"And how is that going?"

"It's been slow getting started. I'm working on one case now." I suddenly realized that the professor might be able to provide background on Corbin Masters. "You know Beau, if you can tear yourself away from that book, I'd be happy to meet up for a coffee. You might be able to help me with what I'm working on."

"That sounds mysterious. Are you busy right now?"

✻ ✻ ✻

An hour later, we were sitting in a near-empty college cafeteria, sipping hot chocolate. I thought Snyder had aged five years since we'd broken up.

"You look beautiful, Rachel. You're becoming more and more special every time I see you. You know you broke my heart."

I found his comment a little creepy. "You look good too, Professor Snyder," I lied, and changed the subject quickly. "What do you know about Corbin Masters?"

Snyder sat back and rubbed his chin. "Not much. We don't travel in the same social circles. He's an older man who lives in a mansion north of Biloxi. I read an article in *Forbes*. He's very wealthy. I believe he made his money in the lumber business but has since diversified."

"I understand he was heavily involved with the America First movement before the Second World War."

"That is true, along with many other successful business people."

"What can you tell me about that movement?"

"Our President at the time was Roosevelt, and he was at odds with Congress over America joining the war. Congress wanted the United States to stay neutral and to keep our soldiers out of harm's way. Roosevelt, on the other hand, felt we had a moral responsibility to help England. The America First movement supported the notion that America needed to have a strong military but that we shouldn't get involved in fighting other people's battles. The movement was started in 1940 and became widespread, with support in many parts of the country. I think at its peak, it might have had close to a million members. There was a faction of the movement led by people like Charles Lindbergh, Henry Ford, Avery Brundage, and others who felt sympathetic towards Nazi Germany. There were demonstrations in major cities led by German immigrants and sympathizers. These were mainly fascists groups and ultra-right-wing conservative types. Like the Nazis in Germany, some of these demonstrators carried swastikas and anti-Semitic signs. Lindbergh argued that the Jewish elites in America were ruining the country."

Snyder paused for a minute to take a sip of hot chocolate before continuing. "Some scholars believe that if the Japanese had not attacked Pearl Harbor, then we might not have sent troops to fight in Europe. If you believe that, you might also believe that there could have been three major political parties in America. The Republican Party, the Democratic Party, and the Nazi party. Getting back to Corbin Masters, of course, he was involved. Participation in the movement was hardly a secret. I could name another ten wealthy businessmen who openly supported the cause. When the Japs attacked, that spelled a change, and the movement faded into the shadows, but they didn't disappear. The same questions haunt America to this day. The people who supported America First are still there. Many of them are looked upon as patriots. They believe in a nationalist view of America and feel that we have no place in foreign wars like Vietnam and Cambodia. As I taught you in class, those who ignore history are doomed to repeat it."

"You sound sympathetic."

"It's like I say about the Civil War. With the benefit of hindsight, it's easy for academics to be scornful. It would be facile to say, 'had I lived during that period, I'd have…. blah, blah blah.' My point is that had you lived at that time and needed to cast the deciding vote to send so many of our young men to certain death, it might not have been as easy."

"I guess not," I agreed. "Have you heard about the White People's Party?"

"The White People's Party is as it sounds. A party of people who feel that the white race is being threatened by legal and illegal immigration. In the sixties, there was the Confederate Knights of the Klu Klux Klan. The seventies saw participation in the Klan start to die off. Recently, however, what is left of the Klan has been melded with Neo-Nazis, the Aryan Nation, and other skinhead groups. Membership I understand is up significantly. I heard that in Mississippi alone, there are over one thousand members and many more sympathizers. The White People's Party is an attempt to resurrect a true white supremacist movement. As for Corbin Masters, he's pretty old, but I wouldn't be surprised if he weren't involved somehow."

I put the pen down and smiled at Snyder. We talked about his classes, his students, and more books about the Civil War. After about ten minutes, I said, "Thank you for the information Professor."

"Are you going to tell me what this is all about?"

"Maybe someday, but I can't now."

"Have I been helpful enough to have dinner with me?"

I gathered my purse and coat. "I like you, Beau, and I appreciate your help. But no, I'm seeing some-one else."

Beau looked down at his hot chocolate for a moment before saying, "Glad I could help."

Chapter 22

December 25th, 1984

Saucier, Mississippi

Gordie opened the trunk slowly with all the anticipation of a young boy on Christmas morning. "Ho, ho, ho, I wonder what Santa brought me?"

When the lid opened, Adrienne Green gave him a wild-eyed look. The bruise on her head had swollen to the size of a golf ball. She started to scream at the top of her lungs, a look of horror now on her face.

Gordie stood back, his hands on his hips, a smirk on his face. "Settle down, girl. Ain't no one around here to hear you."

Adrienne continued to scream for help. Gordie slapped her hard, not because he feared she'd be heard, but because she was giving him a headache. Reaching for her cheek where she'd been slapped, Adrienne started to whimper.

"Pull yourself together, and hush the fuck up." He looked up at the old deserted fishing cabin. His daddy used to bring him here for what he would call 'A real man's weekend.' Gordie's attention was drawn back to the woman who tried to sit up too quickly, only to fall back down into the trunk. He looked down in admiration at her. "You're finer than a frog's hair split four ways."

The woman's eyes were closed as if she was praying that he'd be gone when she opened them. When she opened her eyes, he smiled down at her and said, "Merry Christmas."

Gordie tried to get her out of the trunk, but every time he reached in, she'd kick her legs wildly at him and resume screaming. Finally, he got hold of her hair and pulled her out of the trunk. "Now we gonna go into that cabin and have us a merry good time. If you promise to be good and quit screaming, then I'll let you go when I'm done."

"I'd rather die than be with you."

"So be it then." He started to walk towards the cabin, pulling her by the hair. It took six feet before she relented and stopped screaming. "Let my hair go, and I'll ....do what you want."

"That's better. Daddy done taught me a few tricks in that cabin. I'm going to show you some things, I bet that Jew boy never taught you." He pulled her to her feet and pushed her towards the cabin.

"You're not going to let me go, are you?"

"Sure, why not? I might need to borrow your car, though. If you can find your way out of these woods, then you deserve to live." They reached the door, and Gordie told her to turn the knob and open the door.

"I can't, it's stuck. Maybe it's locked," she said, holding the knob.

Gordie reached around her to grasp the doorknob. "Doubt it, who'd lock this shit hole?"

As he was reaching around her, Adrienne jammed her right elbow into his face as hard as she could. The blow stunned him, and he fell backward into the dirt. Adrienne seized the opportunity to make a run for it. She ran along the side of the cabin, looking for something to use as a weapon. When she made it to the back of the cabin, she stopped abruptly. There was a series of hastily built graves, each with a little cross made of twigs tied together. There had to be a half dozen. Chills ran up her spine. She didn't hear the twig snap behind her. She turned around just as Gordie threw himself on her. They fell to the ground and struggled. Finally, he got his hands around her neck.

Chapter 23

Pass Christian, Mississippi

Bacchus on the Beach was a popular bar and hangout for dockworkers, fishermen, and people like Bubba Lange. Don let his eyes take in the place. It wasn't anything special, a small crowd for a Friday night. Through the cloud of cigarette smoke, he could see maybe a dozen tough-looking rednecks spread out at tables, and another four crowded around the bar. Don asked a Willy Nelson look-alike for a Bud and looked around the room for a man that fit Bubba's description.

Dr. John was on the jukebox singing about being in the right place at the wrong time. Don let his mind flashback to Rachel. They'd been supposed to get together over the holidays while she was visiting her parents. But when he'd called her parent's house and spoken to her mother, he'd been given a number at the Howard Johnsons and a lecture about lying to her daughter. When he'd called the motel, a man at the front desk had told him Rachel had already checked out, and practically hung up on him.

He wondered what kind of a mess she'd gotten herself into this time. Last summer, there had been a close call with her boss getting involved in a shoot-out. Don's pleas that she find another job had fallen on deaf ears. He'd put a list of suggested jobs on her fridge. Tops on the list were cocktail waitress, then school teacher followed by secretary, and then exotic dancer. She hadn't commented on the list. Instead, she'd doubled down and volunteered to run the *Eye on You Detective Agency.*

After a couple of beers, Don's attention was drawn to a big man entering the bar. Two other large white men came in behind him. They all wore camouflage clothing. Don was sure the leader of the group was Bubba Lange. He looked as if he was in his mid-thirties, and about as wide as he was tall. All three men sported handlebar mustaches and wore their long hair in a style called the mullet. The trio nodded to people as they sat down at a table in the corner. Don watched in the mirror over the bar as Willy Nelson went to their table with a pitcher of beer and glasses. Don's assignment was to infiltrate the group, gain their trust, and report back to Fred on what they had cooking. Fred had also added, almost as an afterthought, to avoid getting killed.

One of the handlebar mustaches got up and put some coins in the jukebox. Moments later, Freddie Fender was wailing about wasting his nights away. About five minutes later, the door to the bar opened again, and a middle-aged black man staggered in. It was clear the man had been drinking as he stumbled and bumped into the bartender, causing the man to spill a beer. The black man apologized profusely, belching at the same time. "Maybe you've had enough." Don heard Willy say.

"Nonsense," said the newcomer, veering off at an angle to the bar and landing in a spot beside Don. "I'll have, I'll have," he repeated, trying to form the words. "Whatever he's having." He pointed to Don's beer. "Hey, if you don't mind me saying … like I'm just saying, but that's a fucking stupid hat." He slurred, nodding to Don's ball cap.

Don snuck a peek at Bubba and saw that the commotion had caught his attention. He took off his cap, showing his newly shaved head. He turned the hat around and ran his fingers over the lettering, 'Make the South Great Again.' "You have a problem with that?" Don said, stepping closer to the man.

Willy put the drunk's beer in front of him. "Just calm down, folks, no need to get all riled up over a hat."

"The South's never been great, pal." The drunk sprayed saliva as he spoke. He was reeling, holding onto the bar, trying to steady himself.

"I think you'd best drink that beer somewhere else," Don said in a menacing tone.

Rather than back away, the man pushed Don and said loud enough for the whole bar to hear, "Get the fuck away from me. I'll drink wherever I want."

Don shook his head and took a sip of his beer, then returned the push. "Last warning, get out of here, now." He took a glance at Bubba's table in the mirror. The good old boys were standing, watching the action.

"Fuck off, hillbilly," said the black man, shoving Don again, causing him to spill his beer.

Don took a deep breath, "Listen, man, don't get angry." He extended his hand to the man, but once he was a couple of feet away, he launched a left that landed on the man's jaw. The man fell back a few steps and held onto the bar for support. Don followed up with a hard right to the side of his head. The blow caused the man to stumble and fall into an empty table. "Now, get the fuck out of here, nigger."

The man was hurt but not stupid. He quickly got up and stumbled back out of the bar. Once the door closed behind him, there was a round of applause from the other people in the bar. Don was shaking hands with one of the men at the bar when he felt a hand on his shoulder. His reflexes made his muscles tighten, and his fist clenched.

"Relax, man, just wanted to buy you a drink and tell you how much I enjoyed that." It was one of Bubba's crew.

"Sure, thanks."

The man gestured to the bartender and held up two fingers. Somehow Willy Nelson knew this meant whiskey. "My name's Fender," the man said, holding out his hand.

Don grasped his hand and thanked him for the drink. "Kittyburg."

"To making the South Great Again," Fender said as they downed their drinks. "Why don't you come over to the table, and I'll introduce you to my friends."

Don followed the man to the table. Bubba kicked a vacant chair towards him and gestured for Don to sit down. "Sure taught that boy a lesson."

Don shrugged his shoulders as he sat. "Guy was pretty drunk." Fender poured him a glass of beer.

"Makes you wonder, doesn't it, Mr. Kittyburg," said the man sitting to Bubba's left, "Why a coon would come into a place like this. Let alone start mouthing off."

Don took a long sip of beer. "He was as drunk as Cooter Brown."

Bubba chuckled and nodded. "My name's Bubba Lange, y'all met Fender," he pointed to the man to his left, "And the one that keeps playing with his balls is my half-brother Parker." Don nodded to each man, in turn, making sure he kept his expression deadpan.

"What kind of a name is Kittyburg?" asked Parker.

"German, my dad was a U-boat captain."

"Y'all from Louisiana?" Fender asked, downing the rest of his beer.

"Been lots of places, but I was born right here in Mississippi, up in Natchez."

"Judging by the prison tat," Bubba said, pointing at Don's neck, "I'd say you might have spent some time in Angola."

Don's hand went to the tattoo, and he wondered if they could tell that the ink was fresh. "Fuck, don't get me going on that place. Yeah, I've been a guest for a spell."

"Haven't seen you in here before. You new?" asked Parker, a suspicious look on his face. The song mercifully ended, and Fender got up and went over to the jukebox. Moments later, *Wasted Days and Wasted Nights* started up again.

"I get it, that's why you call him Fender because he likes the song," Don said, snapping his fingers.

"Nah, it's because a few years back, he was working at a boneyard and put some wetback in the hospital by bashing his head in with a rusted-out fender." Bubba poured more beer in his own glass and topped up Don's. "The guy has the worst fuckin' temper I've ever seen."

As Fender came back to the table, Parker repeated his question. "I asked you why we haven't seen you in here before." Parker, who had been peeling the label off the beer bottle, looked up and glared at Don.

"That's right, you did." Don took a long drink. When he finished, Bubba was sizing him up. If it came to blows, Don would put money down on the redneck kicking the crap out of him. "Just rolled into town from Louisiana. I was involved with someone and overstayed my welcome. I thought I'd mosey on down the road."

"What kind of work do you do?" asked Bubba.

"Gruntwork. I've got a degree from the road gang at Angola, and a diploma on shit shoveling from Parchman farms."

"Who did the ink?" Fender asked.

"Some guy named Amos…. I don't remember the last name." As part of his briefing package for the undercover role, Don had shaved his head and gotten a bunch of tattoos. Anyone checking his prison record would see that Don Kittyburg had spent three years for auto theft plus another two years at Parchman for assault. He was told that if he was asked about the tattoo, he was to say the guy's name was Amos.

"Amos does good work," said Fender lifting his sweatshirt to show off a massive Iron Cross that took up his whole chest. Bubba then put his leg on the table and showed off his swastika.

"You know Kitty; can we call you Kitty, or would you prefer Pussy?" asked Bubba, lighting a cigarette. "I'm currently looking for someone with experience in those things. Doing what they're told, handling themselves, minding their own fucking business, that kind of thing."

Don smiled and nodded his head. "I'm good at that."

"I run a seafood business down here. It's hard work, but we can always use an extra hand."

Don nodded again. "Not sure what kind of trouble I want to get into here, but I'll keep it in mind."

Chapter 24

"Where have you been?" Dietz asked in a menacing tone.

"I had some things to do," Gordie replied.

There was silence on the line for a few seconds. "What the fuck happened, Gordie?"

"What do you mean?"

"Don't play stupid. You've made the wrong people pretty upset. Since I hired you, it doesn't speak well for me. Where's the wife?"

"Dead, like I told you."

"Why didn't the cops find her body?"

"What's with all the fucking questions? You said dead, so she's dead. I got rid of the body."

"Why didn't you leave her in the house?"

"Listen, it's no big deal. She got away, okay? I thought she was dead, but she gets up, and before I know it, I had to pull a Rambo on her."

There was a sigh on the phone. "And then you lost the suitcase?"

"That I can explain. Yep, that I can explain. Some bitch named Henderson took my suitcase at the airport. I guess there were two blue suitcases. Or maybe she's just dumb as shit. But not to worry, I got it back."

"Was there something about a disk that you forgot to tell me about?"

"Disk? Oh, I thought I did. I got it off the guy's desk. I thought it might be important."

"Gordie, this girl, Henderson, walked into the Sheriff's office and gave him the disk. Either you got it back as you say, or you're fucking lying."

Gordie took a deep breath. "When I picked up the suitcase, it had pretty well everything in it. You know my shaving kit, my clothes, my razor…"

"Gordie, answer the question," the man interrupted.

"What was the question again?"

"How the hell did the girl end up walking into the Sheriff's office with something that you were supposed to have left in the locker?"

"I…I don't know. I must have left it in the suitcase. By mistake."

"You made a lot of mistakes, Gordie. Let me explain something to you. This woman must know what's on the disk. Otherwise, she wouldn't have brought it to the Sheriff. We can't have her opening her big mouth."

"I can fix this."

Chapter 25

I got home after the meeting with Professor Snyder feeling like I was starting to form an outline of Corbin Masters. I still had no idea how I was going to convince him to do a paternity test. I decided to call Larry Bremmer at the Biloxi Herald, knowing full well that he likely wouldn't be in the office on a Sunday. Sure enough, I called the number on his business card and ended up leaving him a stupid voicemail. "Hi Larry, It's Rachel Henderson. I was in to see you the other day, and well, I thought we could discuss working together. Can you call me on Monday when you get a moment?"

I munched on a dill pickle as I looked up the number for Jayla Lowe in the white pages. The call was answered by a man who said his wife was on a business trip in Florida.

"Maybe you can clear something up for me, Mr. Lowe. My name is Rachel Henderson, and I operate a private investigations agency called *Eye on You Detective Agency.* A case I'm looking into involves the murder of Hartley Green." I paused for a moment to gauge his reaction.

There was a sigh on the phone. "This is getting ridiculous. We went over all this with Deputy Weber."

"I know you don't know me, but I would really appreciate your help. If you could explain what happened, I'd be grateful."

"My wife is an African American woman who just happened to be on a flight out of Biloxi on Christmas Day. She's a buyer for a major retail company that is having a Boxing Day trade show in Orlando. The deputy thought she was this Adrienne Green. Despite Jayla having all kinds of identification, they brought her to the Sheriff's office in Orlando and interrogated her for an hour. This Deputy Weber said he was some kind of expert in forged identification. He kept on demanding to know the name of her lover and threatening to bring her back here to stand trial."

"What finally convinced them to let her go?"

"She doesn't look like Adrienne Green. Anyone with half a brain can see that. For one thing, Jayla is six inches taller and fifty pounds heavier. It took one of the Orlando cops to point that out."

"So, your wife has been released?"

"Finally, but I have yet to hear an apology or see anything in the papers."

"I'm going to be talking to the editor of the *Herald* tomorrow. Would you mind if I speak to him about this?"

✳ ✳ ✳

I had no sooner hung up from the call with Lowe when the phone rang again.

"Hey, I got your message," said Don cheerfully. "I'd be happy to get together on Monday night. Want me to bring anything?"

"Maybe something to drink. We're having steak, so whatever goes with that." I said steak as if I'd never heard the word before.

"Steak? Wow! Like real steak, as in cow?"

"Did you get that job?" I asked, changing the subject.

"I'm a full-time apprentice with the Bubba's Seafood Emporium."

"Sorry, but this all seems kind of weird to me. I know what you said to Arnie, but you were pretty excited about the Senior Agent position, and next thing I know, you're working as an apprentice in a shrimp business."

"It's more than shrimp, they harvest oysters too. Bubba has plans to open a chain of restaurants starting right here on the Coast. If I play my cards right, this could really lead somewhere."

"I'm sure it will lead somewhere..." My voice trailed off into uncertainty.

Don paused for a moment. "Are you going to tell me what's going on and why someone broke into your apartment?"

It was my turn to pause, still not sure he was entitled to the story. "Maybe if you're nice to me tomorrow night, I might tell you something."

After taking a quick shower, I called Arnie and asked if he had heard from Gabriel.

"Yes, they were leaving the island to visit Gabriel's parents in Detroit. He said he had tried to call you a few times, but you were out."

"It's been quite the day." I told him about having coffee with Professor Snyder.

"You're gathering a lot of information. What conclusions have you made, and how does this help our case?"

"Corbin Masters is a fascist who yields power with his money and connections. I believe he's involved in this White People's Party."

"Let's say that's true. How does this help us?"

"I'm getting there, not to worry. I'll come up with something," I said, with as much braggadocio I could muster.

Chapter 26

After the call with Arnie, I settled in for a quiet evening at home. Jacob had given me an autographed copy of Stephen King's Pet Cemetery for Christmas. I figured I'd try to get my mind off the case. Thankfully the book was an engaging read, and I was able to suspend my disbelief. After a couple of hours and three more dill pickles, I was on the last chapter. I thought about Bourbon and what Arnie would do if something happened to him. I was still deep in thought when I was startled by the phone ringing.

"Hello?" There was silence on the line, but I sensed someone was there. Maybe it was what I had been reading, but my mind leaped to something evil. I repeated. "Is someone there?" When there was still no answer, "Listen, whoever this is, I'm going to hang up."

"All alone tonight?" asked a male voice.

"Who is this?"

"Help me out. I'm trying to get a mental image. I can see your living room light is on. Are you lounging in some sexy negligee, watching something on the box? Maybe you could come to the window and show me."

Fear grasped me as I realized who it must be. I fought the impulse to hang up, "What do you want?"

"Are you sitting on that ugly couch? Did you replace the pillows? They didn't match anyway."

"What do you want?"

"Just thinking about you." He yawned and took a deep breath. "I hope you don't mind, but I took a few souvenirs. I'm wearing a pair right now."

I ignored him. "Did you kill Green?"

"What do you think?" There was some dead air before he continued. "I read in the papers that his nigger wife did that. You have to be careful about getting involved in these inter-racial relationships. You wouldn't do that, would you, Rachel?" I tried to answer, but I stumbled on my words. "I could be your boyfriend. Maybe I'll come over…"

I didn't let him finish and hung up. People often say that they're paralyzed with fear, well, I was scared to death, but also angry. The anger fueled me. I turned off the light and went to the living room window, pulling the drapes closed. There was a payphone down the street. I could see from the glow of a streetlight that it was empty. Was he coming for me? Panic kicked in, and I sat in the corner on the floor. Trembling, I jammed my fist into my mouth, stifling a scream. My legs were frozen in place.

I'm not sure how long I sat there, but I heard the apartment doorknob rattle, sending my heart racing. My thoughts were going a mile a minute. I crawled across the living room, taking Arnie's gun out of my purse. I felt for the safety in the dark. My hands were shaking as I sat back down on the floor and pointed the gun at the door. A memory of Gabriel saying he didn't know if he would have the courage to shoot someone. At this point, I was positive that if Rat-Face were to walk through that door, he'd be dead meat.

The rattling stopped. I picked up the phone again and dialed 911.

* * *

"I got a prank call. An obscene call." I said to Deputy Weber, trying to catch my breath. "He must have been calling from that phone booth down the street because he said he could see the light from the living room window."

Weber nodded and walked over to the window and looked out. "Were these curtains closed?"

"No, I closed them after."

"Do you normally have them open in the evening?"

"No, of course not. I just hadn't got around to closing them."

Weber nodded as if he was considering what I said. I didn't care what he thought. "What else did he say?" Weber had his little spiral notebook in his hand.

"He asked me what I was wearing and wanted me to come to the window."

Weber pointed at my flannel nightie and raised an eyebrow. "You say it was the same guy that broke in here. The suitcase guy?"

"I recognized his voice. Plus, he asked me if I still have the ugly couch."

Weber looked at the couch and nodded, "Kind of ugly."

I shook my head, "Then, he said he took some souvenirs and that he was wearing a pair."

"What do you think that was?"

"I don't know, and what difference does it make?"

Weber shrugged again and made a note in his book. He stopped his writing, and his face grew serious as if he finally clued in on something. "That's messed up." He looked down at the Stephen King book on the coffee table. "You reading this?"

"Yes."

"You're obviously a different person, but I find that reading things like that scare the shit out of me. Have you ever read any John Jakes; he writes those books about the Civil War?"

"Can we get back to the call, please? I asked him if he'd killed Green. He didn't answer and asked me if I wanted him to come over. That's when I hung up and turned off the lights and closed the drapes."

"This man, Gordie Howe," he started to chuckle to himself. "Didn't admit to killing Green, right?"

"No, he just repeated the same fairy tale you guys are floating about the wife."

"Hmm, then you called 911?"

"No, I sat there for a while. I'm not sure how long. I was scared. That's when I heard someone outside my apartment rattling the doorknob."

"Who was that?"

"Obviously, the guy."

"How do you know that? Did you ask who's there?"

"No, I didn't do that. I was sitting in the corner, freaking out. I wasn't going to go to the door and ask who's there."

"I see the locks have been changed, that's a good thing. Still, we'll be having one of our cruisers keep an eye for a while. Is there someone you can call to stay with you?"

"Are you going to take this seriously now?"

"I have always taken you seriously, Miss. Henderson. I have no doubt you stirred up a hornet's nest by stealing someone's suitcase."

I thought about calling Arnie, but it was after midnight, and the danger hopefully had passed. I was rattled and started to pace. I told myself that being distressed was precisely what the killer wanted. Instead, I got the mop and bucket and washed the floors. I windexed the windows, dusted the furniture, and made a list of groceries to buy tomorrow. By the time I was done, it was almost 2 AM, and I crashed on the couch.

Chapter 27

After six hours of sleep, I got up and showered and put on a black velvet mini skirt and a hot pink, flowery, off the shoulder blouse. It was one of the sluttier outfits that Don had bought. Looking at myself in the bathroom mirror, I decided that I had better buy some new clothes.

I splurged on a box of Krispy Kreme doughnuts on my way to the office, thinking that somehow it would alleviate my feeling of being alone in the universe. When I got to the office, I found a steady stream of reference checks had come in but discovered that I had the focus of a gnat. It dawned on me that Travis would be on a Christmas break, so I dialed his number.

It took a few tries, but eventually, a sleepy Travis answered. He lived with his mother, who worked at the Tivoli hotel and had likely gone to work.

"Good morning Travis, did I wake you up?" I said, cheerfully.

"It's barely 9 AM. Where are you? I can call you back like, in a …couple of hours." I laughed and told him that I was at the office enjoying a box of Krispy Kremes.

"Krispy Kremes, huh? Is everything all right?".

I took too long to answer, and he cut me off, saying he would be over as soon as he got changed. "Don't eat all of those doughnuts!"

✳ ✳ ✳

When Travis arrived, I told him about last night's adventure over bites of a doughnut.

"Holy crap! You must have been frightened out of your wits."

"Scared, angry, frustrated; I shift from one emotion to another."

"Pretty clear, the cops aren't going to do much."

"That's the frustrating part. They're off chasing the wife when I practically handed them the killer."

"Maybe I should hunker down on your couch for a few days."

"That's very nice of you to offer, Travis. You being here today is more than enough. Plus, Kittyburg is coming over for dinner tonight." We were interrupted by the door opening and Larry Bremmer walking in. "Good morning Larry, want a Krispy Kreme?" I asked, smiling at him.

"I got your message. I thought I'd visit and check out the place." Larry looked around the reception area. I introduced Travis and escorted him to my office. Travis came in a few minutes later with fresh coffee for us.

"Wow, coffee, Krispy Kreme, and beautiful women." Larry took a sip of his coffee. "I like that blouse, it's very …"

"Slutty?" I volunteered, taking a bite out of my doughnut.

"I was going to say the flowers look good on you, especially for December."

I smiled at the compliment. "I shouldn't eat so many of these."

"Did you know the founder and owner of Krispy Kreme was a Nazi during World War 2?"

"Is that true?" asked Travis.

"The family name is Reimann."

I put the doughnut down. "I had a conversation yesterday with a man named Lowe." I watched Larry's face and saw no recognition. "He's Jayla Lowe's husband."

He shrugged his shoulders.

"Jayla Lowe is the woman the police arrested in Florida on suspicion that she might be Adrienne Green."

"I get it now."

I told him about the conversation with Mr. Lowe. "He has yet to hear an apology from the police, or read anything in the paper.

"I can put something in the paper today once I get the official word from Pardy. But I'm confused;

you mentioned in your message about working on something together. Is Hartley Green's murder the case you're working on?"

"No, my client hired this agency to look into a paternity suit against Corbin Masters."

"A paternity suit? From who?"

"I can't disclose that, at least not without the client's okay."

"Corbin Masters.... can't say I'm surprised. There've been rumors."

"Anything you can share? I'm doing a lot of research."

"I honestly don't remember any names. There's something about him getting involved with some of the local talent. Is that what you meant by being able to help you?"

"Corbin Masters' name is on the list I showed you last week."

"The list that came from the disk? Right, I remember seeing his name. Are you any closer to figuring out what that's all about?"

"I've looked into Masters and a few other names on the list."

"And?" Larry prompted, taking a bite of his doughnut.

"There's an organization named the White People's Party. I still have a lot of research to do, but they're a white supremacist organization with connections to the KKK. I don't want to jump to a conclusion, but I'm positive that Hartley's killer stole that disk when he murdered him."

"You're suggesting that Corbin Masters and this white supremacist group had Hartley killed?"

"I can't prove it."

"Pardy thinks Adrienne Green killed her husband."

"I know the theory, but it's predicated on the Greens having marital problems. I spoke to someone who knew the couple very well, and that's bullshit, just like with Jayla Lowe. I'd like your readers to know the truth."

"That's very noble of you. I'd be happy to put this in the *Herald* once you cough up the proof."

I looked at him and decided to show him the schematic of the garage door opener. "On this same disk, there was a file containing the specs for a device." I handed him the drawing.

"A garage door opener?" He looked at me over the top of his glasses.

"True, but it can also be used as a wireless trigger. The bit at the bottom left is the makings for homemade C-4. Before he was murdered, Green said he had found out something big was about to happen."

Larry picked up the drawing and took his time before putting it down. "Who have you been speaking to about the Greens? It must be someone at the *Herald*."

"The person said the Greens would never have had an affair. They've asked me not to disclose their name."

"Another deep throat…you should be an investigative reporter."

"I don't know what has been planned or when it might happen. But I feel certain that Corbin Masters knows something about this."

Larry put his hand on his forehead as if trying to massage away a headache. "What does this have to do with the paternity thing?"

"That's a separate case that just happens to involve Masters. His estranged son, my client, has sent letters asking him to take a paternity test. So far, the man has rejected all requests. Which makes me think he's hiding something."

"Or he just doesn't want to part with his money. What other proof does your client have?"

"Before she died, his mother gave him her diary, which mentions Masters around the same time the client was born."

"That's hardly conclusive. I can't imagine how many people come out of the shadows each year to claim some millionaire is their father. Masters might have rejected the request just out of the sheer volume of claims."

"That might be true. But I met with his ex-wife, Gladys Mayview, and she knows Masters had sex with the staff at his mansion."

"Background information, but not enough to compel the man to have his DNA analyzed."

"Maybe so."

"Do you have anything else?"

"Not yet. I'm just looking for a way to get Masters to want to have his DNA tested."

"If you come up with something, let me know. It would be an interesting story. And if Masters is behind the death of my star reporter, I'd like to help."

* * *

Once Larry Bremmer left, Travis and I worked on the reference checks until Arnie called. I thanked him again for the gun and told him how I had almost used it the night before.

"That must have scared the bejabbers out of you. Had you called, I would have been over in a flash."

"I know. It was late, and Deputy Weber said patrols would be keeping an eye."

"Why is it always Weber that responds? They have other deputies."

"Good question," I replied. "The positive, if you can call it that, is he's willing to concede that this wasn't some drug-crazed punk."

"So he believes that the guy that broke in was Hartley's killer?"

"I wouldn't go that far. He still thinks this is a case of me angering the wrong man by taking their suitcase."

Chapter 28

On the way home, I stopped at Piggly Wiggly and picked up supplies. Putting everything away, I opened up a bottle of red wine and poured myself a large glass. I was expecting Don at 7 P.M., so I had an hour or so to kill. After taking a quick shower, I changed into another one of the outfits Don had purchased. This time it was a leather mini skirt with a zipper up the front and a see-through green top. I put a Boz Skaggs cassette on the stereo and busied myself in the kitchen with the meal. I was still thinking about Don and how strange he had been acting when there was a knock at the door. It was barely 6:30 PM. I was just about to open the door, ready to greet him when my hand froze on the doorknob. Don was usually late for everything. I went to my purse and got the gun. When I returned, someone was rattling the doorknob. Maybe Rat-Face had been watching me and seen me come home with the groceries. I held the gun in both hands like I'd seen in cop shows on TV and yelled out, "Who's there?"

"It's me, Don…open up."

I opened the door and said, "You're early."

"That's hardly a reason," he looked down at the gun in my hand, "to shoot me. I'm trying to turn over a new leaf."

"Like with that goofy hat," I said, letting him into the hall and closing the door. Don was wearing a flattering green turtle neck and jeans. He took off the hat, showing off his newly bald head.

"Oh my God, Don. What did you do?" I asked, shocked by his new look. "Are you sick? Are you getting chemo?"

"No, it's all part of my new look." He handed me a bottle of wine. "Best wine that money can buy."

I looked at the bottle of Two Buck Chuck wine. "Wow, thanks. I didn't expect you to break the bank."

"I haven't gotten paid yet."

"Oh, that's right, the seafood thing. Are they paying you in shrimp?" I asked as he walked into the living room and sat on the sofa.

He ignored my question. "You know, I've always liked this sofa. Classy."

"Is that right?" I thought about the conversation last night. "How's the new job going?"

"Pretty good. I was telling Arnie, it's a ground floor thing right now, but Bubba has plans for a chain of restaurants."

"Bubba? You work for a man named Bubba? What does Bubba have you doing?"

"Today was my first day. They took me out on the boats, handling the nets and stuff. The shrimp season is coming to an end on account of the colder water temperatures. So next week, we start harvesting oysters." He picked up a pillow and admired the duct tape he had used to repair the rip as if he was admiring fine artistry.

"Thanks for the clothes. It made my day." I twirled around, displaying the outfit. "Do you like it?"

He gave me a lecherous look. "You've got great legs. I think they're your best feature. How did you like the other stuff?"

"Oh, the skirts and blouses are nice. I'm impressed."

"What about the other thing?"

"What other thing?" I asked, cocking my head.

"You know the ..." he pantomimed, holding a pair of large breasts.

"Hardy har har, maybe I'll let you judge for yourself if you tell me the real reason you shaved your head." I unscrewed the cap on the wine and poured him a glass.

"It's just the new me. It's kind of a cleanse."

"And what about the hat?"

"You live and work in the South, don't you want to see it proper?"

"Of course, but that's not what that hat suggests."

"Yeah, what's that?" he asked, taking a sip of his wine and grimacing.

"It suggests a rise of a new Confederacy that promotes white supremacy."

Don took the hat off and looked at it. "It doesn't say that. Say, do you have any pretzels?"

"No, I don't. It may not say that, but that's the message conveys. The little Confederate battle flag on the back clinches it." I sat down on the couch beside him. "What's gotten into you, Don? You quit the MBI, shave your head, then take some job, eating shrimp with a guy named Bubba. Have you lost your marbles?"

"It's nothing."

"What comes next? Are you going to get a swastika tattooed somewhere?"

"As a matter of fact," Don rolled down the turtleneck and showed his ink. "You'd likely see it sooner or later."

"Oh, my Lord!" I said, touching it. "Now, I know you're sick. That's deplorable, Don. Is that real…does it come off?"

"It's real."

I gave him a serious look. "I'm not going out with a guy who wears a swastika tattooed on his neck."

"I think you're overreacting."

"It's a symbol of hatred, just like that hat. Who the hell is this Bubba creature?"

"Settle down. You're making too much of this."

"No, I'm not, and don't try to dismiss how I feel."

"Let's enjoy the wine, maybe put decent rock music on the radio. What is this crap?" Don was a classic rock guy and had little patience for anything else.

"Boz Skaggs. He's very popular. This isn't going to work Don, I'm sorry. I guess I didn't realize what kind of man you were. I can write you a check for the clothes, then I think you should go find yourself a little fraulein." I stood up, arms crossed, and pointed to the door.

"Is this because I don't like Boz, whatever his name is? You can listen to him."

"Oh, I can? I have your permission?" I gestured to the door.

Don's expression did a 360 when he realized I was serious. "Can we back up a little? Did you find out who broke into your apartment?"

"It doesn't matter. This can't be fixed with shrimp."

"Come on, Rachel," he reached for me, but I brushed his hand away. "Just tell me who broke in."

"For all I know, it was some friend of yours... some Neanderthal named Bubba."

"I love you. I never wanted to lie to you. If I could find the creep that broke in, I'd ..." he stopped when he saw my eyes cloud over with anger. "I'm going to make a suggestion I want you to consider seriously."

"Is this where you tell me I should quit my job and be a cocktail waitress?"

"I just worry you'll get in over your head."

I rolled my eyes and sat back down. Closing my eyes, I hoped he'd get a clue and leave.

"I'd like you to consider going to Jackson for a month or so. Visit with your parents…"

"I have a job, Don. People depend on me. I can't just leave for a month. Besides, what's going to happen in a month?" I suddenly remembered that Masters and his crew were planning something. A look of horror must have crossed my face as it occurred to me that Don might be involved. "Don, what are you mixed up with?"

"Listen, do you remember when we were working together on the stolen car ring? There were certain things that I couldn't tell you."

"That was when you were working undercover, not for some shrimp factory. Don, are you undercover?"

He shrugged and closed his eyes as if trying to dispel an evil image. "They fired me. Even though I was infinitely more qualified than…well, it's bullshit. It's called affirmative action. So, I lose the promotion because I don't have a vagina. I admit I didn't take the news very well. That's when they told me they needed me to go undercover again. An agent I had trained had been inside a group suspected of being domestic terrorists. He went missing earlier last month. My boss wants me to infiltrate this group and find out what happened to him and what they're planning."

"So, the hat, the tattoo, the job is all just a cover?"

"That's right. We staged a fight in a bar, an idea I got from watching an old Alan Ladd movie. Bubba was impressed with how I handled myself. He asked me to join his crew. Say, do you have any peanuts?"

"No, and you're such a convincing liar. Is this the truth?"

"You can't tell anyone about this. Now, your turn. Who broke into your apartment?"

I stood up again and started to pace the room. I was still not entirely convinced, but holding it all in was becoming too hard. I told Don about the mix-up with the suitcase, the murder of the reporter, the rat-faced man, the disk with the list of names, and the phone call I'd received last night. I pulled the copy of the list and the drawing for the garage door opener out of my purse.

"Have you figured out what this is?" Don asked as he scanned the pages.

"To be honest, I'm not sure. It appears to be the makings of a plastic explosive and a detonating device. The list might be people who are either part of this plot, or who are supporting it."

Don put the papers on the coffee table. He stood up and put his arms around me. This time I didn't push him away. I wanted to be held. I wanted someone to tell me that it would be all right. Then he brought me back to earth. "You're dealing with some bad people here."

"How am I 'dealing' with them?" I pushed him away again. "It's not like I'm asking for someone to break into my apartment. It's not like I'm inviting people to come in and pee on my clothes."

"But you're running around asking questions. Sooner or later it's bound to get back to them. Who did you tell about this list?"

"Professor Snyder, Arnie, Gabriel, the editor of the *Herald*, the pastor at my church, some architect downtown."

"So pretty much everyone. Well, one of them told someone that you looked at, or took a copy of this list. That makes you a problem. They don't know that you haven't figured it out. But if you keep asking questions, then the easiest way to deal with you is just to get rid of you."

Chapter 29

I finally relented and cooked Don the meal I had promised. I even let him play his beloved Creedence Clearwater Revival cassette. Multiple glasses of wine led to a little of this and a lot of that, and before I knew it, I was parading around the apartment in a red satin bustier.

It was after midnight, and he was lying face down in bed while I turned on the lamp and carefully examined him for more offending tattoos. "So, what now, Don?" I asked, poking him in the bum.

He opened an eye. "You're insatiable. You want round two already?"

"No, silly. What do we do about this group of terrorists?"

Don rolled over and mumbled, "It's just my first day. Let me work my magic. Before you know it, I'll hav…." His voice trailed off into a snore.

I shook him awake. "Don, I met a lady at the *Herald*. She told me that Hartley had discovered they're planning something big."

He said something that sounded like, "Put on that bustier, and I'll show you something big."

That earned him a slap. "Come on, Don. Work first, play later."

He lifted himself onto his elbows. "Did this person have any idea of what was being planned?"

"No, but I have a theory, want to hear it?"

"I'm all ears. Start with, why kill Hartley on Christmas morning?"

"Green was Jewish, in an inter-racial marriage. At precisely the same time, two synagogues were set on fire in different parts of the State. I think all of this is coordinated. I think this is about making a statement, just like wearing that stupid hat."

"Sheriff Pardy said the wife killed him."

"That's what they want you to believe. I think the real reason he was killed was that he got too close."

"Too close to what?"

"To whatever they're planning. Listen, Martin Luther King Day is January 21st. I was researching some of the people on the list, and I found a reference to a man named Steve Schaffer. He's argued against honoring Martin Luther King. He maintains that Robert E. Lee is more deserving. I'm thinking that planning an attack, or an explosion on that day might be just the statement this group would like to make."

"The theory makes sense. Maybe you're right. In any case, it'll take some time before I can gain Bubba's trust. I can't just start asking questions."

"What can I do in the meantime?"

"Other than put on that outfit again?"

When I gave him a frown, he suggested, "Look into what the city has planned for that day. Are there any parades? Speeches, that type of thing?"

I nodded and got out of bed, wrapping a sheet around me. I was passing the window and looked out at the full moon. I gasped when I saw a man looking up at me.

"Don, Don…. get up! He's out there. The rat-faced man. He's watching my window."

Don jumped up and went to the window. "That guy? That guy with the jean jacket?"

"Yes, that's him!"

"Are you sure? We're eight flights up."

"Yes, hurry."

Don put on his jeans and looked around for his top. As he ran out the door, I watched from the window. The man took a last look up at my window, and we locked eyes before he walked out of sight.

About ten minutes later, there was a knock on the apartment door. After confirming it was Don, I opened the door. He was standing there wearing his jeans and my see-through top.

"What the hell?"

"I just grabbed what I could. I put it on because it was cold outside."

"Did you catch the guy?"

"Yes and no. I caught up to the guy we saw. He showed me a badge. He's undercover, working for the Harrison County Sheriff's Department. He said he'd been assigned to look in on you."

"No, that's the killer! Gordie Howe!"

"Gordie Howe?"

Chapter 30

Robert E. Lee, Stonewall Jackson, and Jeb Stuart. Those were the names of Bubba's shrimp boats. Don was told to shadow Fender and help out as a deckhand on the Jeb. Before that, they needed to unload massive blocks of ice from a truck into an ice chipper. Fender was leaning against a wall smoking a cigarette while Don struggled with the blocks.

"So, your daddy was a U-Boat captain?" Fender asked, chuckling.

Don thought he might drop the block onto the dock, which likely would spark Fender's legendary anger. "Yeah, U-Boater," Don said straining.

"What was the name of his boat?"

Don finally managed to get the block over to the chipper. "They didn't have names, just call numbers. He was the captain of U-107.

"What happened to it?"

"No one knows for sure. It disappeared in August 1940. They told my mother that the RAF bombed it. Sank with all souls." If Fender was trying to catch him in a lie, he didn't know who he was dealing with. Don took a breather for a moment and leaned against the long hull of a wooden dinghy.

"Well, you know that's interesting shit. You told Bubba the other day that you were thirty-six years old. Now I ain't no mathematical genius, but how could a man who died forty-four years ago be your Daddy?"

"That's just the story my mom told me. After the war, you see," Don 's mind was racing a mile a minute, "she moved and settled in Natchez. She continued to go by the name Kittyburg. Later she got married again to a guy named… Longbottom and I was born. Since my mom never took his name, neither did I."

"Longbottom, Kittyburg…got any other names?" Fender asked, his eyes squinting.

"Nope."

"So, your daddy, your real daddy, wasn't a U-boat captain."

"He was a con. He wasn't around much."

"What's that saying about an apple not falling too far from a tree? Better grab another block of ice."

* * *

An hour later, they were on the Jeb lowering the outriggers. Don was conscious of Fender standing at the helm, watching him. He wasn't sure if he'd convinced Fender with the story about his family. He decided to meet the challenge head-on.

"You checking out my butt, Fender? You a homo?" In Mississippi, even the faintest suggestion that a man might be gay was asking for trouble.

Fender scrambled down the ladder and approached Don, his face beet red. Don held his fists by his side, ready.

"Bubba told me to keep an eye on you. Seeing you're new and all."

"Yeah?" Don smiled at him, diffusing the tension. "Well, I can handle myself. Say, Fender, if Bubba needs my help with anything else, you make sure to tell him all he needs to do is ask."

Fender nodded, "You got something in mind?"

"No, just want to earn my keep."

* * *

Later that day, Bubba was sitting in his office with Parker, who had been burning up the phone lines, digging up what he could on Kittyburg. "You know how Dietz hired that undercover cop? If the state cops are onto something, I don't want to repeat the same mistake. What did you hear from our friends at Harrison County?"

"The arrest records show Kittyburg did a stretch in Angola for car theft. He got let out on parole just like he said. Here's the funny thing though I asked a couple of guys from the Brotherhood about him, and I got nothing. It's not exactly the kind of name you'd forget."

"What else?"

"I confirmed he spent time at Parchman Farms. He was convicted of assault, but his lawyer appealed.

The nigger he beat up changed his story, so they had to release him. Once again, I asked around, and no one remembers him."

"Smells like another cop with a made-up story. What did Fender have to say about him?

"Good worker, does what he's told. Anxious to help. Fender said he might have caught him in a lie about his father, the German U-boat captain. But the guy spun another one."

Bubba shook his head and let out a deep sigh of frustration. Thankfully Parker had the sense not to say 'I told you so.' The brothers had had a huge argument after the fight in the bar. "I'm going to invite him up to The Camp. If you think he's legit, then fine. If you don't, you know what to do."

Chapter 31

December 31, 1984

Gulfport, Mississippi

When I got to the Agency, I reflected on what had happened the night before. I was having doubts that the man I'd seen from my apartment window was the same man I'd met in Jackson. It couldn't be. He had a Harrison County badge? I had stopped to pick up a copy of the *Biloxi Herald*, and true to his word, Larry had included a short piece about the hunt for Adrienne Green.

Harrison County Deputies got a free ride to Disneyworld last week. All at taxpayer's expense. A source connected to the Sheriff's office confirmed that a woman allegedly matching the description of Adrienne Green had been on a Christmas Day flight from Biloxi. Working with their counterparts in Orlando, they were able to find the woman at a local hotel where she was attending a convention. The woman was brought in for questioning, and she was able to prove that she was not Adrienne Green. Police report no leads on the where-abouts of Mrs. Green, who is wanted for questioning in the murder of her husband, Hartley Green.

At 9 AM, I called City Hall and asked to speak to someone about Martin Luther King Day.

I was connected to a woman in the Civic Affairs Department. "I was wondering what type of celebrations are being planned for Martin Luther King Day?"

"On January 21st, the Governor will be in Biloxi. He'll be holding a press conference on the steps of City Hall commemorating Great Americans Day. He will then lead a procession of people down Beach Boulevard to Stonewall Jackson's heritage home."

"What does this have to do with Martin Luther King?"

"We are celebrating all of our nation's great heroes. Including Stonewall Jackson, Robert E. Lee, and of course, Dr. King."

"Do you know of any other celebrations planned that might be more specific to Dr. King?"

"If there were such a thing, it wouldn't be a sanctioned event, so I wouldn't have any information to share with you."

* * *

My next call was to Deputy Weber. "It's Rachel Henderson, and I want to know who you assigned to watch my place."

"Oh, Miss Henderson, nice to hear from you. Has something else happened?"

"Just answer the question. Did you assign a plainclothes deputy to watch my place?"

"No, but I did ask that your apartment be included in the routine patrol. As far as I know, there have been no incidents reported."

"There was a man outside my apartment last night looking up at my window."

"He wouldn't have been able to see into your apartment from the street. Maybe it was just a guy waiting for the bus."

"At midnight? Not likely. Anyway, Kittyburg was here and ran down and confronted him. The man told him he was a Harrison County Deputy and showed him a badge."

"Is Mr. Kittyburg sure? I'll have to ask around. But that would be very unusual."

"You're the unusual one. This is the same creep who trashed my apartment and who threatened me the other day."

"Can you ask Mr. Kittyburg to come in and give us a description of the man?"

"Weber, if you want a description of the man, just pull out the sketch that I did for you. Why don't you do a little police work instead of chasing your tail down in Orlando?"

Chapter 32

Rachel Henderson's comment about chasing his tail in Orlando nagged at Weber. Together with the recent tongue lashing, he'd received from Sheriff Pardy, it made him question the investigation. Initially, it had all made sense. They'd found Adrienne Green's BMW at the airport, and one of the ticket agents identified a woman traveling under the name Jayla Lowe as Adrienne Green. Looking at the pictures later side by side, he had to admit there wasn't much of a resemblance.

He picked up another sketch that had appeared in the *Herald*. This one was of the man identified by the neighbor as the black man seen lurking near the Green home. Pardy had been against putting the sketch in the paper, suggesting that they'd just waste time chasing all the crazy leads which would come in. When Pardy had called him into his office, he had shown Weber what he called his nutjob tally on the blackboard. So far, Eddie Murphy had a slim lead over Michael Jackson and Prince. One caller said they were sure that it was Martin Luther King. When told that King was dead, the comeback was, 'That's what they want you to believe.'

The crime scene had been dusted for prints, but to no avail. It likely meant the killer had worn gloves. They'd found a gun at the scene. It had not been fired and was probably an antique that Green had collected. A neighbor a couple of blocks over had reported hearing a car with a bad muffler on Christmas morning. A routine patrol found an abandoned Chevrolet Caprice that had been reported stolen; they dusted the car for prints and found nothing but cigarette butts, bubble gum wrappers, and an empty Coke bottle. They'd gone over every scrap of paper in Hartley Green's offices, both at home and at the *Herald*. They'd spoken to the employees and got nothing. No one even knew what story he was covering.

Weber looked over at the deputy that had passed on the tip about Jayla Lowe. "Hey Barry, where's that floppy thing the Henderson woman brought in last week?"

"The disk? Why, is she bugging you about that again?"

"Yeah, just get it for me. While you're at it, get me the sketch she did too." Weber sat back and took a sip of his coffee. Ten minutes later, Barry handed him a folder containing the sketch that Rachel had done. "Does this guy look familiar to you?" asked Weber.

"No. You know, she looked at every mugshot we have."

"Remember a few years ago, there was a guy, a recruit right out of the academy?" Weber held his hand over the man's hairline in the sketch. "I think his name was George or something. He had a weird last name."

"I don't remember anyone like that."

Weber looked in the file folder, "Where's the disk?"

Barry shrugged, "I don't know. I suppose someone might have put it in the property room. There was nothing on it anyway. There was just a list of names — no one you'd recognize."

"I'd like to see the list anyway. Can you go find the disk, please?"

Chapter 33

Saucier, Mississippi

Corbin Masters looked out over his mansion's circular lane from his second-story bedroom window. He drew his robe closer against the morning chill. Lately, he was always cold. He watched as his younger brother got into his green Mercedes coupe. He wondered if Chester's stupidity was God's way of balancing the scales. The man was simple-minded, going through life as if he didn't have a care in the world. In his rare waking moments, he was either on a coke-induced binge or out God-knows-where trying to score more. Corbin understood that drugs helped alleviate the pain of some people's pathetic lives, but for idiots like Chester, who had everything they could want, it was just stupidity.

He picked up the latest corporate report he'd been reading and made a note to ask his accountant about the second straight lousy quarter for the mill up in Natchez. He lit a cigarette and thought about the likely issues; cheap out-of-state product, spiraling labor costs, weak-kneed management, bureaucratic regulations that did nothing to help businesses thrive. He'd suggest hiring another boatload of illegal Vietnamese refugees. Those people worked twelve hours a day, didn't complain, and were willing to work for rice.

Masters started coughing violently. The hacking and wheezing were happening more and more frequently and always left him feeling disoriented and seeing stars. When it finally ended, he held onto his desk for support and tried to calm his breathing. He looked down at the *Herald* and saw that he'd once again coughed up blood. He blamed the disease for his short temper, his lack of appetite, and the complete loss of sex drive. He'd started and stopped Chemo; he'd had radiation, and he'd tried experimental cures prescribed by quacks. There was mistletoe, milk thistle, and now shark fin extract, presumably because sharks didn't get cancer.

As he was looking down at the blood-smeared paper, he caught sight of an article about Jayla Lowe and was reminded of the whole domino of events brought on by Dietz's stupidity. First, they had to deal with the cop. Then they found out he had spilled his guts to this Jew reporter. Now, the police had a disk with some very damaging information.

Luckily, he had one of Lange's men inside the Sheriff's department to misdirect the investigation. Corbin picked up a copy of the list. Dietz's name was second only to his own. He was the link to what was left of the old guard, the Klan. Dietz had made a name for himself when the struggle had been one dimensional - the superiority of the white race. *Christ, he still spews that crap about rounding up the niggers and marching them to some state like Idaho. We might have been able to do that a hundred years ago to the Indians, but times are different now.* The struggle had become much more urgent. Weak immigration laws had led to the mongrelizing of America. It was a fight to preserve their heritage, culture, even their language. This fight would require both political savvy and strength. That's where the third name on the list came in. Steve Schaffer was a politician with connections both in Washington and in the State Capital.

Corbin closed his eyes when he saw the next name. Bubba Lange was the power behind the youth movement. He was the link to the Aryan Nation, the skinheads, and Neo-Nazis that had breathed new life in the organization. He and his brother, Parker, ran the militia camps. His thoughts were interrupted by a knock on his study door. "What?" he croaked.

Elizabeth stuck in her head, "Are you all right, Father? I heard you coughing."

She's doesn't give a damn about me. She just wants to know if it's time to collect her inheritance. She has none of her mother's beauty or grace. "I'm fine. What do you want? Can't you see I'm busy."

"Your lawyer is here. He says he has an appointment."

Without telling his children, he had ordered Canyon to change his will. Elizabeth and her dim-witted brother Andrew would, of course, receive attractive allowances, but the bulk of his estate would go into a trust to help the movement. If he could ever catch Chester in a sober moment, he was going to convince him to do likewise.

Chapter 34

"Something wrong, Jim?" Deputy Weber asked, taking a seat in front of Sheriff Pardy, who was sitting at his desk reading the newspaper.

"Damn true, Weber. Jesse Jackson has come from nowhere to take first place in your nutjob poll." He shook his head, his lips pressed together. "You're in charge of this investigation, how could you let it get so off the rails?"

Weber took a deep breath. He had hoped his boss might have calmed down from his earlier tirade. "Hear me out, Jim, there's something wrong."

Pardy sat back, the chair groaning under the weight of his bulk. He gestured to his deputy to get on with it. "What?"

Weber pulled out the sketch the Henderson woman had done and passed it across the desk to his boss. Pardy picked up the sketch and immediately put it back down.

"You said this was nothing."

"I know I did. Do you remember a recruit that washed out a few years back named Gordon Bones?"

"Yeah, the state cops were looking at him because his name came up in a missing person

212

investigation." Pardy reached into his desk for a package of Fig Newtons and put two in his mouth at once. In between chews, Pardy continued, "In the end, they couldn't make it stick, so I took him for a walk out back by the dumpster and suggested he resign."

Weber put the file picture of Bones beside the sketch on the desk. Pardy looked at the sketch again this time, his eyes flicking back and forth between the two. "Okay, maybe…he does look a little rat-like."

"On another note, Deputy McGloyn tells me that the disk that Henderson brought in has been misplaced."

"Deputy McGloyn," Pardy repeated.

"Remember, it was McGloyn who told us there was nothing on that disk. Just a bunch of people donating to some charity." Pardy shrugged his shoulders. "And, he's the one that found the witness who said she saw the black man." Weber nodded to the sketch on the nutjob board. "I think Barry might be fucking with us."

"You think he just made it all up? Why would he do that?"

"I don't know,"

"You realize his daddy's a pastor?"

"Yes, I do."

Pardy stood up and went over to the blackboard, munching once again on a couple of cookies. "I thought it looked a bit like Flip Wilson." He shook his head, looking back at Weber. "What are you waiting for? Get the fucker in here, and we'll talk to him."

"He didn't show up for work today, and there's no answer at his apartment." Weber looked away in embarrassment. "I think he might have overheard me talking to his witness about her statement."

"So, all this business," Sheriff Pardy said, pointing to the blackboard, "is just horse-pucky?"

"I'm supposed to see the witness this morning. I'll get it straightened out."

Pardy's shoulders slumped, and he looked up at the ceiling. He took off his glasses and rubbed his eyes. A sure tell for Weber that his boss was about to blow. "Rachel Henderson was right, then?"

"I don't know," Weber said, wondering if his boss was contemplating another dumpster run.

Pardy glared at Weber, and barked, "Send a patrol to Barry's apartment." As Weber got up to leave, Pardy added, "And maybe you'd better apologize to Miss Henderson."

Chapter 35

Gulfport, Mississippi

It was a cold, windy morning with temperatures expected to get no higher than the mid-fifties. I reluctantly put on my leather mini skirt again, paired with another see-through blouse, and drove in to work. I decided to pass on the Krispy Kremes this time.

When I got to work, I brewed myself a coffee and started wading through a stack of bills. I was wondering just how I was going to pay for a computer on top of everything else when the phone rang. My mood picked up when I realized it was Gabriel. "How is everything in the Great White North?" I asked.

"Beautiful, it brings back memories of growing up in Detroit. You know, snow forts, snowball fights, and lots of hot chocolate. Any more on the case?"

"I thought I saw the suitcase guy down on the street looking up at my apartment, but when Kittyburg ran downstairs, it turns out it was a cop ..."

"Did you say Kittyburg?" Gabriel interrupted.

"I'm sworn to secrecy, but it turns out he's still with the MBI working undercover. He's looking into the disappearance of an agent who was investigating a domestic terrorist organization."

"So, are you guys….?"

"I guess so," I said, biting my lip. There was silence on the line until I asked, "Anything new on the trial?"

"Baxter's lawyer has put two motions forward. One for a change in venue. With all the publicity in the *Herald,* he's arguing that he wouldn't get a fair trial in Biloxi. The second motion is to move the trial ahead to next week. He must be getting sick of prison food. The DA said that the Judge is likely to approve both motions. She wants to make sure that Ben and I are ready to go on Monday."

"I'm sure you'll be happy to see an end to this."

"You can say that again. The time away has been good for us. Jacqueline and I have had a lot of time to talk about things. Listen, Ben's waiving to me. We're all going ice skating today."

I didn't get a chance to feel melancholy after speaking to Gabriel; I had no sooner hung up when the agency door blew open, and Deputy Weber walked in. "Look what the wind blew in."

"Good morning Miss. Henderson. I've been doing some thinking about the case, and I was wondering if we could start over."

"Thinking? I didn't think you were capable of that."

Weber shook his head and looked up at the ceiling. "Maybe I was mistaken about …. you know… the guy and the suitcase. Can we do a reset?'

"A reset? You mean, get into a time machine and go back to when you weren't such a knob?" I come from a long line of people who like to rub it in.

"Look, I'm trying here. I was going to go pay a visit to Fern Hooper and thought you might like to come along?"

"I might if you told me who Fern Hooper is."

"She's the woman who said she saw a black man lurking around the Green's place on Christmas morning."

It took me all of ten seconds to grab my coat and purse.

* * *

On the way over, Weber showed me a picture of Gordon Bones. "Do you think this could be your guy?"

"He's not my guy, and yes, his hair is longer, but it could be him."

"This guy was fired a while back," he said, pulling onto U.S. 49, leading to Saucier.

"Why was he fired?"

"It's kind of sketchy, but Sheriff Pardy asked him to resign when his name came up in an investigation being conducted by the State Police." I didn't say anything. I was looking out the window, waiting for an apology. "He might have kept his badge."

"You believe me now?" I asked, turning towards him.

"I always did."

"Sure you did," I said. "What about that disk? The one that you said was nothing."

"I never actually saw what was on it. One of our more tech-savvy deputies was the one who said it was nothing."

"So maybe you …the new and improved, 'thinking' Weber should look at it."

"I would, but apparently, it's been misplaced."

I had given my copies of the disk to Don. Otherwise, I would have flashed them in Weber's face and gloated about doing his police work for him. Plus, Arnie and I had told Sheriff Pardy we had no idea what was on the disk. I wasn't quite ready to trust my new friend.

The Hoopers had a massive home elaborately decorated for Christmas with a nativity scene. It was in a predominantly white part of town. As we were getting out of the cruiser, I said, "Seems to me, a black man in this neighborhood might stand out."

Weber ignored my comment and went to the wrap around porch to knock. "Better let me handle the questions. This is an official police investigation," he said in his bossy, big boy tone.

No sooner had he knocked, than the door was opened by a middle-aged woman wearing a navy-blue dress, white hair piled up on top of her head.

She had cat-eye glasses hanging from a chain around her neck. "Are you Deputy Weber?"

"Yes, and this is a Private Detective by the name of Rachel Henderson. Can we come in?"

Judging by the woman's gaping mouth, Mrs. Hooper hadn't expected anyone but the deputy. She gave me a once-over before recovering and directing us into the living room. The room smelled of lemon pledge, and a couch and chair were covered in plastic.

"Thank you for seeing us, Mrs. Hooper," Weber said as we sat down on the couch.

"Have you caught him?" She turned to face us.

"You mean the man in the sketch?" asked Weber.

"The nigger…" she caught herself and then looked at me, "I'm sorry the black…man."

"No, we haven't, Ma'am. I'd like to go over your statement, but before we do, I looked up some police records this morning." Weber put a copy of the sketch of the black man on the coffee table. "You've called the station several times to report seeing black men lurking about."

"I've caught them looking in my window a few times."

"You reported seeing a black man six times during November."

"Maybe it was more than a few times."

I thought Weber was going to leave it there, so I jumped in. "Mrs. Hooper, has it always been the same black man?"

"Yes," she said enthusiastically as if she had just realized it. "He looks a little like Flip Wilson."

I pointed to the sketch. "You said you saw this man on Christmas morning."

The woman nodded, her eyes sparkling, "I saw it in the paper," she said proudly. "I bet you've had a lot of calls."

"A few," Weber replied, giving me a look suggesting that I leave the questions to him. "Interestingly, none of your neighbors reported seeing a black man in this neighborhood."

"That's not right," replied the woman. "The deputy said there had been many other sightings. He asked me whether I'd also seen this black man."

"He showed you a picture of the man?" I asked.

"Of course. He said that the man was very dangerous and preyed on white folks."

"So, you saw a picture of a black man. Did you see him coming out of the Green's house on Christmas morning?" I repeated, trying to maintain eye contact.

"The deputy said it was Christmas morning."

"You also said that you knew the Greens were having marriage problems," asked Weber, raising his voice and looking at me while asking the question. "Did you know the Greens very well?"

"I know their type." She turned to me, giving me a once-over again before turning back to Weber. She lowered her voice as if I couldn't hear. "She was always dressed like a harlot. Wearing miniskirts, showing off everything the good Lord had given her. My Lord, she was half his age! They always had parties. Wild parties, playing loud music at all hours of the night. I believe you call them orgies." She pronounced orgies with a hard G. "Well, I'm sure you've heard the stories. They just weren't decent folk."

✳ ✳ ✳

"This was a big set up. You need to get rid of that deputy," I said as we got back into Weber's cruiser.

"I said to leave the questions to me." He put the cruiser in gear.

"You brought me. What was I supposed to do, just sit there and look like a harlot?"

"Yes, just sit there." He backed out of the lane and then added, "As for Deputy McGloyn, he has gone off the reservation. We have an APB out for him."

"My pastor's name is McGloyn."

"Barry is his son."

"You don't get it. Reverend McGloyn's name is on the disk. The one you can't find."

"You said you didn't know what was on the disk?"

Chapter 36

Bubba called early to wish Don a Happy New Year. "I understand you're willing to do just about anything to help out?"

"Within reason, I guess. Fender tell you that?"

"Yeah, he said you were a pretty good worker. He also reminded me that you did a tour in 'Nam."

"Fucking place, mind my French. I enlisted to do my part for America, but if you ask me, we should never have been fighting in that shit hole."

"Amen to that brother. What drives me crazy is we were fighting with one arm tied behind our back. We should have nuked the fuckers. You know your way around weapons?"

"Yeah, M16, mortars, claymores, whatever's needed."

"Do you know where Saucier is?"

"Sure, north-west of Biloxi."

"There's a training facility up there called The Camp. Some ex-military guys run it. They'll make sure you are up to speed so you can be … more help to us."

"Ex-military?"

"A group of concerned patriots, like you, who train people to be ready in case they're needed."

"Needed for what?"

"Anything from helping to patrol the southern border, right up to a race war. It's about five miles north of town on Highway 5. You'll see a church on the left called the Sword and Arm of the Lord. Look for my brother, he'll get you up to speed."

A half-hour later, Don was in his truck on his way to the militia camp. According to his briefing, similar camps had been popping up all around the country. Many were well-financed and had access to sophisticated weapons. A sense of unease came over him as he recalled how rookie MBI Agent William Morrison had been planning to attend the camp before he'd mysteriously disappeared.

He thought about Rachel and the list. She was playing a dangerous game with deadly people. She was convinced that there were plans afoot to use homemade C-4 at the upcoming Martin Luther King Day. Once Don had understood the risks she was taking, he'd counseled her to let it go and let him do his job. He also suggested that they not see each other for a few weeks just in case they were being watched. She'd reluctantly given him the copies of the lists and blueprints, which he planned to fax to his boss Fred Moller at the earliest opportunity.

Don turned the truck into a long lane bordered by a thick pine forest. He could see a dilapidated clapboard church at the end of the lane. A hand-painted sign indicated he was approaching the

Church of the Sword and Arm of the Lord
Pastor Parker Lange

When he pulled up next to the church, he saw a group of men in camouflage khakis hanging around out back. As he got out of his truck, one of the group approached him. "Are you Kittyburg?"

Don nodded, and the man who'd spoken extended his hand. "Barry McGloyn, welcome to the camp. Parker just went into the church to make a call. He said to look out for you." Don nodded again as his eyes took in their surroundings. He counted over a dozen scruffy looking men wearing fatigues that looked like they'd come from an army surplus store. The men all carried sidearms. A couple of them were walking towards a shooting range carrying M16s on their shoulders. "Heard you were in 'Nam," said Barry. "I was too young to enlist. My background is in law enforcement."

Don nodded. "Care to give me a tour, Barry?"

"Sure, can do. Over to the left, we have the rifle range. Everyone here has to be certified on not just handguns but also automatic rifles. To the right is the parade ground, that's where we work on our drills. You see that cliff just past that?" Barry asked, pointing to a rock cliff that rose about a hundred feet. "That's where we learn to rappel. And over here," he said, pointing to a sandy area the size of a boxing ring, "We do hand to hand training. We have a guy with a black belt do the training. If you follow this dirt road, it goes up into the hills for miles. Parker likes everyone to do their running. The church basement is where we conduct classroom instructions in patrolling, land navigation, radio communication, and things like military strategy. There's a couple of outbuildings on the other side of the church; one has bunks for those of us who live here and take care of the place."

"Who's in command?"

"Parker pretty much runs things and sends..." Barry stopped in mid-sentence as a bulky man sporting woodland camo and wearing army boots came out of the church and started walking towards them.

Don recognized the barrel-chested man as Bubba's brother. "Hey Park, Barry was just going over the lay of the land with me."

A grim-faced Parker nodded, looking at Barry. He gestured in the direction of the church. "He's on the phone. He wants to speak to you."

"Say, Park, is this a real church?"

"Yeah, and I'm a fucking pastor." Don nodded. He had a hundred questions but needed to be careful with Parker. He had the impression that the man hadn't wholly bought the fight in the bar. "Bubba says you know your way around weapons."

"That's true, but I've been cooped into a dark cell for a spell, so I might be a little rusty."

"Let's walk over to the range. You can show me what you can do," Parker said.

They walked the hundred yards to the range with Parker trailing behind a couple of steps and answering Don's questions with grunts or one-word answers. When they got there, Parker gestured to one of the men with an M-16 to share his weapon with Don. Don took the rifle and looked down the field to where a bunch of beer bottles were balanced on a fence rail about forty yards away.

"Let's see what you can do, Kittyburg."

Don assumed a firing position lying down on the ground and flipped the firing selector to semi-automatic. It was a windy, cold morning, and he figured the likelihood of hitting a bottle at about a hundred to one.

"What're you waiting for?"

"Just getting a sense of the wind." Don aimed and depressed the trigger, feeling the barrel of the rifle rise as it bucked against his shoulder. Sure enough, none of the bottles were damaged. "I said I'd be a little rusty."

"Here, give it to me." Parker stood as he sighted the rifle. He picked off two of the bottles in succession before handing the weapon to one of the other men. "More than a little rusty, I think. Come on, you would have learned how to rappel down a building in the Marines, right?"

* * *

They walked to the other side of the camp, with Parker again walking a couple of steps behind Don. "How's Kirksey?"

Don turned around and said, "I'm sorry, who?"

Parker gave him a sly grin. "Kirksey Nix. Just about the most famous guy in Angola."

"Oh yeah. We traveled in different circles."

"I guess that's right. He told me he never heard of anyone named Kittyburg. Thought it sounded like a Jew name."

Don stopped and stared at Parker, "Look, there's got to be over 6000 people there, I heard of him, but I'm a small fish. As for being Jewish, I was christened in a Methodist church up in Natchez."

When they'd climbed up the hill to the rocky outcrop, Don could see that a heavy rope had been tied to a pine tree and lay dangling off the cliff. Sensing Don's hesitation, Parker asked, "Do I have to show you how to do this too?"

"No. Just looking for the safety line, the carabiners, gloves, the proper equipment."

"Just fucking get on with it."

Don grabbed the rope and gave it a good tug. "You sure this rope is strong enough? When was the last time you replaced it? I can see it starting to fray." Parker responded by pulling his Colt sidearm and gesturing towards the cliff. Don was confused. If they wanted to kill him, then why didn't they just shoot him? It was like they wanted to stage an accident. He'd be lucky to get out of this alive. He started to tie the rope around his waist.

"No, no need for that," Parker said, waving his gun. "Just grab hold and rappel. Like they taught you in 'Nam."

Don had taken a basic rappelling course at the police academy, but never eight stories high. He remembered being scared to death even with a safety line.

Chapter 37

Gulfport, Mississippi

I didn't have a good answer to Weber's question, so I stayed silent for a minute. As he drove back to the agency office, he kept looking over at me. Finally, I returned his gaze. "Remember how I told you what hotel room I was in, and you sent the killer?"

"I didn't send the killer…"

"Right. Someone in your office did because I told no one else. Listen, Weber, I'll say this slowly so you'll understand. I didn't want to say I had seen the file because I didn't know if somehow this information would get back to the killer. They'd already killed a reporter because of what's on that disk."

"McGloyn said the file just had a list of names and addresses."

"There are about twenty names. I think they're either involved or, in some way, support what is about to happen."

"And what is about to happen?"

"I don't know for sure, but I believe that they are planning to blow something up on Martin Luther King Day."

"How did you come to that conclusion?"

"It isn't a conclusion, just a hunch. One of the names on the list is Steve Schaffer, the politician. He maintains that instead of honoring King, Mississippi should be commemorating Robert E. Lee."

"So what? Lots of people probably think that."

"There was another file on that disk. It had a drawing of a remote detonator and the ingredients on how to make C-4."

Weber almost drove off the road, and I heard horns behind us. "Are you saying that this Steve Schaffer is going to blow people up?"

"It's a hunch, but I think a good one."

"I need to see this stuff for myself. Do you have a copy?"

"I gave it to Kittyburg."

Chapter 38

The worst part of rappelling is letting go and trusting that you aren't going to plunge to your death. Don locked his feet around the rope and used his left hand to hold the rope over his head. He used his right to guide the rope behind his back. Slowly he fed the line down and lowered himself. By the time he had dropped ten feet, pain was radiating through his arms. The rope was tearing the skin from his hands. He looked down and wondered if this was how Morrison had died. He started back down but hadn't gone another foot when he stopped and saw a grinning Parker looking down at him. The muscles in his shoulders were burning. He thought about swinging the rope towards the cliff and maybe catching hold of something. He could hammer a spike into a crevasse, except he had no spike, no carabiner, and no hammer. Don looked down. Directly below him, there was an outcropping of sharp rocks. If the fall didn't kill him, the jagged rocks surely would.

He continued his descent, his hands leaving a trail of blood on the rope. His mind was racing in panic. He was still a good seventy feet from the ground. Out of the corner of his eye, he saw Parker rushing down the trail, accompanied by Barry.

Another ten feet, and he didn't think he could go any further. He wasn't scared of falling anymore. So be it. If he had to die, then he'd done his bit. He thought about Rachel. She was convinced that something big was in the works. The homemade C-4 was meant to do major damage and to call attention to what these guys want. But what do they want? Let's stay out of foreign wars...I can live with that. Do away with affirmative action...now you're talking. Kill all the Jews....no, that's not right. Moving all the Mexicans and blacks to some remote state, well, that's just messed up.

* * *

While Don was trying to hold on, Parker ran into the church to talk to his brother.

"What's up, Bubba?"

"There's an APB out for Barry. They know he's been misdirecting them about the investigation. It's too risky having him involved. Besides. I have another little job for him."

"That's going to leave us down one man."

"How's the new guy?"

"He talks a good story and has answers for everything. I left him dangling from a rope just now so he might be dead."

"I have an idea."

* * *

Don looked down. Only thirty feet to go. *Great, I can look forward to being a cripple for life.* His hands had grown numb. Pain seared through his shoulders like a branding iron. He took his right hand off the tail end of the rope and put both hands above him in a desperate attempt to not fall. He was no longer rappelling. He was holding on for dear life. He called out, "Help!" He didn't expect anyone to help him. He was pretty sure this was Parker's plan all along. He wished he could have one more chance with Rachel. At least they'd had last night, and a chance to set the record straight.

He took a look around; a crowd of people had gathered at the base of the cliff. They were yelling at him. "Let go…let go…let go."

Bloodthirsty bastards was his final thought as his hands lost their grip, and the rope started to slip through his fingers.

Chapter 39

Don closed his eyes, somehow believing that would lessen the agony. He felt the world rush by in a blur and prepared himself for pain. When the collision came, he started screaming. He heard laughter around him. Slowly he stopped bellowing, realizing that the onlookers had been yelling at him to let go so they could catch him with the bedsheet they had been holding. He ran his hands over his body, realizing he was unhurt.

"Looks like you might have to borrow a pair of jeans," a voice yelled.

"They teach you how to fall like that in 'Nam?" another voice asked.

The guys brought Don into the church, where a smirking Parker greeted him. "Funniest thing I've seen in a while. Help me," Parker mocked, windmilling his arms.

It took a good hour before Don's nerves settled down. A pastor wearing a gray tunic and looking like a southern version of Cary Grant showed up and led them in a short prayer service. A couple of people served sandwiches. Introductions were made, and Don was able to say thank you to Ace, Joe-Bob, Brodie, Jethro, and Zeke for catching his fall.

* * *

While he was finishing his sandwich, Parker came and slapped him on the back, asking how his hands were. Don looked at his hands, which had been bandaged crudely and looked like oversized oven mitts.

"They'll be okay. I'm thankful that one of the guys knew a bit of first aid."

"That's good."

"Say, where did Barry go?"

"He needed to go to one of the other camps."

"You guys have more than this place?"

"We have militia and paramilitary camps throughout the state."

"Why so many?"

"The Church of the Sword and Arm is one of the fastest-growing ministries in the South." Before Don could ask another follow-up, Parker asked, "Are you ready for this afternoon?"

"This afternoon?"

"Yeah, we've scheduled an impromptu briefing on explosives. I believe you told Bubba about having some experience with explosives."

"I didn't realize I was on the agenda."

"Got to be prepared for the unexpected."

* * *

After lunch, Parker got everyone's attention and introduced Don as a munitions expert who was a specialist on claymores and other anti-personnel mines.

Don reluctantly stood up, "Two-thirds of the American casualties in Vietnam were caused by land mines planted by the Viet Cong." He had no idea if that was true, but it sounded good and got everyone's attention. "Any type of explosive has to be handled with care and respect. There were lots of situations where people had their hands blown off." For effect, he held up the oven mitts.

The rest of the afternoon went quickly, and Parker said he had done well in leading the discussion on explosives. "We might have a job for you."

"Sure, I told Bubba I'd be willing to help out."

"Great, we'll get into specifics later."

Chapter 40

Gulfport, Mississippi

I took a deep breath, sighted the gun, and slowly squeezed the trigger. In my mind's eye, I saw the head explode in ribbons of bright orange brains. I hadn't been planning on spending the day killing pumpkins. When Arnie picked me up that morning, he'd had four good-sized pumpkins sitting in the back seat that he'd decorated with a magic marker to look like the rat-faced man.

What I had wanted to do was to spend the day with Don, now that he was back in my good graces. However, he had been adamant about no contact for a few weeks. With him being undercover, and people watching me, we had to be very careful.

"Well done, Rachel." Arnie was standing behind me. "You're a natural." We had been at it for over an hour, and I was just now getting comfortable with the .38's kick. "That's a pretty heavy gun for a beginner, so you're doing well. If you decide to buy a gun of your own, you might look at a lighter weapon, but you'll find the recoil is worse. In terms of stopping power, the .38 does the job. How do you feel?"

"Kind of exhilarated. It helps like you said, to visualize someone. Wearing this mini skirt doesn't help, though."

"Now there are going to be times when your first shot either misses or doesn't put the man down. So, let's practice a rapid-fire, double shot."

He placed a fresh pumpkin on the stump, but after twenty minutes, my double shots were still hopelessly off the mark, and I thought my arm was going to fall off.

"It doesn't matter. If you have to fire your weapon, you'll be a lot closer. Let me give it a try." Arnie took the .38 and fired four shots in a row, emptying the chamber. Pumpkin brains flew everywhere. "That was fun. We should do it again next week." Arnie handed me back the gun.

As we were walking back to the van, he asked what other plans I had for the day. "I thought we could take a drive up to Saucier."

"Weren't you just up there yesterday with Weber?"

"I thought we could do a drive-by of Corbin Masters' house. See how rich people live," I answered.

"I've seen it. We'd never get past the guard. "

"Yeah, but maybe just being near might inspire me."

* * *

The Masters' home was what you'd expect of a mansion in Mississippi. The first thing I noticed was the eight-foot-tall metal fence that surrounded the property. There was a gate with a rent-a-cop, just as Arnie had said. As we idled in front of the house, we looked up the long laneway to an enormous white antebellum three-story mansion.

While we were looking at the house, I brought Arnie up to date on Weber's turnaround and our visit to Fern Hooper. "I need to get the copies of the disk back from Kittyburg. He promised to do some checking on the names."

"Do you think you can trust Weber?"

"I'd already told him about the files. I pretty well had to, once he told me about Deputy McGloyn."

Arnie nodded. "Speaking of Kittyburg, why did you give the list to him?"

"The seafood job is a cover. He was sent here by the MBI to look into this white supremacist group, and to find out about an agent who disappeared. He left me a message yesterday to say that his boss asked him to go to a militia training camp today."

We were interrupted by the guard rapping on Arnie's window. It was a heavy-set white man wearing a uniform. "Deliveries have to go through the servant's entrance."

"Yes, siree, sir," Arnie said enthusiastically. "Now, we ain't delivering today. The missus," he said, looking over at me, "well, we wanted to do some house hunting."

The guard bent down and looked through the window at me. "Now you listen here. Y'all best be getting along. These here homes aren't for you."

"Well, thank you, sir. That is one mighty fine house. Could you tell me who the owner is?" Before the guard could reply, the front gate opened, and a green Mercedes coupe rolled out. The driver waved to the guard and turned right onto the street.

"Mr. Corbin Masters own it, and he don't want your company."

"One last question, sir, was that him in the green coupe?

"That was Chester Masters. Now get out of here before I call the police."

Arnie rolled up his window, and I pointed in the direction the coupe had gone. "Follow that Mercedes and step on it."

We almost lost the Mercedes but found it again after twenty minutes, parked in front of a bar called Stonewalls in downtown Saucier. We parked down the street, and I said, "I'm going in. Gladys Mayview told me I should talk to him."

"You're dressed kind of…"

"I've been to lots of bars before. I'm just going to go in, get him interested and find out everything he knows about his brother."

"If you aren't out in thirty minutes, then I'm going in and shoot some pumpkins."

Chapter 41

Ocean Springs, Mississippi

Gordon Bones (aka Gordie Howe) had a room at the Good Night motel in Ocean Springs. He thought the place was a dump and ought to be condemned. There was a for-sale sign on the front of the property. The TV didn't work, the toilet continually backed up, and there was never any hot water. Who in their right mind would buy the place?

Of course, there was no working phone in the room, so any time he needed to make a call, he had to use the payphone in the strip plaza across the street. The creepy guy had told him to call at precisely 7 AM on Mondays and Fridays to check-in.

The weather at 7 AM was cold, and he blew hot air on his hands as he stepped into the phone booth. The last call with the creep had not gone well. The man had been obsessed with that Rachel Henderson. He'd planned to take care of her last night, but she wasn't alone. He'd almost put his switchblade up her boyfriend's ass, but he killed people for money, and the guy wasn't part of the deal. Gordie picked up the phone and dialed the number.

"I presume you have taken care of things," said the familiar voice who answered. It wasn't really a question, so Gordie didn't feel obliged to answer. Finally, the creep got tired of the dead air, and asked slowly, as if he was talking to a two-year-old, "Have you taken care of the matter we spoke about on Friday?"

"No. I tried a couple of times, but she was with someone."

"I thought I had made myself clear."

"Clear enough, but I didn't think you'd want the witness. I'll get it done, don't worry." The truth was Gordie had enjoyed speaking to the girl. He'd been watching for an opportunity to get her alone. That would make up for the nigger...he felt he was owed.

There was a pause on the line for about ten seconds before the creep started speaking again, "Listen, I have another job for you. It needs to be done today. You need to drive up to Hattiesburg. There'll be a meeting with someone at a place called Dan's Diner at 10 AM sharp. It's on Perry Street. Park your car in the lot behind the restaurant. Our man will meet you in the diner."

"How will I know him?"

"He'll be wearing a dark blue windbreaker and a John Deere hat."

"I get my money upfront, remember?"

"Same deal as last time. He'll have it with him."

"What's the job?"

"The man will explain it to you." Almost as an afterthought, he added, "Don't screw up again."

"Fuck you," said Gordon after hanging up. Hattiesburg, what the fuck is in Hattiesburg?

Gordie got to the diner in plenty of time. He was driving the shiny new red Chevrolet S10 pick-up he'd stolen in Ocean Springs. No doubt by now, it had been reported stolen, so he'd swapped plates with a car at the Publix Plaza.

He parked the truck at the back of an empty lot and checked his Timex; it was still a few minutes before 10. His stomach grumbled. He hadn't had anything to eat yet. Getting out of the truck, Gordie made his way into the restaurant. A few people were sitting at the counter. He selected a booth in the back where someone had left a copy of the *Hattiesburg American* on the table. The waitress came by to take his order, and he asked for the 99-cent breakfast special. The front page of the paper was about a trial taking place at the courthouse, located across from the diner. The article was about former Biloxi Mayor John Baxter and a rumor that he was expected to turn state's witness against the gangster Frank Reznikov. Gordie wondered if the job had anything to do with the court case. Why else was he meeting someone across from the courthouse? Was Reznikov paying to get rid of Baxter?

When the waitress brought his food, he folded the paper and read the rest of the coverage while he ate. The reporter had written that the jury selection was flawed. After all of the legal hoopla, they ended up with a jury of 12 old white guys. The reporter compared the jury to a meeting of the local Rotary Club. *What the fuck did he expect in Mississippi?* Gordie looked over at the courthouse and speculated how he might take out Baxter. He had his switchblade in his pocket, but he figured that whoever he was meeting would be bringing him a gun.

By 10:45, there was no sign of anyone wearing a John Deere hat. Gordie decided to charge the creep a day's pay for hauling his ass to Hattiesburg. Plus, he wanted to be reimbursed for breakfast. That'd be only fair. He paid the waitress at the cash, leaving what he thought was a generous 10 cent tip. Walking back to the truck, he thought about catching a peeler show, but it was likely too early for the ladies. He lit a cigarette and got in, putting the key in the ignition. When he got back to Gulfport, he'd pay a visit to the *Eye on You Detective Agency*. Maybe he'd get lucky, and she'd be alone. He cracked his window and flicked his butt out onto the pavement. He noticed a man standing amongst a group of pine trees looking at him. He wondered if this was the man he was supposed to meet. He was holding something in his hand. Gordie was about to call out when all of a sudden, a smile washed across the guy's face.

* * *

They said the explosion could be heard for miles. Over at the courthouse, the whole building shook. Someone looking out the courthouse window pointed to the flames rising from behind the diner. Moments later, a second explosion erupted. Former Mayor Baxter, fearing for his life, slid under a table.

The few people who were at the diner ran out, but there was nothing left of Gordie and his little red truck. No one saw Barry McGloyn watching from the pine trees.

Chapter 42

Saucier, Mississippi

It took a few moments for my eyes to adjust to the darkness in the bar. A smattering of people sitting at tables were listening to the Moody Blues on a jukebox. There was a bar off to the right with a tattooed woman drying glasses. I looked around for the man who'd been driving the green Mercedes. The only likely millionaire was sitting at a table in the back, talking to another man. I decided to wait up at the bar and see what happened.

"Evening, what'll ya have?" asked the bartender as I walked up. She was attractive in a no-nonsense, take no prisoners sort of way.

"Can I have a glass of red wine?"

"Sure can, princess. I happen to have a half bottle of Two Buck Chuck in the fridge. I drank the first half myself."

I guessed it was my week for cheap wine. "Sure, that'll do. Care to join me? My name's Rachel." I parked myself on a barstool.

"Patty, and that's the best offer I've had all day." She fetched the bottle from under the bar and looked surprised that it only contained a quarter of the bottle. "I guess I must have drunk a little more than I thought." She poured two glasses and put one in front of me. "You working this neighborhood?"

"I'm sorry?"

"You're a pro, aren't you?"

"Oh, no." I laughed as Patty took a sip of her wine, waiting for more. She finally wandered down the bar and poured a Bud for a man. I sensed him looking my way.

When Patty came back, she said the man was interested and want to know the game.

"My game?"

"Listen, princess. You come into a bar in Mississippi, looking like you do, you must have a game. What is it?"

I took a sip of wine and looked back at the man I thought could be Chester. He was still deep in conversation with the man at his table.

Patty caught the look. "Looking to score some drugs? You don't look the type."

"What kind of type do you think I am?"

"I don't know," she smiled. "You have a game, I just don't know what."

"Do you know the white man sitting back there?" I nodded in the direction of the back table.

"Oh, I get it. You prospecting for gold? That's Chester Masters. He comes in almost every couple of days to meet with that man. I don't know why, and I don't want to know." She started to wipe the bar down with a dishtowel.

"What's he like?"

She shrugged. "He doesn't have much to say." A pretty good tipper. He likes to drink Jack and Coke. I only know who he is because he pays with his American Express card." As Patty was talking, I noticed in the mirror behind the bar, that the other man had got up from the table, leaving Chester all alone. "There you go, Princess, he's all alone." I took another sip of wine, and Patty added. "He doesn't strike me as the type to approach a woman."

I finished the wine, put a ten on the bar, and said thanks for the advice. I slid off the barstool and made my way to Chester's table. Chester's eyes followed me to the table. "Do you mind if I sit down?" I asked. Chester gestured to a vacant chair as the song on the jukebox changed to Lynyrd Skynyrd, wailing about three steps. Once I sat down, I smiled at him. He looked away and seemed to be studying the Civil War decorations on the walls. "Red wine."

"Sorry?"

"You were going to offer to buy me a drink, Chester."

He gulped, blinked, and then waved to Patty. "Do I know you?" He asked as I crossed my legs seductively.

"Do you want to?"

"I ...., yes, what? How? Where?" His mouth was out of control, but his eyes were riveted on my legs. Chester had the Jay Leno chin, and his clothes hung on him as if they belonged to a larger man. His eyes were sunken, and he sniffled every twenty seconds. I finally pulled a tissue out of my purse and gave it to him. I felt sorry for him. Patty brought me a glass of wine and another Jack and Coke for Chester. As she was leaving, she gave me a wink. "What's your name?" Chester asked.

"Rachel - and I'm not a whore." I took a sip of my wine. Patty must have opened a fresh bottle. The wine went down way too smoothly.

He took a long drink and seemed to settle down. "How do you know my name?"

"I was speaking to Gladys the other day."

"Gladys…" He looked confused for a moment before asking, "My sister-in-law?"

"She goes by Mayview now. Gladys Mayview."

"I don't understand." He pulled his brows together in confusion. "How do you know Gladys?" Chester asked my legs.

"I'm a private investigator working for a client who wants to prove that your brother is his father. Gladys suggested that I speak to you." Chester sat stone-faced. I wasn't sure he had understood. "Do you know what a paternity test is, Chester?" He shifted uncomfortably in his seat and shrugged. "What about DNA?" He shrugged. I couldn't remember what it stood for myself, so I repeated the line about a genetic fingerprint. "Tell me about Corbin."

He took a long drink before asking, "What… do you want to know?"

"How does he treat you?" It must have been the right question. His face dropped like a boulder falling off a cliff. Maybe he was the kind of guy that needed a speaking prompt.

"He's not a nice man. Daddy gave the business to both of us, but Corbin tells me that I'm too stupid to be trusted. He calls me names, bad names all the time."

"That must be hard for you." He finished his drink as I watched him. "Do you think he might be my client's biological father?" Once again, he shrugged, "Does the name Candy Boyle ring a bell?" He shrugged again. "Do you remember many of the women Corbin has been with?" He shrugged again, and I decided if he did it one more time, I'd have to slap him. "Are you involved in the business?"

"No, Corbin thinks I'm a retard. He says I can't be trusted with my own money."

"Corbin has a reputation for being a lady's man. Is that true?"

"He'd fuck the grandfather clock… if it had the right parts, I mean." Chester's face broke into a grin.

I laughed, not at the comparison, but because it reminded me of Gladys' comment about fifty percent of the town. That's the moment I decided I liked Chester.

Chapter 43

Gulfport, Mississippi

The sun was out the following morning, although the wind still brought a wintery chill to the air. When I arrived at the Agency, Arnie was already there, and the coffee was brewing. Bourbon was basking in the sunshine on the mat by the doorway.

"I thought Bourbon could guard the place while we go computer shopping." Arnie handed me a coffee.

"Good idea." I took off my coat. "I heard an update on the court case on the ride here."

"The bombing?"

"Yeah, what do you make of that?" I asked.

"It's going to take days, maybe weeks before they can determine who the driver was."

"Think Reznikov is sending Baxter a message?"

"Seems likely, why else would it happen outside the courthouse just when Baxter was about to make a deal?" Arnie took a sip of his coffee.

We were interrupted by the front door opening and Jimmy Hopkins walking in. "Good morning. Hey, is that your cat?" he asked, stepping over Bourbon.

Bourbon reached out and slapped Jimmy's leg. "That's Bourbon, he lives with me," said Arnie. "He doesn't like people who ignore him."

Jimmy bent down to pet the cat, which encouraged Bourbon to purr and sashay around his legs.

"Are you all set to guide us in our purchase?" I asked. "I think Arnie might want one too."

"Absolutely, I've done some research. Apple just released a unit called the MacIntosh, it's a little pricey, but it's state of the art. It comes with a big 9-inch screen, and it'll play your floppy disk. You'll need to buy a few things as well, like a printer and a mouse."

"A mouse? As in mice?" I asked, horrified.

"No, a computer mouse. I think it got its name because of its shape, but you move it, and it will move the cursor on the screen. It'll be easy to show you."

I shook my head, and Arnie asked. "You said pricey…how much are we talking about?"

"The Mac will run you about $2500 plus there are the other things, so figure on $3,000 all in."

"All in?" I asked, "Is there a less expensive option?"

"Commodore makes a unit called the Amiga. But you have to buy the monitor separately, and the reviews are not as good."

✳ ✳ ✳

A couple of hours later, we were huddled in a booth at the Friendship Café drinking hot chocolate.

The computer store said they would have both computers ready early that afternoon.

"I'm worried that I just put $3,000 on my credit card, and that I'm too stupid to know how to use it," I said.

"I'm a little worried about that too." Arnie sipped his drink.

"That I'm too stupid?"

"No, silly, that I'm too old."

"Not to worry, guys, I'll teach you everything you need to know."

"Thank you, Jimmy." The waitress came to take our orders, and I added, "Seriously, we wouldn't have known what to buy if it wasn't for you."

"It's nothing. I'm happy to help." Jimmy's modesty led him to change the subject. "Your business card said you're private detectives?"

"Yes, it's still a small business," I answered, "But we're poised to grow quickly now that we are computerized."

"What kind of work do you do?"

"We have a case where a man has hired us through his lawyer to help prove that a very wealthy man is his father," replied Arnie.

"Like in that Michael Jackson case?"

"Yes, but in this man's case, he genuinely believes this man and his mother…well, you get the picture," I replied.

"How do you prove something like that?"

"Have you heard of DNA?" When Jimmy shook his head, I explained that it was kind of like a genetic fingerprint. "If there's a match to the client's DNA, then the courts have found this to be sufficient to prove paternity. In our case, though, the man doesn't want to have the test done, so we're kind of stuck. There's no way to compel him."

"That's too bad. I wish I could help you. I kind of understand how your client feels. I was adopted, and I have no idea who my birth parents are. My adopted parents are cool, but it's not the same. They say they treat all their kids the same, but they don't."

"Have you ever thought about trying to find your real parents?" I asked.

"I lie awake dreaming about it."

"Maybe we can help."

Chapter 44

Later that afternoon, I was hard at work with Arnie in the office, learning from Jimmy how to use the new equipment. By the close of business, everything was hooked up, and they both knew enough to be confused.

Jimmy was showing them how to use the word processor function when he asked, "I've been thinking about what you said earlier about finding my parents, how do you go about doing that?"

"Birth mothers are usually easier to find than birth fathers. Is your adopted mother on your birth certificate?" I asked, thankful for the break.

"Yes, her name is Donna Hopkins."

"That's normal, once an adoption takes place, the name of the birth mother is amended to show the adopted mother's name. Have you discussed your desire with your parents?"

"Dad said they didn't have anything to tell me. My adopted mother couldn't have any more kids naturally, so they wanted to adopt."

"If we got involved, they might be more willing to share things like the name of the adoption agency, the town you were born in, maybe the hospital where you were born. Some states have an adoption reunion registry that connects people to their birth parents, assuming all parties agree. Mississippi currently doesn't, but once we have the details, then it's a relatively simple process to track them down."

"How much would I have to pay for this?"

"If you want to proceed, then the first step is to talk to your parents and tell them how you feel. If your dad has already shut you down, then maybe ask your mom if she would meet with me. As for cost, you helping us with the computers is good enough."

"I would help you anyway."

"That's sweet, Jimmy. Before we do anything, I'd like to meet your mother."

Chapter 45

Don worked hard to win over Bubba, Parker, and the crew over the next week. He congratulated himself on having turned a corner with his bravery in the rappelling exercise. Since then, he'd balanced his time either at the militia camp or on the boats with Fender.

One militia day had been all about arm to arm combat. He'd felt his police training and physical condition would work in his favor. He told himself to play it cool and not to show off by hurting anyone. He'd acquitted himself well in the practice stages when the instructor was demonstrating takedowns and holds. Parker had been observing the session and told the instructor to have the boys take turns sparring to see if they'd been paying attention.

When it was Don's turn to fight, Parker selected a big man from Appalachia named Jethro, to be his sparring partner. The kid seemed friendly enough and a little simple. Everyone was sitting around the ring, and a man named Brodie leaned over and told Don to watch out, as Jethro was a southpaw and sneaky fast.

Even before Parker said go, Jethro charged. Don easily dodged out of the way, moving to the left of the larger man to avoid his left hand. He then got in close and grappled with him, executing a perfect leg sweep takedown. He let Jethro back up and extended his hand only to have the man bat it away with his left and then punch Don in his shoulder with his right. The blow came as a surprise and knocked Don back a few feet. While he was rubbing his shoulder, Jethro charged again, and Don barely had time to duck another right fist. He flashed a quick look at Brodie, who was laughing. Jethro charged again, leading with his left and swinging wildly with his right. Don could have easily dodged Jethro's punches all day but wanted to demonstrate his skills. He allowed Jethro to get in close and once again grappled with him, holding on to his camouflage tunic, aiming to flip him. The maneuver backfired, and the larger man started swinging Don around like he was a ragdoll, finally flinging him to the sand. This move brought a lot of hoots and cheers from the onlookers. Don got up and once again ducked another right and grabbed Jethro's shirt, trying to tie up his arms.

Shouts of, "Watch out for his feet Jethro" came from the crowd.

While it hadn't been covered in training, neither had punching, so Don felt totally justified in head butting Jethro's nose. He heard the crunch of cartilage as Jethro stumbled backward, blood spurting from his nose. A chorus of boos rang out as Parker called an end to the fight.

"People," Parker said, trying to quiet the crowd. "Let's say you are up against it, and a Spic is kicking your ass. You've got to be prepared to throw the rule book out." Parker slapped Don hard on his shoulder and whispered, "You fight like a pussy."

✳ ✳ ✳

The next militia day had started with a five-mile hike. This was followed by a session on a march that was planned for the twenty-first. "The rally is in celebration of Great Americans Day," Parker said.

"Aren't we celebrating Martin Luther King Day?" Jethro asked, his nose all bandaged.

"No, we ain't celebrating that, numbnuts," replied Brodie. "The Governor says we gonna celebrate all our heroes, especially the white ones like Stonewall and Robert E. Lee." This brought giggles from the crowd.

Parker raised his hands, calling for silence. "I have more to share with you about some special preparations for the 21st." He put up a detailed map of downtown Biloxi on a makeshift board. Parker had drawn the streets, the buildings, and cars in the parking lots. Some cars had an "X" drawn on them. Next, he and Billy-Bob handed out signs that said things like, "Immigrants go home!", "God Hates Gays" and "Diversity Equals White Genocide."

"All of the proper permits have been obtained, and you have every right to march that day. The police will be there on account of a rumor that some left-wing pinko groups might try to cause trouble. Our right to public protest is in the constitution of this here U.S. of A. Our right to bear arms is protected, so everyone needs to bring their sidearm as a show of force. We will not stand down when we're exercising our rights." Parker then led everyone in a rousing chant of, "You will not replace us" and "Blood and Soil." In ten minutes, he had them all whipped up like rabid dogs.

Chapter 46

I found the separation from Don very difficult. I picked up the phone several times to call, each time putting the phone back down, wondering if someone could be listening in on his phone. I had the feeling of being watched, and drove back and forth to work with one eye on the rearview mirror, looking for a tail.

Over coffee, I read the latest update on the trial in Hattiesburg. Because of the bombing, the judge had ordered a continuance. Baxter now refused to discuss any further plea deals. He demanded round the clock protection, his own jail cell, separate meals, and a private shower. The warden quickly said, no, no, and no.

Gabriel's call was a welcome relief, breaking the silence in the office.

"Anything new from your end?" he asked.

"A couple of inquiries, but I'm not sure they'll amount to anything. There have been quite a few reference checks to keep me busy, plus I'm trying to learn how to use this computer. Oh, and I had some good news yesterday, my brother, Jacob, got the job at the DNA laboratory, and he's excited about doing real science for a change. And it gets better, his company is located in Mobile, so I'll have him nearby."

"That's great news. With Arnie moving to New Orleans and things heating up down there, I've been worried."

"Hattiesburg is only ninety minutes away."

"True, but the US Marshall Service have booked us into a hotel, and we're under strict orders to stay put."

"Anything further on the truck that blew up?"

"A witness walking by said that they saw a greasy-haired white man sitting in the driver's seat, smoking a cigarette. But no luck in coming up with an identity. They did discover the truck had been reported stolen. Not a big surprise, with a courthouse across the street."

There was an awkward silence before I suggested, "Maybe I can take a day this weekend and drive up there."

"That would be great, I'd love to see you. We all would," he added quickly. "I'll ask the Marshalls, but since they won't even let us order Chinese food, I think having visitors might be hard in case you're followed."

We discussed Baxter's demands, and Gabriel advised that the D.A. had arranged for Baxter to see a psychiatrist.

* * *

True to his word, Jimmy came in every couple of days, working around his shifts at the library. He taught me how to set up invoices using Lotus.

"You're picking this up pretty quickly, Rachel."

"Any more thoughts on what we discussed the other day about finding your birth mother?"

"I'm waiting for Dad to go out of town. Mom said he has a job hauling stuff up to Jackson."

"Are you scared to talk to your Dad?"

"He's made it very clear that he doesn't want to talk about it."

* * *

Later that afternoon, Weber called, and I asked him about preparations for Martin Luther King Day.

"Good news, Sheriff Pardy has authorized HSM, that's heightened security measures, for the Governor's parade."

"That's great. Have you alerted your bomb squad to look for explosives?"

"I'll have to ask Pardy about that. By the way, we're not allowed to call it…" he lowered his voice to a whisper, "What you called it. We are under strict orders to call it Great Americans Day."

"Bullshit. What's going on with this missing deputy?"

"He's vanished. I even called his father. He has no clue to his whereabouts."

"Did you think he would tell you?"

"He's a man of the cloth."

"Yeah, the white sheet type," I added under my breath.

"I have a lead on Gordon Bones, AKA, the rat-faced man. Sorry, AKA means ...."

"Also Known As. I know, Weber."

"After he left Harrison County, he got a job with a security company up in Jackson. It looks like he left them a year ago. We have a call into them for an LKA, that stands for Last Known Address, by the way," he added officiously.

"BFD."

"BFD?"

"Big Fucking Deal."

* * *

As I was about to leave for the day, Donna Hopkins called and asked if I knew the diner on Pass Rd.

Chapter 47

"Thank you for agreeing to meet me, Mrs. Hopkins." I figured the woman sitting across from me was in her late forties. She was slim and dressed professionally in a navy pantsuit. She wore her curly brown hair in a ponytail.

"Jimmy is quite taken with you, and your offer to help him." She looked over at her son. "That's pretty much all he talks about."

"Have you had a chance to discuss his desire to connect with his birth parents?" I took a sip of my coffee.

"I know it's been a dream of his for a long time. I'm afraid my husband is a little tired of discussing it. I didn't tell Fred we were meeting today. He's a good man and tries his best with Jimmy." She served up a plastic smile, adding, "Sometimes he can lack a little empathy."

I nodded, "Can we discuss what happened around the adoption?"

"Of course, I have no secrets from my son." She put her arm around Jimmy's shoulder. "Isn't that right, Jimmy?"

"Yes, Mom."

"I understand that you were unable to have more children naturally?" I asked softly, wary that I might be dredging up painful memories.

She nodded. "I gave birth to twins, Jimmy's older brother and sister. It must have been too much for me. We desperately wanted another, but I kept miscarrying." Her voice quivered as she spoke, and she took a sip of the coffee the waitress had brought.

"How old was Jimmy when you and your husband adopted him?"

"He was a newborn, six weeks, I guess. He was a wonderful baby."

"Do you remember the name of the adoption agency that you worked with?"

"It was through the church. I figured you'd ask about that, so I looked it up before coming." She passed a folded piece of paper across the table. Across the top of the form was Southern Baptist Adoption Services. It had Baby Boy Jimmy, and his date of birth as April 10th, 1968. The letter was signed by Reverend McGloyn, Pastor of the Church, as well as Witness Elfriede Goran.

I was surprised to see McGloyn was the Reverend at that time. "I see Reverend McGloyn signed this. Did you deal directly with him?"

"Yes, he was new to our Church, and the adoption agency was just being set up."

"Did the adoption cost you money?"

"My husband handled the details. I'm sure it did, though. We had money in savings for a new car and then we didn't. I don't know how much."

"Did you ever try to find out who Jimmy's real parents were?"

"No, I remember Reverend McGloyn saying it was best not to know. He said birth mothers sometimes have remorse over giving up their child and might try to take them back. He assured me that Jimmy was healthy and that there was no history of illness in the family. We were just so happy to have Jimmy."

"Elfriede Goran is the witness. Did you deal with her?

"I have a vague memory of her being helpful. She worked for the adoption agency."

"When did you tell Jimmy he was adopted?"

"I didn't. I suppose I always planned to, although Fred said it would be a mistake. Jimmy's older sister, Markell, broke the news when he was eight. You know how kids can sometimes be. There was an argument. I don't remember what it was about."

"I do," said Jimmy, speaking up for the first time. "I was doing my homework, and she came in with her friends and wanted to watch *Happy Days*. When I said I was there first, she told her friends not to worry about me because I was adopted."

"She felt bad about it afterward," said Donna. "Jimmy came and asked me if it was true. There was no point lying."

"Do you have any other records we could look at?"

"That's all I have. Maybe my husband might know more, but I don't want to ask him if I don't have to."

"Was Jimmy born in a local hospital?"

"I guess so, I don't know for sure. I guess I'm not much help."

"That's okay. We have found people with less. So, we have the name of the Southern Baptist Adoption Agency, we have the witness, the Reverend, the date, we should be fine." I said, talking through my hat. I had never actually worked an adoption case. I turned to Jimmy and smiled. "What are you going to say when you finally meet her?"

"I don't know. I'd like Mom to come with me."

"That would be nice. Leave this with me."

Chapter 48

Don was getting used to early morning wake up calls from Bubba. If he was to be on the boats, he was expected to be at the docks by 5 AM with two coffees. Since there was no phone call, Don scrunched down under the blankets. He felt he'd done a good job of fitting in with the others, but sensed that Parker still wasn't convinced. It was little things like a stare, a sarcastic comment, and then last night when he got back to his apartment, he could have sworn someone had been there. He'd chalked it up to paranoid thinking until he went into his kitchen and found an empty bottle of Bud with its label peeled off.

The phone rang at 6:45. Don answered with his head still under the covers. "Yeah?"

"Wake up, Li'l Kitty." He had expected Bubba, not Parker. "We've got some work to do."

Don sat up and looked out the bedroom window. The day looked overcast and cold. "Who is this?" he asked jokingly.

"Fuck off. Grab your gear, we're going to Gautier. I'll be downstairs in the parking lot in five minutes."

"I don't mind driving myself," Don said quickly but realized that Parker had already hung up.

Five minutes left no time to shower. He would have liked to call Fred to tell him about Gautier but worried that if Parker were to call back and get a busy signal, he'd be suspicious.

✳ ✳ ✳

They drove in silence for the first five minutes. Gautier was about twenty-five minutes away, off Highway 10, near Pascagoula. "What's the plan for today, Park?"

"Name's Parker, and you'll find out soon enough." Parker pulled onto the two-lane highway heading east.

"What do you think about Reagan's upcoming inauguration?" Don asked, detecting that Parker wasn't in the mood for small talk. Parker's reply was to grunt as he lit a menthol cigarette. "Say, have you read any good books lately?" No response, Don cracked a window. "Don't suppose you follow ice hockey?" Still no response, so Don tried another tactic. "You owe me a beer."

"How do you figure that?" Parker accelerated and passed a car, swerving back wildly, barely avoiding an oncoming transport truck. Don tensed and looked for a seatbelt.

"Did you find what you were looking for in my apartment?"

"I couldn't find my lighter, thought maybe you took it," Parker said as he pulled out to pass another car.

"The lighter you just used?"

"Yeah, I guess I was wrong." Don saw an oil truck bearing down on them.

"Uh! Park, Park…you'd better get back in the right lane…Park!" This time there was an angry blast of an airhorn as Parker pulled back just in time. "Want to slow down a bit, Parker?" In response, Parker sped up and started tailgating another truck, weaving erratically back and forth. Don looked behind them, hoping for a Sheriff's deputy car with lights ablaze. "Well, where do you live, Park? In case I ever misplace something."

Before they got to Gautier, Parker slowed down and turned into a gravel lane leading to an old farm-house. The house was a two-story red brick home with a confederate battle flag hanging as a curtain in the front window. The place was poorly maintained, the roof was bowed, the front porch looked like it was rotting away, and broken window shutters were hanging down.

"Nice place, Park. This where the Lange clan grew up?"

Parker ignored him and drove the truck along the side of the house. The backyard looked like a garbage dump with a half dozen abandoned and rusted out vehicles. A couple of bloodhounds chained to a picnic table started to bark wildly. Parker turned off the ignition and got out, saying, "Come along, Li'l Kitty, it's showtime."

Chapter 49

Thankfully my new computer proved to be a distraction from the lack of business. I pulled out the notes that I had taken earlier and thought I'd spend the morning checking into Jimmy's birth parents. Calling Reverend McGloyn and asking for a favor was out of the question, so I looked up Goran in the phone directory. There were two listings in the metropolitan Biloxi area, one was in Port Christian, the other was in Picayune. I flipped a coin and called the Picayune number. A young woman with a baby screaming in the background picked up.

"What?"

"I'm sorry, I might have called at the wrong time."

"There's never a good time. What do you want?"

"I wanted to know if Elfriede Goran lives at this number?"

"Elfriede? That's my husband's Nana, and no, she doesn't live with us. She's in a nursing home."

"Oh, okay, my name's Rachel Henderson. Do you know what nursing home she's in?"

"Yes, I know, but you'd best explain why you want me to tell you."

"It has to do with when she worked with the Southern Baptist Adoption Services."

"Oh well, have at it. She's a resident of the Dixie Nursing Home in Picayune. But if you go see her, you're likely wasting your time.

"Why?"

The woman let out a long sigh. "Elfriede started losing her marbles a few years ago after her husband died. Somedays she's lucid, at least for an 83-year-old. Other days she doesn't know where she is. She says she hears things, has hallucinations, and is paranoid the staff is trying to poison her."

"I used to work in a mental hospital. I've seen my share of dementia. What kind of hallucinations does she experience?"

"Last spring, we brought the kids to see her for Mother's Day. She said she hadn't been sleeping because of the Nazi stormtroopers marching up and down the hallways."

Chapter 50

Don followed as Parker led the way past the barking hound dogs and onto the back porch. A middle-aged man held the door for them. The man had long unkempt gray hair that had been hand combed off his forehead. His face was stubbled, and his cheek had a large gin blossom, a sign of someone who liked to drink. He nodded to Parker and eyed Don suspiciously. "Who's this? My hounds don't like him. They only howl like that when the cops come around".

"He's with us, Steve," answered Parker.

Steve pointed to a staircase leading down into a cellar. "I've got everything you need down there. He's already at it."

The basement was cold and damp but had new fluorescent lighting. A man with his back to them was hunched over a workbench.

"You remember Barry?" asked Parker.

"Of course. Hello, Barry. I was wondering where you went." Barry nodded to Don and then resumed his work with a soldering iron.

"You said you were pretty comfortable around explosives, so you and Barry have some work to do."

Don looked around the cellar. It had concrete walls, a dirt floor, and little windows. The wooden steps leading upstairs were the only visible way out.

"You being a munitions expert," explained Parker, putting his hand on a plastic bin containing a light brown putty-like substance, "must know what this is."

"uh…Silly Putty?" Don said, looking at the material.

"That's a good one." Barry turned around. "Homemade C-4. There's enough here to blow this house and everything in it to the moon." His eyes were gleaming with excitement.

"I knew that," Don replied, turning to look at Parker. "What's the plan?"

"We need some pipe bombs. We have everything you guys need. I want thirty of them so you'd best be getting on with it. They all need to have remote timers. Barry can show you the ropes."

Once Parker retreated upstairs, Barry turned to look at Don. "Ever build a pipe bomb before?"

"No."

"I heard you did a whole presentation on explosives up at the camp."

"I never had to make the grenades. I just needed to know how to throw them. I'm a quick study. Just tell me what I need to do."

Barry gestured to some rusty four-inch pipes on the floor. "First, we need to cut the pipes into one-foot lengths. There's a hacksaw over there." He pointed to another workbench.

"What are you working on?"

"Remote triggers."

"And what are we planning to blow up?"

"If Parker wants you to know, he'll tell you. For now, start cutting. I'd like to get this done today."

Don's mind raced as he walked over to the bench. He didn't want to be part of whatever these nutjobs were planning. He'd heard of C-4 and knew of the damage it could cause. He could stall, take his time, but in the end, Parker would get pissed and even more suspicious. He needed to call Fred and tip him off, but he'd likely just want more details. He saw no alternative other than to do what was being asked. Don put the first piece of pipe in a vice grip and grabbed the rusty hacksaw. He measured out a foot and started to cut.

It was hard work. By noon, Don had thirty pipes all cut into one-foot lengths. "Sure seems like a lot of bombs," Don said, hoping Barry would volunteer something.

"They get fastened in threes with wire. It will only make ten bombs."

Somehow that didn't make Don feel any better. "Where did you learn all this stuff, Barry? I thought you said you were in law enforcement."

Barry turned back to his soldering and paused as if he was weighing how much to say. "Someone taught me the ropes. There was a time I was planning on joining the bomb squad. I figured I should learn as much as I could."

"Do you know how these are going to be used?"

Barry got up and handed Don a can of silver spray paint. "Make sure you coat them well. We'll let them dry over lunch."

Lunch was red beans and rice along with cornbread and a mason jar half full of what Steve, the capillary guy, called his magic tonic. Don took what he thought was a cautious sip and felt the corn-tasting liquid burn down his throat. He started coughing uncontrollably, which, of course, made everyone laugh. Parker called him a pussy and asked Barry how much progress had been made.

"We got the pipes cut and painted. I'm just about done the electronics," said Barry in between mouthfuls of beans. "After lunch, Don will thread the pipes and drill the holes. Then we just have to fill up the pipes and wire everything up. We should be finished by 5 PM at the latest."

"I'll take the pipes with me, so we have them for the march." Parker gave Barry a nod and smiled.

He wants them for the march. Don thought. Congratulating himself for finally learning something useful, he decided to push the envelope. "How do you plan on using them, Park?"

Parker gave Don a tired look and said, "Finish your lunch, boys, best be getting back to work." He walked out in the backyard, accompanied by Steve.

The rest of the afternoon dragged on. While Don had never been that handy with tools, Barry had led him to believe that the pipe threader was simple. Barry lost his patience with him at one point and vented his frustrations. "I told you…full revolutions otherwise, the caps won't fit snug. It'll affect the blast size."

By the end of the day, Don was tired of cutting, threading, and drilling. He was also tired of Barry moaning about his work. Also, the red beans were giving him gas. Barry didn't say anything, but after a particularly loud and smelly eruption, he got up and opened the windows. Together they filled each pipe with the C-4, then Barry topped off each pipe with ball bearings.

When they were finally done, Parker took the crate holding the bombs and put it in the back of his pickup under a tarp. He told Don to get in. Parker tuned the radio to a country and western channel.

"So, the pipe bombs are for the march? They're going to make one hell of a mess." Don laughed uncomfortably.

Once again, Parker ignored his question. Don decided if Jackson was going to give him the silent treatment and make him listen to this God-awful music, he'd try to amuse himself. "I bet your parents never let you play with firecrackers, right, Park?" Don waited a moment then asked, "Is that guy back there, the one with the map of Mississippi on his cheek, your old man?"

Don thought he detected a twitch, but Parker continued driving, stone-faced. Don frantically pressed a bunch of presets on the radio, only to find that they were all playing the same crap. "Do you like the Stones, or are you more of a Beatles guy?" No reply. "Stones? Yeah, I like them better too."

"Fuck off, and shut up."

"You got a gal, Park? A short dumpy guy like you, I bet the girls are all over you. Or do you like boys?" Don asked, winking. Parker responded as expected by turning into an Amoco station, and pulling up alongside the building. "Come on," he said, getting out of the truck. He walked to the front of the vehicle and gestured for Don to get out. When Don shook his head, Parker started pounding on his truck in anger. "You been looking for a beating for a while, your times up, Pussyman."

Don was under no illusions that in a fair fight, the much bigger man would clean his clock. "Geez, I thought you could take a joke," Don said, finally sliding out of the truck. He then wasted another couple of minutes doing stretches.

"Are you ready for your beating?"

They circled each other for another minute before Parker couldn't stand it anymore and charged. Thankfully, Don was big on self-preservation and was able to sidestep him. He danced around, displaying his Muhammed Ali moves.

"Watch my feet, Park, they're lethal. Remember, Jethro?" Parker faked a right and threw a wild left, which brushed against Don's cheek. He backed away and shook off the blow. "Don't forget about the head butt. That's a killer."

The thing about big men is that they can often be slow. Parker threw another left, which Don was able to block. He hit Parker with a quick right jab to the chin, barely fazing him, and the man chuckled. While he was laughing, Don rammed his knee into Parker's nuts. That wiped the smile off his face. Parker made a strange "ugh-oh-groan-whoosh" sound and bent over.

A knee to the head would have finished him off, but instead, Don went to the pop machine and got him an ice-cold root beer. After a few minutes of holding the can to his balls, Parker said, "You fight like a pussy."

He didn't say anything else until they got to Don's apartment. The fight might have been a mistake. But Don figured he wasn't building any relationship with the man anyway. When Parker pulled into the parking lot, he turned off the ignition and turned to Don. "All right, you worked hard today, and you're going to know soon enough, so keep this to yourself. We're going to use them as car bombs to kill some left-wing pinkos at the march. Kind of a deadly fireworks display."

Chapter 51

Port Christian, Mississippi

I opened the door to the Dixie Nursing Home and was immediately transported back to all of the nursing hospitals I'd ever visited. It was the old people smell. A urine odor, although they all say it isn't. Before I started working as a nurse, I hadn't liked old people. Mostly because a lot of them are cranky, but also because they kinda scared me. Saggy skin, poopy diapers, veiny hands, and scraggly hair gave me the willies; I just couldn't help it. It made my stomach turn to think that one day I'd be like that. Then I started working with seniors and learned that most were sweet, lonely people who spent a lot of their time living in the past.

I asked at the desk if Mrs. Goran would be up for a visitor, and was directed to a room down a long hallway. She was sitting in a chair by the window. In the bright daylight, her hair was snowy, and her skin was taut, resembling a crudely carved wax dummy. Her head was in constant motion as if agreeing with sentiments no-one else could hear. On her dresser stood many photographs, including a black and white wedding portrait. A bowl of yellow jello lay untouched beside it, along with a water glass containing her teeth.

"Mrs. Goran, can I visit for a spell?" The woman was either deaf or lost in her own mind. I repeated the question and walked into her field of vision.

"I heard you fine the first time," she gummed. "Just hoping you'd leave."

I told her my name and that I had come about the Southern Baptist Adoption Services.

She looked at me for the first time. "Lots of babies."

"You worked with Reverend McGloyn." I think she nodded her head, but it might have just been a tremor. She repeated the line about lots of babies. A sensation of this being a waste of time came over me. "I've come because of an adoption that took place in April of 1968 when the adoption agency was just starting. It was a Negro child by the name of Jimmy."

She didn't say anything for a few moments, then, "*Jimmy...Jimmy Crack Horn and I don't care,*" she said, her voice barely above a whisper.

I leaned closer, not sure what to make of it. "What was that?"

"*Jimmy Crack Corn and I don't care,*" she repeated, this time singing in a creepy old lady's voice.

"Do you remember anything about that adoption?"

She then gave me a serious look and reached out to grasp my arm with her bony hand, "Don't eat the food here. They put stuff in it. Fuckers."

The conversation with Mrs. Goran went downhill from there. At one point, I thought she was going to give herself a stroke by yelling about the nurses and doctors. It made me think about my father, and I felt terrible on many levels. I'm sure that once she'd been a bright, warm-hearted person who'd cared for her family, the church, and looking after the babies... all the babies.

I called my parent's home number as soon as I got back to the office. Mom answered again and was immediately suspicious that I had done something foolish.

"No, nothing, Mother, I guess I was just missing you."

"That's nice, dear. Did you hear about Jacob's big promotion?" *There it is, he gets another job, and she calls it a promotion. She never once congratulated me when I told her I was taking over the office. She cautioned me about getting in over my head.*

"Yes, and I'm excited that he'll be moving this way. I hope we can see more of each other." I wanted to ask her if she knew about Jacob's sexual preferences, but I didn't feel it was my place to let that cat out of the bag. "I thought I could come up there again soon. Maybe we could celebrate his promotion."

"That would be fine, but you should check that he has the time. With this promotion, he's bound to be pretty busy."

"I'll check with him and set something up. I want to be around for Martin Luther King Day."

"You mean, Great Americans Day."

Mom calling it that annoyed me, and I didn't know why. "Do you think I could talk to Dad for a minute?"

The request made her think for a moment before she said, "Is everything okay, Rachel? Are you sure you're not in some kind of pickle?" She eventually put the phone down and started yelling at him to pick up the extension. The yelling back and forth went on for a couple of minutes before Dad finally said hello. His voice sounded weak, especially for someone who had been yelling a few moments earlier. I couldn't remember the last time I had spoken to him on the telephone.

"Hi, Dad."

"Hello… girl, your mother said you were in some kind of trouble."

I sighed, "No, not at all, Dad. I just want to say that I love you. I'm sorry we didn't get much time to talk over the holidays."

"That's all right, girl. I know how busy young people are. When you're young, there's always tomorrow." Rachel heard her mother harp about something in the background, which led to Dad telling her to get stuffed and not to interrupt him when he was talking. "Listen, if you're in trouble, just say the word, and I'll be there."

A few minutes later, I ended the call and then cried for an hour.

Chapter 52

Don rushed to his apartment and dialed Fred Moller's number. He waited for an agonizing five rings before his boss picked up. "It's on Martin Luther King Day," Don blurted out when his boss answered. "They're going to kill a lot of people."

"Talk to me."

Don told him about the 30 pipe bombs, the C-4, and Parker's admission that they were going to be used along the parade route to kill counter-protestors.

"Pipe bombs?"

"We were in Gautier. There's a guy there named Barry McGloyn who seemed to know his way around bombs. I was being watched too closely to sabotage anything. I can tell you where the house is, and you can go and arrest him."

Fred paused for a moment. "I'll discuss this with Carol George. She's likely going to have questions."

"You're going to discuss this with Carol the Vagina? Carol, the vagina, gets to decide what to do? Now you're just rubbing my face in it, Fred."

"She's the Senior Agent in Charge."

"In charge of nothing," Don said under his breath.

"How are the bombs going to be used?"

"He said as car bombs."

"How are we supposed to know which cars?"

"I don't know. He didn't say."

"What else DID he say?

"That's it. He wasn't chatty. I practically had to beat that out of him."

"January 21st, that doesn't give us much time. Tell me about the rally."

"Yeah, they call it a march. Typical Neo-Nazi thing with signs, and skinheads shouting their garbage."

"I'll talk to Carol, but I can tell you we're not going to let them blow people up. Are the bombs still in Gautier?"

"No, I saw Parker Lange, Bubba's brother, load them into his pickup."

"Maybe Carol will have an idea..."

Don interrupted, "Listen, let's stage a police stop for some busted headlight, bullshit reason, and low and behold they'll find the bombs and arrest him. I memorized his license plate, and I know a deputy who could pull this off, but we have to do this now. Right now!"

They argued about the plan and whether they should wait until they talk to the vagina lady. Finally, Don wore Fred down, and he agreed.

✳ ✳ ✳

Parker's balls hurt. He had just come from a meeting with Bubba and Fender, and it was unanimous, there would be one less Kitty on the planet after the rally. He had tried to give the man the benefit of the doubt.

Bubba had told Parker that he was pleased things were proceeding as planned. What they had arranged was going to rock the country and bring attention to their struggle. A press release had already been drafted to be sent to the *Herald* after the march. His thoughts were interrupted by flashing lights in the rearview mirror. "Fuck, now what?" He hadn't been speeding and was less than a block away from his house. He signaled and pulled over to the curb, slamming his fist into the dash.

"License and registration please," asked the Harrison County Deputy once he ambled his way to Parker's window.

"I wasn't speeding."

"I know that. Did I say you were? Now, license and registration."

Parker pulled the ID out of his wallet, cursing under his breath.

"Sorry, were you talking to me?" Deputy Weber asked.

"No. Why'd you pull me over?"

"Title 63 of the Mississippi Motor Vehicles and Traffic Regulations, Chapter 7," Weber spouted out

officially. "All vehicles must display properly func-
tioning brake lights. Your left light is flickering. As the
nametag says, I'm a Deputy Sheriff and not an electri-
cian, but I'd say you have a short in your wiring, Mr.…"
Weber looked down at the license. "Mr. Parker Lange.
Say, are you related to the actress? I caught her in that
movie *The Postman Always Rings Twice* with Jack…"
he looked up at the sky, trying the remember the name.

"You stopped me for a flickering brake light?
Bullshit."

"The law is quite clear, Mr. Lange," Weber
said very seriously. "I could cite you for driving an
unsafe vehicle."

"Just do what you have to do. I'm late for an
appointment."

"I need to give your vehicle a quick safety inspec-
tion. Can you turn off the ignition, Mr. Lange?"

"The truck's fine. It's recently been serviced."
Parker whined.

"Can you turn off the ignition, Mr. Lange? This
won't take long." Once he had turned off the engine,
Weber walked to the back and made a show of looking at each tire. "Tires look okay, maybe about 50%
wear," he called out. "I see you like Goodyear. I'm a
Michelin man myself."

Parker was watching Weber in his mirrors,
cursing.

Weber stood up and looked in the back of the
truck. "F150, good sturdy vehicle. Do you use it for

hauling? I see you have a tarp back here." After a moment, Weber called out, "Mr. Lange, I'm afraid I will have to ask you to exit the vehicle and come here."

Parker got out of the truck and walked back to where the Deputy was standing. Weber moved the tarp and found an empty crate. No pipe bombs. He looked at Parker, who was grinning, "I should be writing you up for this. With all the wind we get down here, a good gust can blow this lose tarp right out of the cab and onto a car behind you. This is a very serious safety hazard, Mr. Lange." When Parker didn't reply, Weber asked, "Have you been hauling something recently?"

"A couple of weeks back. I just forgot about it. I usually keep all that stuff in the shed. I'll put it back when I get home. I just live a block from here."

"I know that. I saw on your license. Nice neighborhood?"

We were waiting for Weber's call at the Agency. Don had called saying he had important news, and we had agreed to a meeting at the office. While we were waiting, he brought me up to date with what was happening with the pipe bombs and the plan to use them.

A cold shiver ran down my spine, "Oh my God, Don…thirty pipe bombs filled with C4…Arnie and

I checked with someone at Keesler, and the man said the stuff was more explosive than TNT."

"Once they catch Parker with the bombs, they can try to get him to flip on the people in charge."

"I'm glad you called me. I was worried and almost called you a dozen times."

Don put his arms around me. "It'll all be over soon.

We were interrupted by the phone on my desk. I answered, and Weber identified himself as if it was the first time we'd spoken. "I need to speak to Don."

"It's okay, Weber, it's Rachel, you can speak to me."

"No, I need to speak to Kittyburg."

"He's brought me up to date. You can talk to me.'

"I need to speak to Don," Weber repeated.

I reluctantly handed the phone to Don, who listened for a few minutes before grabbing a pen and writing something on a message pad.

When he hung up, he said that Weber stopped Parker on a safety violation about a block from his house. When Weber had looked under a tarp, the crate was empty.

"Ah, shit!"

"He thinks that Parker might have stored the bombs in his shed. He gave me the address. He didn't tell me to check it out, but the way he repeated the address a couple of times, really slowly, suggest that's what he has in mind."

"Let's go." I grabbed my coat.

"You're not coming."

"Just try to stop me. Remember, I started this."

Don looked at me and shook his head in frustration. "We both know this is a really bad idea."

✳ ✳ ✳

Parker's address was on 7th Avenue. We did a drive-by and saw that it was by far the dumpiest house on a dumpy street. It was like two trailers arranged in an L shape pattern. There were no trees or shrubbery in the yard, so we decided to park down the street and wait for the lights to go out. It was just past 1 AM.

"Looks like a shed in the back." Don turned off the ignition.

"I hope he doesn't have a Doberman waiting." I was referring to when we'd broken into Huedunit Painting last year.

"I bet he's in an ice-cold tub, chilling his aching balls."

"That's weird."

"I kneed him in the nuts today. He wasn't pleased about it."

The lights didn't go out until after 1:45 AM. We got out of the truck and slowly made our way to the back of his property. I was wearing another one of Don's slut ensembles, hardly what you'd want for breaking and entering.

"Doubt this dump would have a security alarm," Don whispered.

"Why the shed?" I asked. "Why not in the house. Wouldn't it be safer?"

"I don't know, he said something to Weber about keeping the tarp in the shed." We got to the shed door and found that the door was padlocked. "Okay, no problem, I have my picks. It'll take me less than a minute." Don pulled a sleeve of tools out of his jacket.

"Last time you said that, there was a Doberman bearing down on me that I had to fight off with a broom. Hurry up, this place gives me the creeps," I whispered.

I held Don's flashlight as he worked the lock with his pick. It took more like ten minutes, but he finally got it open and gave me an I-told-you-so look. It wasn't a big shed, maybe the size of a large bathroom. I stubbed my toe on something metal and then pulled a Three Stooges, stepping on a garden rake the wrong way. "Don, shine the light over here before I kill myself."

There were two sets of metal shelving containing garden tools, gasoline cans, and old tires. On one of the shelves, there were a couple of wooden crates. "They were in a carton like this," said Don, waving me over.

All we found were work gloves, mason jars, grass seed, and some spare parts. We took turns sighing, both thinking the same thing. Parker probably had the pipe bombs in the house.

✳ ✳ ✳

"Okay, now what?" I said once we were back in the truck.

"As you said, he probably has them in the house. But I need to get you back to the agency. My boss, Bubba, likes to call me at 3 in the morning to tell me where he wants me for the day." I looked at him sympathetically. "And then, I'll wake up Fred, my real boss, and tell him my great idea was a bust."

"By the time you called Weber, and he'd had a chance to pull Parker over, he could have dropped the bombs off to someone else. When you're talking to your boss, tell him we need a tap on that man's phone, a bug in his car, and round the clock surveillance."

"The march is one day from now."

"Alright, let's look at this logically. What did he say again about using the bombs?"

"He called them car bombs. I assumed he meant along the route. Because the bombs are rigged with remote detonators, I expect he wants to take out some counter-protestors."

Rachel tapped her head against the truck's window. "I think we have no choice but to break into his house. If he tries to stop us, you can just …you know kick him …in the ….

"We can't do that," Don interrupted. "And before you ask, Weber wouldn't be able to get a warrant."

"Alright, but wait a minute. To plant the bombs along the route, they'd have to risk being seen crawling under someone's car. If they planted the bombs on their own cars, then they wouldn't even need to put the bomb under the car, they could put it in the trunk."

"If they stole a bunch of cars in advance and planted them along the route, they could just detonate them at the right moment." Don suggested.

"When you call Weber back, ask him if there's been a spike in stolen car reports. Get a list of every vehicle stolen in the last few weeks."

Chapter 53

I didn't sleep more than a couple of hours after getting home. I stared at the alarm clock until it flashed 6:30, then sat up and reached for the telephone by the bed. I dialed Don's number, but the call went to his machine. I was worried about him after last night. I had begged him to call in sick, but he wouldn't hear of it. Falling back on my pillow, I felt like crying again. I thought about the bombs and how much better it would have been had they caught Parker with them in the back of his truck. I stewed about what I could do for what seemed like hours, but when I looked at the clock, and only five minutes had elapsed.

A burst of energy came over me, and I sat up and dialed the number for the Harrison County Sheriff's Department. When I asked the receptionist for Deputy Weber, I was told he wouldn't be in until later that afternoon. I hung up and quickly dialed Jacob's number. A strange male voice answered.

"Hi, I was calling for Jacob. Is he home?"

"Who be callin?"

"I'm his sister, Rachel."

There was a pause on the line, "Oh, um…, Jake's in de shower. Is dis urgent, o'kin he call ya back?"

I quickly asked him to have Jacob call his sister at her office. Once I hung up, I berated myself for not having at least asked for his name. Arnie had given me the number for his new apartment in New Orleans. If anyone could help pick up my spirits, it would be him. Thankfully he answered.

"Hey Sunshine, you're calling kind of early, aren't you? Is everything okay?"

"I'm fine. I hope you don't mind, I just wanted to talk to someone."

"Sure," Arnie said, his voice sounding more relaxed. I told him about the bombs and the plan to use them on Monday. "Good Lord, Rachel. Is Don sure?"

"Yes, apparently, he saw a map where the bombs will be placed."

"You should call your friend at the newspaper. They need to warn people to stay away."

"I was thinking the same thing, but won't they know that the information came from Don? I don't want to put him in any more danger."

"Maybe, but it doesn't matter. There could be tens of thousands of people down there. We just can't let it happen!"

We discussed the situation further, and he promised to call his cousin at the Sheriff's department while I reached out directly to Sheriff Pardy. Arnie said he'd drive into Biloxi on Monday morning and do what he could. I called the Sheriff and was told that Pardy was out on a call, and they'd give him my message.

Finally, I tried Larry at the *Herald*. When he answered, I blurted out that we had received confirmation that there would be car bombs set to explode during the march on Monday.

"How do you know this?" asked Larry.

"I have a friend who is working undercover with this group. There will be ten car bombs detonated remotely along the parade route. They want to take out the counter-protestors."

"Have you shared this information with Pardy?"

"He's out of the office, and I had to leave a message. Maybe he'll listen to you if you call him."

"I can do that. What else can I do?"

"Put it in today's late edition. On the front page, warning people to stay away."

* * *

When I got to the Agency, I was beside myself with worry. I tried to think about what I could do that might help the situation. Finally, I decided that I needed to keep busy and to spend some time on Jimmy's adoption case. I had the name, the adoption agency, and the date. How hard could it be to find a birth mother? I knew there was a department in Jackson that looked after maintaining the records relating to all adoptions in the state. I tried there first, and after being bounced around and then cut off, I called back and was connected with a woman who I could have sworn was a twin of the woman who'd answered my call at American Airlines.

"Mississippi Adoption Services, how can I direct your call?" the woman said in a tired voice.

"My name is Rachel Henderson. I'm a private detective in Gulfport. I'd like to speak to someone who could answer a couple of questions about an adoption that took place on April 10ᵗʰ, 1968, with an agency called the Southern Baptist Adoption Services."

"Are you the party that was adopted?" she asked in a flat voice as if reading from a checklist.

"No, his name is Jimmy Hopkins."

"Are you the adoption mother?"

"No. Her name is Donna Hopkins."

"Are you the birth mother?"

"No, that's who I'm trying to find?"

"Do you have a court order?"

The question took me by surprise. "No, no, I don't."

"Under Mississippi law, adopted children are prohibited from accessing their original birth records."

"I just assumed that …"

"Assumed?" she interrupted with a harrumph. "Is that what you said? You thought you'd just call here, and we'd roll over and violate multiple statutes and privacy laws just on account of what? You being a Private De-tec-tive?"

"I'm sorry, I didn't realize all that." Before I could ask anything else, I heard the dial tone.

I walked around the office after hanging up the phone, scolding myself for being so stupid. Gabriel would never have made that mistake. I paced the floor, thinking about what to do. Finally, I put the Closed sign on the door, locked up, and drove to the library. I went to the reference section and looked in the abstracts for Mississippi Adoption Laws.

I found pages and pages of references and articles. The first thing I read was that Mississippi adoption laws had not changed since they were written in the 1800s. The archaic laws were from a time when an unwed pregnancy was considered a disgrace. If you were an unmarried mother and didn't take yourself to the unwed mother's home, the Sheriff came and picked you up and took you there. When your baby was born, they would be forcibly taken from you and brought to the Mississippi Children's Society in Jackson. That's where they stayed until an adoption agency found suitable parents.

I knew many other States now offered open adoptions where both sets of parents meet and often can play a role in the child's development. I learned that Mississippi still only permits closed adoptions. The difference is that the adoption file remains sealed unless a court order is obtained. There have been very few instances of successfully opening the adoption file through the courts, except in the case of health issues. If I had known this, I wouldn't have wasted my time calling.

Chapter 54

It was 2:30 by the time Don got home from dropping Rachel off at her car. His mind was whirling, and there was little point in trying to sleep, as Bubba would likely be calling. He decided to call the number Deputy Weber had given him. It took a half dozen rings before he heard the sound of the phone being dropped. Finally, a sleepy Weber answered. "This better be good."

"It's Don. I searched Parker's shed and came up with nothing."

"Did you have a warrant to do that?"

"No. You know I didn't." Don quickly avoided the lecture on proper police procedures by making a request. "I need you to do something."

"As long as it doesn't involve breaking the law."

"I want to know if the incidence of stolen vehicles has picked up over the last few weeks."

There was silence on the line. "That's interesting. Pardy was talking about that very thing yesterday. He thinks there might be another stolen car ring working the coast."

"Parker called them car bombs. If the plan is to detonate them amid anti-fascist protestors, they might not want to risk being seen crawling under cars. Why not steal ten cars and leave them along the route, with the bombs already in the trunk?"

"I guess that makes sense."

"When Parker was drawing a map of the route, he drew pictures of cars with an "X" on them."

"What do you need me to do?"

"We have to move fast, Weber. It's now Sunday morning, and the march is tomorrow. I need a complete list by make, color, year, and license plate of any car stolen in the last three weeks."

Weber took a deep breath. "This will involve multiple counties, Sheriff departments, Biloxi PD. You know that the Gulf Coast is the stolen car capital of the universe. It's going to be a long list."

"I need it by noon at the latest."

When he hung up the call with Weber, Don took a deep breath and called Fred Moller at his home.

"Yeah? Who's calling, Christ, it's not even 3 AM."

"It's Don. I have some bad news." He told his boss that the earlier plan had failed and that he'd violated a bunch of laws to break into Parker's garden shed to search for the bombs. To his credit, Fred accepted the information and said it was a worthwhile attempt. Don told him about the idea of using stolen cars to plant the bombs.

"Stand down for now. I'll brief Carol George when I get to the office and see what she has to say."

Don felt like saying he didn't give a shit what she had to say, but he was too exhausted to argue.

* * *

Bubba called at 5 AM. Don figured he might have gotten a couple of hours of sleep.

"Wakey wakey. I heard you had quite the day yesterday."

A sleepy Don searched his mind. Was he referring to kneeing Parker in the nuts, building the bombs, or something else? "Yeah, glad we got it done. Everything all set for the rally?"

"Pretty much. I got a couple of the guys working on some logistics. Listen, today is going to be a warehouse day. I need you in Port Christian for 8 AM. Fender will meet you and tell you what needs to be done. The weather is supposed to be shit today, so you get to stay in the nice warm, dry warehouse."

After showering, Don drove to Pass Christian and stopped at a place called Daddy's for breakfast. Over a feast of ham and eggs, he read yesterday's *Herald*. The front page was about former Mayor Baxter spurning offers from the D.A. and deciding to take his chance with a jury. Opening arguments were set to start that morning. In an article on page two, there was a black and white picture of a burning truck. The Forrest County Sheriff was quoted saying that the incident involved the death of an unknown male and that the State's Senior Agent in Charge of Fucking Everything, Carol "the Vagina" George, strongly suspected a pipe bomb. No motive was given for the blast. To the apprehension of other diners, Don took out his anger on his fried eggs, spearing the yolk over and over again.

Once he'd calmed down, Don looked for any mention of the upcoming march and found a small article on the back page. In it, the reporter said the Church of the Sword and Arm of the Lord was planning a rally on Monday, followed by a march down Beach Boulevard to the home of Stonewall Jackson. The church, according to the reporter, was one of the fastest-growing denominations, and they sought to preserve their white Christian heritage by following the Gospel of the Lord. Sheriff Pardy was quoted as saying he expected a peaceful event and that a strong police presence would be in attendance to ensure order.

Fender was waiting for Don and took the coffee with a grunt of thanks. They went into the warehouse, and Fender showed him what to do with the remaining shrimp and how to clean all the sorting tables, oil the machines, clean up the garbage, and mop the floors. He also said he'd check-in at the end of the day

"Where's everyone else?"

"The shrimp season's over, so they're off doing other things."

"Where are you going?" Don asked as Fender turned to leave.

"You going to be lonely here all by yourself? I got other stuff to do for tomorrow's big show," he said, pantomiming an explosion with his hands. Don watched him leave, locking Don inside the building behind him.

Chapter 55

The parking garage was drafty. This time Corbin stayed in his car and told Bubba and Dietz to get in.

"Is this car safe?" Dietz asked, reluctantly getting in the back seat.

"Yes, I'm not like you. I take precautions." Once Bubba was in the back seat, Masters added, "I thought it best that we meet one last time before the big event." Both Dietz and Lange remained silent, waiting for Corbin to ask a question. "Have we got the cars?"

"We have twenty nondescript models, as you said," replied Bubba.

"What about the bombs?"

"Parker dropped them off to me last night on the way back from Gautier." Bubba cracked a window as the older man lit up a cigarette.

"Any idea of how much damage this is going to cause?" Dietz turned to face Bubba.

"Depends on how many people are there. With this stuff, I bet it will be in the thousands,"

"What about the cop, has he been taken care of?" Masters asked, coughing, and smoking at the same time.

"Parker has him on ice. We've set up a little additional surprise for him after the parade."

"And the place in Gautier?" asked Masters.

"Schaffer was going to clear everything out today. If anyone goes looking, they'll find an abandoned house with the only fingerprints pointing to Kittyburg. Parker also gave Steve some stuff he took from the guy's apartment."

"Good work, Bubba."

"Last night on the way home from my place, Parker got stopped by a Harrison County Deputy, who looked under the tarp expecting to find the bombs."

"That cinches it." Dietz blurted. "You hired a cop. You need to be more careful, Lange." Dietz was happy someone else had messed up.

"Fuck off, Dietz. They wouldn't have sent a second cop had you not hired the first." Bubba slammed the seat in front of him. He didn't like Dietz, and he was positive the feeling was mutual. "Notice that I took care of your second fuckup."

"Shut up, girls," said Masters. "Don't get your panties in a knot. We haven't come this far to dissolve into a catfight."

Bubba made a rude gestured behind the driver's seat and shared a look with Dietz. He was pretty sure that neither of them cared for Masters.

Chapter 56

January 20th, 1985

Gulfport, Mississippi

When I returned from the library, I tried to keep myself busy and make up for the time wasted in calling the adoption registry. I couldn't help but feel that I had been swimming upstream. I found myself wanting donuts and went looking for what might have been left from the other day. I was about to bite into a stale honey cruller when the ringing of my telephone saved me.

I recognized my brother's voice immediately. "I'm sorry about this morning, Jacob. I didn't mean to intrude."

"That was Louie, don't worry about it. He just told me to call you at the office. What's up?"

"Uh…. I don't know how to say this. It's really none of my business, but…"

"Yes, Louie and I are in a relationship. We have been for over a year. And if you're about to have a heart attack, hold on. He's also black."

"He's black?"

"African American is what he prefers."

"You're in a homosexual relationship with a black man, and you're moving to Alabama!" I cried out, knowing I was being a little theatrical.

Thankfully, Jacob was laughing at my over the top reaction. "I've wanted to tell you for a while. It's just as well you found out. I'm not in a rush to tell Mom and Dad, though."

"My God, Jacob. It's freaking Alabama! They arrest people like you on sight. They believe in electro-conversion therapy."

"Don't worry about it. I tell people he's my male slave. Notice how they don't have a problem with that."

"And he's a Negro - I mean, colored?"

"African American."

Our conversation continued more calmly then it had started. We discussed Jacob's new job, and where they'd be living, His preference was to rent a house on a quiet street, of course with a separate door for Louis. His new employers wanted him to start as soon as possible and were willing to subsidize his move. Louis had been a landscaper in Jamaica and had an interview next week with a company in Mobile. We eventually got around to talking about Mom and Dad. "This isn't going to be easy, Rachel."

"I know, but we have to do something. Mom says he's getting worse…that his mind is going."

"Rachel, that might be true, and it's sad, but Mom's mind has been shuttered for the past ten years. I'm a lot more frightened about telling her about Louie than I am Dad."

I ended the call by telling Jacob that I loved him no matter what, and agreeing to have dinner next week.

Chapter 57

Don was to call Deputy Weber at noon, and his boss Fred had told him to stand down and wait for further instructions. He desperately needed to get to a phone. He tried the metal door before remembering that Fender had locked it from outside. Since he'd left his picks in the glove compartment, he went looking for some other way out. A garage door to the docks where trucks would load the produce had been chained shut.

His eyes scanned the warehouse. Cement cinder blocks, metal roof, and a poured concrete floor offered no way out. The ceilings were at least twenty feet high. About a foot below the ceiling was a bank of narrow windows for ventilation. He could likely shimmy out the window, except for one big problem. He wasn't twenty feet tall.

Kneeing Parker in the nuts might have been a mistake. Like a kid getting a time out, Don was being locked in here as punishment. The rest of the guys were probably distributing the pipe bombs. The bombs he'd helped to make. He needed to get out and call the cavalry. Not only that, but he also needed to get back in before they discovered he'd left. He walked around the warehouse floor, and kicked an empty root beer can, pretending he was a famous soccer player. He kept asking himself, "How can I get out of here?" When he'd tired himself out, he sat down on a pile of shrimp nets that had been tossed in a corner. "How can I get out of here?" he asked out loud.

By noon, I hadn't heard from either Don or Weber. I tried calling Deputy Weber first, knowing that Don was likely to be on a boat out on the Gulf. Weber answered, and I asked if he'd heard from Don.

"No, but I'm expecting to. He was supposed to call me at noon about a stolen car report."

"I'm getting worried about him. He fought with his boss yesterday. What about the stolen cars?"

"It's about double the number we normally have in three weeks, so Don was likely right that they may be planning to put the bombs in cars."

"That was my idea. But it doesn't matter. Can you get people out there tomorrow, checking for those cars? The bomb squad should be on standby."

"I spoke to Sheriff Pardy about this, and he's authorized overtime for everyone and asked for help from the neighboring counties. Everyone will carry a clipboard and be on the lookout."

"How long is the list?"

"Keep in mind this is every vehicle stolen in the past three weeks. We can't separate ones that might have been stolen anyway. There are," he paused for a minute, counting slowly out loud, "at least eighty cars and trucks stolen in the past three weeks."

"That's a lot of vehicles for your people to spot."

"I was hoping that Don could narrow it down."

"Arnie Simms and I will there tomorrow; can you give us a copy of the list?"

"Meet me at City Hall, bright and early."

It came to Don all of a sudden. If he could find a way to string a net from the window, then he could use it to climb up. But how to get a net up to the window? There had to be a way to open those windows. The answer was a telescoping pole that was leaning in the corner. It took precious time, but Don eventually had the netting attached to a window lever used to open the window. He checked his watch - almost noon. The climb up to the window on the net was relatively easy. When he got to the top, he unlocked the window and looked outside. It was pouring rain, and he was at least twenty feet up from the pavement below. Twenty feet was too much. Even if he fell and landed perfectly, he'd likely break one or both of his ankles. Holding onto the window frame, he started hauling the net up and pushing it outside through the open window.

It took time, and thankfully the pier was next to empty on a Sunday. He finally got enough of the net outside and crawled through the window. The rain made climbing down dangerous, and he almost slipped a couple of times, but finally, his feet touched the ground.

I was thinking about my conversation with Jacob about calling Louie his male slave when something occurred to me. During my visit to Mrs. Goran, I had asked about Jimmy's adoption, and she started singing that *Jimmy Crack Corn* song. The song was racist and was about a black slave who killed his master by staging an accident. Replaying the conversation with my mind, I remembered thinking she'd first said, *Jimmy Crack Horn*. Was that the name McGloyn had called Jimmy when he was brought in for adoption? Could his birth mother's last name be Horn? It was a long shot, but I had nothing to lose by checking into it. It was likely that the birth mother was either a member of McGloyn's church or at least someone who lived close enough to be referred to Reverend McGloyn for an adoption.

There were a half dozen listings in the greater Biloxi-Gulfport area for Horn, and another two with the named spelled Horne. I dialed the first number, and when a woman answered, I introduced myself and said that I was looking for a Horn that had given birth to a boy named Jimmy on April 10th, 1968. The woman quickly answered that she had moved to Biloxi from Natchez about five years ago. The second call was answered by a man who said he was a bachelor and knew nothing about a baby boy. I hit pay dirt on the sixth call. I could tell by the tears.

"Are you Jimmy's birth mother?" I asked softly.

She didn't answer the question but continued to cry. Finally, she said, "Tell me about Jimmy."

"He's very handsome. He's bright. Smart with computers. He goes to high school here in Gulfport. He's the kind of boy that any mother would be proud of."

"Has he had a good life?"

"Yes, Mr. and Mrs. Hopkins have brought him up to be respectful and hard working. But something is missing. He asked me to help him find his real parents."

"Oh, my lord, I thought this day would never come."

"Could I buy you a coffee?"

* * *

Don ran to a payphone outside of a 7-Eleven. He noticed that the price had jumped from a dime to twenty-five cents. As he was digging in his pockets for loose change, he saw the front page of the *Herald* in a newspaper box beside the phone.

Credible Bomb Threat Reported for Rally

Harrison County Sheriff's representatives have advised this newspaper that they have received a credible bomb threat for Monday. An individual called the police switchboard, mentioned the white supremacist rally and said that the police should expect a series of large explosions. In reacting to the call, Sheriff Pardy reminded everyone that the organizers of the rally had obtained the proper permits for their march down Beach Boulevard. Counter-protesters are being asked to stay home.

Don dialed Weber's number. When he was put through, an excited Deputy Weber asked where he'd been. "Seriously, you were supposed to call in. You've got people freaking out everywhere."

"Long story, but they locked me in this warehouse in Port Christian. I had to find a way out."

"I guess you haven't heard the news."

"Go ahead."

"I just spoke to Rachel. There are eighty vehicles reported stolen in just the last three weeks. Sheriff Pardy's worried that there might be even more pipe bombs. He argued with the Mayor about canceling the ceremonies. When the Mayor wouldn't do it, he called the Governor, who also said no. Pardy called a friend at the *Herald,* and they were supposed to put something in the paper warning people away. He's got deputies coming from two counties, and from Biloxi PD. He even called your boss at MBI, asking for state troopers."

"My boss?"

"She's here right now, speaking to Pardy."

"She?"

"Yeah, I have her card right here. Nice lady. Very pregnant. Her name is … Carol George, Senior Agent in Charge."

"Ah, fuck her."

"Don…, did you just say you're the father? You had sex with your boss?"

"No, I didn't say that. I meant, fuck, this situation is messed up."

"Yes, it is. Have you learned anything more?"

"I think they kept me locked in the warehouse so that I wouldn't have time to warn people."

"You know that place you told me about in Gautier?"

"Yes, that's where we built the bombs."

"A rapid response team from Parker County went in there this morning. They've recovered some C-4, some Creedence Clearwater Revival cassettes, and a ton of fingerprints."

* * *

Rather than meet at a coffee shop, Deborah Horn suggested that I come to her apartment in Biloxi, where we could talk. When I got there, she was still crying. She had to be in her mid-thirties and must have had Jimmy as a teenager. She invited me into her basement apartment and said she had just put on a fresh pot of coffee. As we sat down in a small breakfast nook, I could see Jimmy in her; she had the same nose and body type. Once we were had our coffee, I thanked her for seeing me.

"I was only fifteen."

"What about the father?" I asked, already knowing the answer.

Her eyes hardened, and she shook her head. "He didn't want to be a father. Just as well. He wouldn't have been good for Jimmy. Last I heard he was in jail."

"Tell me about the adoption?" I didn't need to know this, but I wanted her to talk.

"Underage, unmarried, living with my parents. When I started to show, I told them. Pop took it better than Ma. I don't see them anymore; we've had a falling out. I still think it was Ma that called the cops." Deborah stopped and drank some coffee, which seemed to give her courage. "The cops came when I was ready to give birth and took me to what they called a special place. I had Jimmy there…with a midwife. I got to hold Jimmy. He was so beautiful." She started to tear up again.

"Take your time," I urged.

Once again, her eyes hardened, and she looked away. "Never given birth, have you?"

"No."

"A woman, she said her name was Goran. She was from the Church. She pulled Jimmy right from my arms." The recollection must have been too much for Deborah as she got up and walked to the other end of the room, hiding her face. I waited awkwardly at the table for a few minutes before she spoke again. "I'm sorry, I guess I've never been able to get over it. I've never been able to look at Ma and get past what she did to me."

"Have you ever tried to find Jimmy?"

"No." She looked around the basement apartment. "Look at me. I work at the root beer company, making less than $5 an hour. What kind of life could I provide for him?"

It was harder climbing up the netting than it had been getting out. The rain was coming down horizontally. Don finally made it to the window. He slithered in, turned around, and pulled the netting back inside the window. Once he'd climbed down to the warehouse floor, he used the pole to unhook the netting from the window handle. He looked at his watch. It was 2 PM, and he was exhausted after spending three hours climbing up, out, back in, and down again. He suddenly realized that if Fender were to walk in, he'd find that Don hadn't done anything.

Chapter 58

January 21, 1985

Martin Luther King Day
Biloxi, Mississippi

The weather forecast was for an unusually warm and sunny day. *With intermittent bomb blasts in the downtown area*, I thought as I made my way to City Hall. It was a majestic pillared building with a large courtyard in front. At 9 AM, there were already twenty or so people gathering on the steps. I spotted a stressed-out Deputy Weber talking to Arnie and a couple of state troopers. Thankfully the Governor wasn't scheduled to speak until later that morning. The deputy's face was flushed, and his sleep-deprived eyes were like a searchlight, in constant motion. Nodding to Arnie, I asked if anyone had seen Don.

"No, I was going to ask you the same thing," said Weber. "I spoke to him yesterday afternoon, after you and I talked. Did you call him last night?"

"I called his apartment about a hundred times last night. At midnight I couldn't take it any longer, so I drove over to his apartment. His truck wasn't there. What did he say when you spoke to him?"

"Don thought they might be onto him." Deputy Weber told me about Don's escape from the warehouse, and that he was going to try to get back in before they returned. Our attention was drawn to a group of five Nazi-helmeted men on Harleys riding into the square to join the others.

Weber's radio squawked, and a voice said that they hadn't found any of the stolen cars. "Keep looking, and then when you're done, start over again." He rolled his eyes, "I'll look like a hero even if they find one bomb and take it out. If, on the other hand, they don't find any bombs, then Don and I might be looking to come work for you."

"Give us one of the clipboards and tell me what hasn't been checked."

"Better than that," he said, handing us each a clipboard. "I'll drive, you spot."

Arnie went with another deputy. The clipboard had five pages of sheets, divided into columns - one for the owner, another for make and model, another for color, and a final column for the license plate. Weber drove down Beach Boulevard to a spot he said hadn't been checked yet. There were maybe forty vehicles in the lot - likely tourists wanting to shop on a beautiful sunny day.

It was mentally tiring work checking each vehicle against all five sheets. It took a good half hour before we concluded that none of these cars were on the list. We were about to leave when something dawned on me. "Stop. Back up to that green Pontiac." It was a Pontiac 6000 with Mississippi plates. I had initially discarded it because the license plate didn't match.

"Is it on the list?" Weber leaned over to look.

"We busted a car theft ring last year. You know what one of the first things they do when they steal a car?"

"Swap the license plate," replied Weber.

"Exactly. You need to have every car that matches the description on these sheets check that the license plate matches." Weber radioed the other teams and then dispatch for the make and model matching the Pontiac's license plate. It came back minutes later that the license plate belonged to a white Toyota. He then radioed the Sergeant on the bomb team and gave the specifics of the Pontiac.

We continued checking the other cars in the lot. There were a couple of other model matches. An old blue Chrysler K car and a white Suburban, but when we checked, they both had the correct plates.

The bomb squad arrived a few minutes before 10 AM in a large black van. The sergeant came over and talked to us, and we pointed out the car. They started out using a long mirror device to check the undercarriage. When that search yielded nothing, the sergeant came back and stood by my window. "There's nothing under the car, nothing connected to the ignition. Other than what looks like a baseball glove, there's nothing suspicious in either the front or back seat. There is, of course, the trunk. There's a trunk release by the driver's seat, but I'm kind of reluctant to release it because it might be the trigger switch. What can you tell me about the explosive device?"

"Homemade C-4, in a pipe bomb," I said, remembering what Don had told me. "Oh, and they have a garage door thing as a remote control."

"What type of pipe?"

"I assume metal," I blurted out, immediately regretting it.

"You assume?" He shook his head and leaned down to look through the car at Weber. "Deputy, there's different kinds of metal, and then there's PVC. We can get equipment that can detect C-4 by the trace vapors but not if it's encased in a lead pipe. Our best bet is to use a portable x-ray machine to see what we can see in the trunk. As for the trigger device, most garage door openers only work if the person pressing the button is within fifty yards of the device. Unless, of course, the remote has been modified."

It took the better part of half an hour before the Sargent walked back and said there were long cylinder objects in the trunk that looked more like aluminum baseball bats than pipe bombs. "I'm going to unlock the trunk. We need you to stay outside the perimeter just in case."

Weber drove to the far end of the lot, and we watched as the sergeant walked by wearing a bomb suit and gave us a thumbs up.

A few minutes later, the sergeant shook his head and held up a kid's Louisville slugger.

"They tried to throw us off," I said.

"What do you mean?"

"That car was stolen and parked in plain view, and it just so happened to have baseball bats in the trunk."

"Why would they do that?"

"I don't know, let's hope Don does."

Chapter 59

One day earlier,

Saucier, Mississippi

Don finished the chores he'd been assigned by 5 PM and waited another two hours for Fender and Parker to arrive. They unlocked the warehouse door. "Geez, about time you come back. Why'd you lock me in here, Fender?"

"Lock you in? Shit, was the door locked? It must do that automatically." Parker gave Fender a smirk then nodded to Don.

"How are the nuts, Park?" Don returned the smirk.

"Let's not start that again."

Don bit his tongue and smiled. "Can I go now? I need to rest up before the big show." Don repeated Fender's earlier gesture of an explosion.

"Speaking of that, we're all driving up to Saucier and getting together with some of the others. Kind of a dress rehearsal."

"Mud and oil, right? I got it."

"It's blood and soil, and get in the truck. Fender, you drive. I don't think Pussy likes my driving."

* * *

"Yeah, I'm telling you, he was pretty much shitting bricks when we drove to Gautier," Parker said, looking back at me from the front seat. "I thought he was going to wet his diaper. Ain't that right, Pussyman?"

"Can we listen to some decent music?"

"You're such a little wimp, aren't you Pussy?" repeated Parker.

"I know you are, but what am I?" It occurred to Don that Parker was trying to provoke him into a fight, just like he had done to Parker. This time, however, Don had to consider Fender, a much different issue.

"I don't suppose you've heard the news?" Fender looked at Don in the rearview mirror.

"What's that?"

"Some fucker called in a bomb threat for tomorrow. Imagine that, here we are exercising our freedom of speech, and these lefty pinkos are threatening to blow everything up." Parker turned around again and was watching Don's expression. Weber had said that Pardy had called in the bomb threat. Don thought something was wrong. *Why are they dragging me to Saucier, they could just as easily have killed me today? I must still figure in their plans, and why aren't they concerned about the bomb threat?*

"How does that change our plans for tomorrow?"

"It doesn't," replied Parker. "I bet those pinkos won't be able to stay away. All we have to do is press a button, and kaboom, pinkos to heaven. Hey, that sounds like a Willy Nelson song, doesn't it? *Mamma, don't let your babies grow up to be pinkos.*"

"Not great, Park."

"What's great, Pussy, is that while the bombs go off, you'll be leading our little peaceful march down Beach Boulevard."

Parker doesn't know that we know about the stolen cars. Hopefully, Weber can find the cars and the bombs before they can be detonated.

Chapter 60

January 21, 1985

Biloxi, Mississippi

After the incident with the bomb squad, we heard over the radio that two other stolen vehicles had been found in various parking lots in the downtown area. They were being checked out by the bomb squad. Sheriff Pardy radioed Weber, telling him to get back to City Hall as things were getting out of control.

When we got there, the crowd had swelled to well over a hundred. An older man, introducing himself as Steve Schaffer, was speaking into a microphone about the importance of culture and heritage. "The Governor has decreed that today be celebrated as 'Great Americans Day.' Friends, we should all welcome that. The South needs its heroes. But what do those northern liberals have to say? They say your heroes aren't good enough. They say wonderful people like Robert E. Lee, Stonewall Jackson, and let us not forget George Wallace, just weren't good enough. They want us to tear down the monuments of our heroes and put up theirs. Well, we will not be replaced." He repeated the phrase in ever-increasing volume and encouraged the crowd to say it with him. Finally, he put up his hands to quiet the crowd. "Not on this soil. The soil of our forefathers, of our heroes who died for this land. They spilled their blood to save us from those who wanted to tell us how to live. Blood and Soil," he led the chant, with an almost hysterical crowd repeating his words.

I found myself looking at the crowd for a sign of Don, and wondering if the other men from the list were here somewhere. Or were they just the enablers, the money men? A group of counter-protesters was gathering in the parking lot, their signs calling for an end to hatred.

When Schaffer stopped talking, a large man with his hair in a mullet started marching everyone in twos out of the square. Shouting "Death to all the Jews," they walked right by where I was standing,

Weber came up to me and winced. "I'll never make it to Sheriff because of this. Pardy is incensed. He wants me to order those counter-protesters to disperse. Look at all of the television cameras."

"Weber, I'm sorry I called you those names a few weeks ago. I was upset about people not believing me. I don't think you're stupid."

He smiled. "No need to apologize for calling me Mr. Big Brain, I thought it was a compliment."

I laughed. "Have you heard back from the bomb squad?"

"Both stolen cars we found had their license plates switched, but the bomb squad found nothing."

"This is starting to look like a hoax."

"Yep. Any sign of Don?"

"Nothing."

Chapter 61

The night before

Saucier, Mississippi

It was after 8 pm when Don and the others arrived at the camp. Parker motioned for Don to follow Fender into the church. When they walked in, Don saw Steve, now wearing a black sports coat and ranting about immigration policy.

"I am calling for the complete closing of our southern border. We need to stop the flow of rapists, killers, and drug dealers coming into our homeland." Steve continued until he noticed that Parker and the others had arrived, and then led the applause saluting what he called true American heroes.

Don looked behind him, thinking he was referring to someone else. Parker gave him a dirty look and a shove forward. There had to be a hundred people listening to Steve's rant. Don saw that half the audience was either skinheads or were wearing some type of Nazi paraphernalia. The scary part was the other half of the audience. They all looked like clean-cut ordinary people. They could be the trucker you met at a truck stop, the mechanic that fixed your car, or the guy at the store bagging your groceries. There was a sprinkling of women, but the crowd was overwhelmingly angry white men.

They found a seat at the back of the church and settled in to listen. Steve was doing a masterful job of inflaming the crowd. He had a gift for knowing when to raise his voice and when to slow down his delivery. Every few minutes, his speech would hit a high point, and the crowd would be on their feet. At one point, Parker looked down and saw Don wasn't seig-heil-ing like everyone else. "What the fuck is your problem, Kittyburg?"

"I've been locked in a warehouse all day with nothing but rotten leftover shrimp to eat. I think I'm going to puke." Don started gagging, acting as if he was going to throw up in Parker's lap.

A look of horror washed over Parker's face. "Get the fuck outside."

When Don stepped outside under a porch light, he found the cold night air invigorating. He was nauseous, but it wasn't because of the shrimp. How easy it was to promote hatred. Of all the times he'd gone undercover, he had never felt this vulnerable before. He was wondering how long he'd be permitted to stay outside when he noticed the ember of a burning cigarette beside one of the sleeping cabins. Don walked over, and as he got closer, he recognized Jethro.

"Couldn't take all the bullshit?" asked Jethro.

Don ignored the question. "What are you doing out here?"

"Having a smoke."

"That's funny, I thought you'd be eating that stuff up."

"Might have before." Jethro took a drag from his cigarette. "I don't much care for killing people, even if they're niggers."

Don thought about that for a moment. "Going to be a big day tomorrow." Don was hoping Jethro would take the bait.

"We had a cop here before. He asked a lot of questions, just like you. I told him some stuff about their plans. One day he just stopped coming. Rumor has it he was told to fix the ice chipper and had an accident."

"You think I'm a cop?"

"Ah shucks, Kittyburg. They know. They're just setting you up. Lots of niggers are going to die tomorrow. If I were you, I'd hightail it out of here before you end up...." Just then, the door to the Church opened. Don slipped into the shadows behind Jethro.

"Hey, that you, Jethro?" Fender called out from the doorway?

"Just having a breath."

"You seen that Kittyburg guy?"

"Ain't seen shit out here." Jethro took a final drag and threw his cigarette into the grass.

Don faded into the dark behind the cabin, trying to make sense of what Jethro had just said.

Don sprinted through the pine forest adjacent to the Church as fast as he could. His plan was to put as much distance between himself and the church as possible. He was sure they'd be out looking for him now. He ran for twenty minutes. It was slow going in the dark, and he fell a couple of times before stopping to rest against a pine tree. His hoodie was drenched in sweat. He looked behind him and saw flashlights heading in his direction. At this rate, they'd be on him soon. He was traveling east away from the church. That would make the highway about a mile off to his right. He was about to set off at another sprint when he heard the howling of bloodhounds.

Don took off his hoodie and dropped it on the ground about ten yards further east. Retracing his steps, he branched off towards the highway. Looking back, he saw the flashlights getting closer, and he could hear someone yell, "Over here."

Another ten minutes and he stopped again, leaning against a tree trunk trying to catch his breath. The shouts seemed to be further away off to the east now. He guessed the time was around 11 PM, a little more than ten hours before things were going to start blowing up.

* * *

Don got to the road ten minutes later. He was out of breath, bruised and scratched from running into trees. He could no longer hear shouting or the dogs. Maybe they'd decided to get in their pickups and were out on the roads looking for him.

He needed a ride. Biloxi might only be thirty minutes by car, but on foot, he didn't think he had the time or the energy. At this hour there wasn't much traffic on the highway. He started walking south, only hiding if he saw a pickup headed his way. Over the next half hour, he saw seven vehicles - all pickups.

It was almost midnight when he flagged down a Chrysler K car. An older man, wearing a straw hat, who was barely visible over the dash, had no choice but to stop as Don was standing in the road waving his hands frantically back and forth. Don approached the driver's window.

"Is there an emergency?" The man looked as if he was in his eighties.

"I'm with the State Police. I have to get to Biloxi. There's going to be a bombing."

"I ain't going that far."

"Then, I'm going to have to take your car." Don opened the driver's door. The old man was surprisingly strong and tried to pull the door closed. He put his foot on the gas, and the car lurched forward with Don holding on for dear life.

"Listen, I'll arrest you for obstructing a state investigation," Don yelled. "You know what they do to people like you in prison." Somehow that must have gotten through to the man as he put his foot on the brake.

"What do they do to folk like me in prison?"

"I don't want to say. Can you just drive me? Please?"

The man looked at Don suspiciously. "All right, all right, get in. But I want to hear about those prisons." Don sensed that the man was going to take off on him again, and quickly hopped in the back seat behind the driver.

"What ya'll sitting back there? I'm not gonna make a pass at you."

Don ignored the question. "My name's Don Kittyburg. I'm an agent for the Mississippi Bureau of Investigation."

"Where's your badge?" The man finally put the car in gear, checking his mirrors a half dozen times.

"I'm undercover. Do you know what that is?"

"I watch Miami Vice every week. Folks say I look like Sonny Crockett. I even bought me some clothes like him. You know, pastel-like. I think it makes me look younger." A pickup truck passed them on the left, blasting its horn. Don realized that the old man was barely going twenty-five miles per hour. "Now tell me again about what they're going to do to me in prison."

"Tell you what, I will if you speed up a little."

Chapter 62

January 21, 1985

Biloxi, Mississippi

My nerves were fraught, and I expected to hear a bomb blast any minute. I kept scanning the crowd looking for Don. For him to miss this meant that something terrible had happened. The Governor was on the steps of City Hall trying to be heard over the chaos in front of him. Both the marchers and the anti-fascist protesters were waving their signs and trying to drown out each other. The marchers were making their way onto Beach Boulevard. The deputies had formed a line trying to keep order between those marching, and the counter-protestors.

Weber ran to catch up. "So far, so good, but I'm worried that if one person throws something, things could get crazy fast. Any sign of Don?" I shook my head and asked for an update on the bombs. "Nothing. I took teams off the parking lots and redeployed them to keep these groups separated."

At one point, there was a scuffle with a bunch of Nazis getting into it with the bystanders. Deputies quickly rushed in with batons to keep the two groups apart. My attention was drawn to a car honking madly up ahead. It was someone in a sedan, driving against the flow of the crowd. "Jesus, Weber, that car is going to run people over."

Weber yelled to a deputy and started running towards the car. Thankfully the driver of the vehicle was going at a relatively slow speed, blasting his horn when people wouldn't get out of his way. All of a sudden, the car came to a stop about twenty feet from me. I watched as Don Kittyburg got out.

"Did I miss anything?" He laughed as I ran over and hugged him.

"I've been so worried. Where have you been?"

"Long story and not important. Have any bombs..."

"No, it looks like one big hoax," I said, interrupting. Weber ran back when he saw Don.

"Listen," Don yelled over the sound of the crowd. "There's something wrong. They should have killed me. There was a guy up at the militia camp, he told me everyone knew I was a cop, and that this was a big setup." He went on to explain how he had escaped. Don looked around at the counterprotestors. "Jethro said he didn't want to go along with a plan that would kill that many Negros."

I looked around at the crowd before turning to Weber. "There are no colored faces here."

"Most of them are probably over at Hiller Park," replied Weber. "The NAACP is gathering there to celebrate Martin Luther King. I understand Coretta Scott King is going to be there."

"Why didn't you mention that?" I looked at him in confusion.

"It's not a sanctioned event. The Governor ordered everyone to promote Great Americans Day."

I looked at him, dumbfounded. "I've changed my mind again. You're stupid." Weber didn't hear what I said, on account of a massive explosion.

Chapter 63

Hiller Park was five miles away, but the blast was so powerful, people scrambled, running in all directions thinking they were in danger. Another explosion followed the initial one. Anti-fascist protestors threw down their signs and ran crazily. The marchers continued as if nothing had happened.

"It started," I yelled at Weber, who seemed to be mesmerized.

"Listen, Weber, we have to get to Hiller Park. I might be able to stop this," said Don, shaking the deputy.

In the end, it was the sirens that prompted Weber to move. "Follow me. I have a cruiser."

"Is there a back street you can take?" Don asked as he was getting into the front seat. Several emergency vehicles passed us.

"I was born and bred here. I know a short cut." Weber yelled, putting the cruiser in gear as I piled into the back. "What's the plan, Don?"

"The bombs are all hooked to remote detonators, and you have to be close enough to detonate the bomb. I might be able to recognize some of these people before they press the button."

Weber pulled a quick left and then another right with the car fishtailing behind him. "I need a gun," Don yelled to him as he held onto the dash.

"All my weapons are property of the Harrison County Sheriff Department and can only be used by properly deputized officers."

"But I'm a cop," Don yelled, letting his frustrations show. "Can you not take a risk for once?"

Rather than wait for Weber to reconsider, I reached into my purse for Arnie's .38 and handed it to Don. We arrived at Hiller Park and saw a flood of people running towards us. "How did so many people hear about this gathering?"

"I heard about it from my church," said Weber. "The Reverend at Bay Vista even rented a bus to pick people up and take them to the park."

As we got closer, I noticed that the lot full sign was up in the parking lot and that people had parked their vehicles on the lawn. Just then, we heard another blast that rocked the cruiser. A fiery yellow flame billowed to the sky. There were too many people running towards us. Some were climbing onto the car, yelling and screaming for help. Don yelled and got out of the cruiser, running towards the blast.

I ran after him. I saw a familiar face in the crowd, Sergeant Geiger. His eyes were tearful, and he was carrying the body of a blonde woman in his arms. He recognized me as I approached. Without stopping, he yelled that Mrs. King was on the grandstand. I ran as best I could in the direction of where I thought the grandstand was located. There were hundreds of panicking people, many with cuts to their faces, stampeding in the opposite direction.

A fourth explosion rocked me off my feet. The sound was deafening. My ears were ringing. I had seen the blast raise a car off the grass, 6 feet in the air. I saw huge plumes of fire and a secondary explosion. The air was filled with pieces of metal. I stayed down and shielded my face from the falling debris.

Don ran towards the blast, leaving Weber and Rachel behind. He held his gun, pointing up, shouting, "Police, get down." A man was walking away from the blast headed towards the grandstand. It was hard to see through the smoke, but Don thought it was Barry McGloyn. A green Cherokee was parked near the stage where a bunch of people were huddled together. Don quickened his pace and yelled out to him, "Stop, Barry!"

The man looked back and then sneered at Don. "Are you proud of your work, Kittyburg?" He saw Barry reach into his camouflage vest.

"It's over, Barry. Put the detonator down, and you can still live."

Barry took a last look at Coretta King and then went to press the thing he'd taken from his pocket. A split second before he could press the button, Don shot him in the chest.

I started running again, looking for Weber or Don. An African American man was lying on the ground, blood pouring from a leg wound. I knelt beside him. He was saying something to me, but I couldn't make it out over the ringing in my ears. Blood was flowing thickly from his wound. The metal in his calf was about 4 inches long. I took my sweater off. A moment of indecision struck me. Should I pull the shrapnel out of the wound, or would the blood just flow faster? I looked at the man. His eyes seemed to be imploring me to take it out. I took off his belt and wrapped my hand around my sweater. I pulled on the metal, and it came out with a gusher of blood spurting over me. I used the man's belt to tighten the pressure above the wound. I used my sweater to tie off the wound, hoping that I had saved at least one life.

Don ran over to where Barry lay on the ground and kicked the remote out of his hand. Barry's chest wound looked bad. He wasn't going to last long. "Where are the other bombs?" Don asked, kneeling beside him. Barry's eyes opened, and a spittle of blood bubbled up from his lips. He was trying to speak, and Don leaned closer.

"It's too late. Blood and Soil," Barry said, just before he closed his eyes for the last time.

Don sat on the grass and looked around the park for anyone else he recognized. His ears were ringing, and he found it hard to see through all of the smoke. Multiple bodies were littered around the park. A small group of deputies and paramedics were on the scene trying to help people. There had been four explosions, leaving six more bombs. Before Barry had been shot, he had been heading towards the car parked close to the grandstand. Would someone else try to detonate that bomb?

He got up and started running towards the Jeep. He made it two feet when he was tackled from behind. The force of the hit sent him sprawling, and he lost his grip on his gun. He was momentarily stunned but recovered enough to realize that Parker was sitting on him punching him. They struggled, and Don tried to throw the heavy man off, but there was no use. The man was too heavy. Parker then got his hands around Don's neck and started to choke him. Don clawed desperately at the big man's hands, trying to breathe. He knew he had only a few moments before he'd blackout. He looked up and saw the hatred in Parker's eyes.

All of a sudden, Don heard a scream, and a body flew into Parker, knocking him off.

"What the fuck?" yelled Parker as he tried to recover. Don crawled away and was trying to catch his breath. He looked back and saw that it had been Rachel who had barreled into Parker.

Parker was now getting up off the ground, ready to exact revenge. "You're going to wish you didn't do that." A revolver suddenly appeared, and Parker looked over at Don and smiled as he pointed it at Rachel. "A pussy saved by a pussy,"

Don leaped in front of Rachel but realized that he wasn't going to be fast enough. A gunshot rang out, and he looked back at Rachel in horror.

I saw a big meatball-shaped man sitting on Don, trying to strangle him. I had nothing to use as a weapon, so I charged the man with everything I had. Luckily, he was so preoccupied with choking the life out of Don, he didn't see me coming. The force of my body hitting him was just enough to knock him off.

I knew the man would turn on me, so I tried to scramble to my feet. He was on his knees now, saying something that I couldn't make out. I looked over at Don and saw he was on all fours trying to breathe. I realized now the man had a gun. He pointed it at me. I saw Don leaping, trying to be faster than the bullet. Even the ringing in my ears couldn't block out the gun blast.

Don fell to the ground, helpless to stop the inevitable from happening. He took a last look at Rachel and then looked back at Parker just as the man's chest exploded.

The force of Weber's shotgun blast knocked Parker back about three feet.

* * *

Over the next several hours, chaos reigned in the park. Paramedics attended to the injured, firefighters put out fires, and police were everywhere. Don spied a man with the same vest as McGloyn had been wearing walking towards the exit, and the police swarmed him. Fender had seen Parker go down, and when he'd realized he was surrounded, he'd given up without a fight. He told Don where to find the other six bombs, which were diffused by the bomb squad.

Chapter 64

In the week that followed, the Biloxi bombings were front-page news. Mississippi and home-grown terrorism became linked as the top story across America. When the dust settled, the *Herald* reported that one hundred and sixty-eight people had died. Dozens more would live the remainder of their lives crippled. The vast majority of the casualties were African Americans. The Governor called it a dark day for the state and demanded a public inquiry into the conduct of the local police. He also sent the National Guard to Biloxi, anticipating that the coloreds would retaliate. The Mayor appealed for peace, imposing a curfew to prevent the rioting that everyone was expecting.

A letter from a group calling themselves the Coalition of Concerned Americans was delivered to the *Herald*. In the letter, they took responsibility for the bombings and said this was the first salvo in the race war that was to come. The letter also included a list of demands it claimed would need to be implemented for the South to be great again. Larry Bremmer refused to put it in the paper. Instead, he decided to pick up the story that Hartley Green had been working on and wrote a week-long expose called *The Politics of Hate*.

I gave a copy of the list that had the names of Corbin Masters and Reverend McGloyn to Deputy Weber. The police brought close to twenty people in for questioning based on information from Fender. In return for a lighter sentence, Fender gave information on both the Green murder and the MBI agent who had disappeared. The killer, in both cases, was a man named Gordon Bones. Fender also said that his remains were in the Hattiesburg morgue, the victim of a car bomb. After meeting with the county prosecutor, Sheriff Pardy said there was insufficient evidence to charge them.

One evening, Don and I went to Mobile and visited with Jacob and Louis at their new apartment. Louis was a big, tall bald African American man with a tinge of an island accent. He had an infectious, unrestrained laugh, and I liked him right away. The evening lasted well into the morning, and Louis delighted us with tales of growing up in Jamaica.

Don told us about having had to sit through hours of debriefs on what had happened with the bombs. Some were skeptical about the story when they found the evidence planted in the house in Gautier. While his boss Fred Moller said he was supportive of what Don had done to limit the catastrophe, the Governor wanted someone to blame. Instead of extending the Senior Agent role to Don as promised, he was invited to apply. This time Don did not threaten to quit but did say he might consider a sex change.

I brought up the family situation and told everyone about my visit to Mrs. Goran and how I was affected by my call to my father. We debated a variety of possible solutions, ranging from Don's suggestion of getting it all out in the open. In his words, it would be like "removing a Band-Aid." Louis and Jacob were for a 'wait and see' approach.

"What about you, Rachel?" asked Jacob.

I took a deep breath. "This is what we should do. I want to spend some time with them. Reconnect and assess their situation. I want to take Dad to see his doctor. Depending on what he has to say, I'd invite the pastor of their church to visit. If we have to make a tough decision, then I'd like you there with me, Jacob. If the doctor feels it's premature, then I'd still like to introduce Don to them, and I suggest you also invite Louis."

* * *

Later that week, Donna Hopkins called and told me about a wonderful meeting they'd had with Jimmy's birth mother. "It couldn't have gone better," she said. "She came over to the house and met everyone, including my husband. Jimmy is thrilled."

"That's great, Donna."

"All thanks to you, Rachel. Listen, I know you're busy, so let me just say thank you."

Epilogue

Rod Smith walked into Mr. Canyon's office. He wasn't surprised to see that Masters had not deigned the meeting worthy enough to make an appearance. Once they were seated, Canyon quickly got down to business.

"I have briefed Mr. Masters about your client's claim, and he, of course, has denied any involvement. On the matter of your request that he willingly submit to a paternity test, he has declined to do so. I can't say I blame him. Wealthy people receive this type of thing regularly. Tell your client, Mr. Brodie, to take his act somewhere else."

"I figured that would be the response." Rod slid another document across to Canyon.

"What's this now?" The lawyer said, letting his eyes scan the document.

"It's a motion that is being filed in Family Court this morning. It recaps our request for Corbin Masters to submit to a DNA test as well as providing the results of such a test done on his brother Chester Masters. If you skip ahead to page five, you will see that the results show a familial connection between my client's DNA and Chester Masters. The results indicate that my client's father is Chester's brother."

"This is crap. Chester would never have agreed to this."

"He's in your waiting room in case you want to depose him. As I'm sure you know, Mr. Canyon, the courts have ruled favorably on this type of evidence as sufficient to compel an alleged father to take a DNA test."

In the end, Corbin Masters never did take the test or admit any responsibility. He threatened to tie the matter up in the courts for years. As everyone knew, he had the resources to do it.

The offer of a settlement conference came as a big surprise. Two significant factors came into play. First, Corbin's health continued to slide to the point where even shark fins couldn't prolong his life. The second was a ruling in another state that a DNA paternity test could be done on a deceased person. Corbin realized he could not elude his responsibility for Michael Boyle even in death.

Through Mr. Canyon, Rod Smith and Brodie were offered a sizeable settlement, in return for renouncing any claim to Corbin Masters and his estate. Brodie, who had claimed he didn't care about the money, in the end, agreed to a negotiated settlement. All of this was good news for Rod Smith, who would be entitled to a sizeable fee from which he would carve off a portion to reward the Eye on You Detective Agency for their excellent work.

— The End —

Note to the Readers

I hope you had fun reading this book. Some might be disappointed with the death toll at the end, and that the white knight didn't totally save the day. As I mentioned at the beginning, this is a work of fiction. I opted for this ending because I couldn't bring myself to gloss over the impact of the recycling of hatred that is happening in America. Without leadership that condemns hatred in all its forms, the world is doomed to repeat it's past.

For those who think this could never happen, you need only to look up the Oklahoma City bombing. One hundred and sixty people fell victim to a car bomb placed in front of the Alfred P. Murrah building by a domestic terrorist named Timothy McVeigh.